1000

D0984292

MINDFIELD

BOOKS BY WILLIAM DEVERELL

MINDFIELD

a novel

William Deverell

M&S

Copyright © 1989 William Deverell

All rights reserved. The use of any part of this publication, transmitted in any form or by any means, electronic, mechanical, photocopying, recording or otherwise, or stored in a retrieval system, without the prior consent of the publisher, is an infringement of the copyright law.

Canadian Cataloguing in Publication Data
Deverell, William, 1937–
    Mindfield

ISBN 0-7710-2659-5

I. Title.

PS8557.E8775M56 1989   C813'.54   C89-094688-4
PR9199.3.D474M56 1989

Printed and bound in Canada

This is a work of fiction and all characters and incidents herein are purely fictitious.

Published simultaneously in the United States by British American Publishing, Latham, New York.

McClelland & Stewart Inc.
The Canadian Publishers
481 University Avenue
Toronto, Ontario M5G 2E9

Dedicated to Montreal, a city unique.

Thanks to Tom Berry, George Mihalka, Jean-Claude Lord, and Tekla Deverell, all of whom gave thoughtful and often inspired advice, and to Allegro Films of Montreal and the film crew, artists and cast who helped interpret this story for the screen.

The CIA was fascinated by LSD and other psychochemicals that they thought might be useful in getting people to talk or in temporarily putting them out of action. There was an urgent need, the CIA argued, to develop techniques to "render an individual subservient to an imposed will or control."

They worked on ways to achieve the controlled production of headaches and earaches; twitches, jerks, and staggers. They wanted to reduce a man to a bewildered, self-doubting mass to subvert his principles, a CIA document said. They wanted to direct him in ways that "may vary from rationalizing a disloyal act to the construction of a new person."

One of their longest-running goals was to develop a way to induce amnesia. They wanted to be able to interrogate enemy espionage agents in such a way that neither the agents nor their superiors would know they had been compromised, and they wanted to be able to wipe clean the memories of their own agents after certain missions and, especially, when they were going into retirement.

They were interested in simple destruction, too. As with the other business that made amnesia so attractive, they wanted to be able to get away with murder without leaving a trace.

New York Times, August 2, 1977

MINDFIELD

Friday, eleven a.m.

Kellen O'Reilly armed himself with caffeine and nicotine at his kitchen table as he waited for Margot. On the phone she'd been breathless, had hinted at menacing secrets. "I'll tell you when I get there."

He stared at, without reading, the Montreal *Gazette*'s front page. CHAOS IN STREETS PREDICTED, said the headline. Alarmist propaganda from the *comité executif*.

Kellen's headache was complicated by a prickly, inexplicable anxiety, a sense of impending *folie* which arrived last night, an unwelcome guest whom he'd tried to drown in vodka and soda, but who stayed overnight and woke up with him in his bed, in his head.

Along with this thirteen-ounce hangover. Drinking. Thinking. Reading. Alone, until midnight, in his own easy chair.

"That's pretty sad, isn't it, Mao?" he said to his old tomcat, who was lying near the radiator, asleep, uncaring.

Yesterday had been bad. Bork the Stork had conspired with the Monster, Kellen's new desk computer, to break his spirit, and he'd returned home enervated, mentally washed out, then began to notice a disquiet growing tumor-like within him. Its source, he thought at first, was loneliness: the monk-in-a-cell pattern he'd got into in recent months, and he'd actually considered dropping into one of the pickup bars on Bishop, in the *Anglais*-Yuppie barrio, but in the end he couldn't face the awful game.

He stayed home and read Camus and drank half a twenty-six of Stolichnaya.

And felt inner tremors all night, fluttery feelings, little bats trapped inside him.

1

Goddamnit, he'd been *well* for so long. Well. Unsick. Mended. For almost twenty years. After five years of crawling from hell.

Could the seams of his mind be unraveling again?

Unthinkable thought. Avoided now, interrupted by Margot's footfall on the stairs outside.

She didn't knock, used the key over the sill, and emerged from the vestibule talking about the cold snap. Kellen tried to rise to greet her, but felt glued to his chair.

"My God, it's even colder in *here*," she said, shucking off a fur coat. "How can you stand living in an igloo?" She went to the rad and turned up the heat, then bent and patted Mao, who stood and stretched and prowled about her ankles.

She looked at the mess in the kitchen, then studied Kellen with a cold appraiser's eye. About a week's worth of blond-gray grizzle veiled the angular planes of his cheeks and jaw. Ragged hair curled over tautly muscled shoulders. The whole unkempt package was hunched into a cardigan sweater, an item of clothing ugly and old, tobacco-smelling, showing his shirt at threadbare elbows.

"You look like hell," she said.

"Yeah, well, we're on job action. Work to rule."

"Job action, eh?" She was looking at the half of Stolichnaya on the kitchen counter, the empty soda cans. "Why don't you and your downtrodden comrades just do it, take to the streets, get the goddamn thing over?"

"Yeah, we're going out. Totally illegal strike. But the executive retained this brilliant lawyer, who happens to be a Communist, and she's painted us into a corner with rhetoric that would embarrass Joseph Stalin. Now we have to walk out to save face."

He jerked upright at her touch.

"Relax." Her fingers traced across a shoulder to the spine, and she massaged him gently there. "Your stupid strike, is that all that's eating at you?"

"You've nothing to lose but your brains, I told them." He shrugged. "I'm almost a lone voice."

2

She patted his cheek, then picked up his ashtray. "Are these just today's butts?" He turned, watched her shake it into the wastebasket. "A single drop of pure nicotine on the tongue will kill a hundred-and-seventy-pound man in three minutes, did you know that? Carcinogenocide, pal."

"She's become a fresh-air fascist. This comes from your new boyfriend, right? Mr. Live-Right."

"Let's not," she said. Her face seemed hidden from him, made up, fuchsia lips, mascara in the morning, red hair for the month of February. The Technicolor woman.

Yeah, let's not, he told himself. "So how'd the audition go?"

She became chatty. "I think I've got a shot. They want me back Monday for a longer look. It's only a movie-of-the-week, but I'd *kill* for that part. Jon Voight's in it."

"What do you play?"

"His scheming ex-wife. Don't say I'll be perfect for it."

A helpless, crooked smile broke through the wall of Kellen's malaise. Margot seemed chirpily nervous, putting off the moment. She was high on something, a legal substance, maybe love. Yuppie-love with Mr. Live-Right, clean and keen and carcinogen-free.

"There's a fresh pot on the stove. You still, ah, do coffee? Or does a single drop of pure caffeine also have incredible stopping power?"

He got up. She blocked his way and brushed his cheek with a kiss. "I'll get it," she said.

"I'll get it," he said.

"*I'll* get it!"

Don't be controlling. He subsided to his chair and watched her move briskly to the stove. She was about as skinny as the fire pole by his office door. She'd become an aerobot: dance those ounces off, ladies. She'd been rounder and softer at twenty-five, when he married her. That was ten years ago. It lasted six.

Too many dark rooms, she'd announced. Too many closets with skeletons unshared, unspoken of. Too many veiled, blank years, his shattered past an opaque glass seen through only darkly. The controlling hadn't been meant for her. The controlling was to keep him whole and sane.

As she poured her coffee, she glanced at him, seemed about to say something, then looked away. Say it, he thought. Give with the bad news.

"You don't like Brad, do you?"

"I've never met him. If you like him, I like him."

"You don't like him because you think he's just a rich jock."

"I don't like him because he sells non-union doughnuts."

"He's not what you think. He's gentle, he has a nice, soft personality, he's shy, really, and he, ah, he . . . "

"Yeah?"

"He proposed," she blurted.

Kellen felt an overwhelming sense of resignation, of failure. "Congratulations," he said.

She couldn't hold his eyes, and looked away. "I, ah, can't seem to find my divorce papers. I looked everywhere."

He lit another cigarette, drew on it deeply.

"And, ah, you know, I need them. The papers. To get married. The lawyer said he mailed them. I don't know, maybe when I moved . . . Anyway, you know how totally scattered I am. Unlike you."

"Totally in control."

"So I thought maybe you could lend me yours. The divorce decree, or whatever they call it."

Kellen nodded, feeling a slow, creeping numbness. He walked into the living room, to his desk. Margot followed.

A map of Montreal was pinned to the wall behind the desk. Papers were scattered on it. *Word Processing Made Easy*, volumes one and two, were open in front of, incongruously, an old Remington typewriter. Telephone and answering machine.

Margot sat on the arm of the easy chair. Beside an open book. Camus. *The Plague.*

"You marrying him for his money or his nice, soft personality?" He began going through the drawers of the desk.

"Please, Kellen."

"I'm sorry. I'm being shitty." He shuffled through some files with personal papers. No divorce decree. "I think I may have put it in a box upstairs."

He found himself staring at a snapshot, he and Margot in happier times, hand in hand, smiling, weekend in Quebec City, *Le Vieux-Port*. More pictures. His mother, posed against a tree, trying to smile, but stern behind it, ascetic. Dead three years, a stroke, she had kept his frangible mind together through many troubled years.

Underneath that, another picture: Kellen at ten, wrestling with his father's leg, his father laughing, in an undershirt on the lawn, 1954. He quickly closed the drawer, feeling more pain, a different kind.

"You'll get a chance to meet him. Brad."

"Where?"

"The wedding."

"Thanks, but I'll take a rain check." He stood up and butted his cigarette into an ashtray. "I'd feel like Banquo's ghost. When is it?"

"In two weeks."

He turned to her. "You're pregnant."

She blushed. "It's true," she said, a little faintly.

A vulnerability about her got to Kellen. And he denied the sadness he felt, and put his arms around her. He felt her shiver.

"It's what you always wanted," he said. "I'm happy."

Kellen tried his best to live that lie until she left. He promised he would find the divorce papers, and arrange to get them to her. She stayed for an hour, talking to fill his silence, sharing her hopes for and fears of remarriage and motherhood, but after she left his emptiness took over him. At the end of a stressful marriage, somewhere beyond love, they'd found friendship, and he was going to miss that, miss her visits, her mothering, her caring.

From his kitchen window he watched her slide lithely into the driver's seat of a shiny red Porsche, pre-nuptial gift from the doughnut king, he guessed. The car pulled away from the curb across the street in front of a park where bundled toddlers romped in the snow, watched by mothers. His street, Avenue Ducharme, Outremont: two-storey duplexes square and squat, winding wrought-iron staircases trellised like butterfly wings, the naked skeletons of elm trees in the park, church steeples beyond, the looming gray mountain, and the brilliant cold-blue sky.

He lit another cigarette from the embers of his last one and felt his anxious self plunging into even a more terrible gloom. He felt the old fear, the fear of falling over the edge.

Why? Why now after twenty years? Maybe it was just a fusion of crises – the forthcoming walkout, Borko on his back all day-shift long, the Monster eating his files . . . and now add to that mix the thought of another man's dividing cells in the womb of the woman he'd loved, still loved.

And maybe, somewhere beneath consciousness, he was still being haunted by his father. He'd never worked through the anger; he'd been told that. Until Kellen did so, the ghosts would keep making their regular visits. But whenever he thought of his father, murderous headaches racked him.

He sat at the table and unfolded the newspaper, tried to escape into it. And he saw, near the bottom of the front page, a photograph of Dr. Gregor Satorius, bow-tied, elderly, and stern, staring directly into the camera. CIA MUST DISCLOSE NAMES, LAWYER SAYS. As he looked into Satorius's eyes his mind went back to Coldhaven Manor, and there was nausea . . .

He was jolted by a vision that jumped like a spark across his brain.

Teeth biting rubber, electrodes in your brain, Dr. Satorius says you are sick and this will make you better, and his finger is on the button . . .

Immediately upon that, another flashback.

The smiling man shatters, his odious face disjoins into shards of broken glass, and all that remains are the padded wall and the spotlights and your fear and your despair . . .

Kellen broke out into a hot hard sweat.

"Mlle Paradis, you seek the usual order under Section 398 of the *Code de Procédure* requiring Dr. Satorius to produce documents."

"My clients' files, yes, my Lord." Sarah Paradis had a feeling of foreboding about this chambers application. She'd drawn a bad judge, a reactionary dinosaur.

"Very well, he must produce them at your discovery on Monday. You have the order. So far, so good. But you also want access to the files of his other patients."

"Yes, I do."

"Well, had you not better obtain their consents? You can't just fish through people's private medical files without their leave."

"It would help if we knew who they were."

"Inquire of your clients."

"As your Lordship *might* recall from the affidavits, the patients were kept isolated. They were never allowed to meet. They were numbered by code and only Dr. Satorius has the key to that code. The court will be aware that my clients have very little recall of their own time at Coldhaven, let alone a memory for others they might accidentally have seen there. I'm sure hundreds of persons would come forward if we could reach them."

Urgent words for dead ears. Judge Martin had been a Mulroney bagman downtown, Sherbrooke to Dorchester, shaking down the big law offices. *Monsieur le Patronage.* He'd peddled too much influence to be electable, even in our corrupt democracy, so he was appointed to *la cour supérieure.*

"I don't see it as the court's function to create more business for your already busy practice, Miss Paradis. I can't see that your clients are entitled to any files but their own. You've made this argument very strongly once already."

"Thank you." A waterhead. *Une tête d'eau.*

"On the other motion, Miss Paradis, what is your answer to counsel for the U.S. Department of Justice?"

"What was his question?"

J'ai mon voyage, Sarah Paradis thought. This cucumber has already made his mind up. He'd listened with tender sympathy to the tearful pleas of the lawyers for the American and Canadian governments, co-conspirators here on behalf of the U.S. secret police. State privilege was their plaintive cry, the security of the Western World was at stake. What the CIA had been up to – three and four decades ago – was still a state secret in 1989.

She felt badly for her clients, several of whom were sitting in the gallery watching their brave lawyer try to keep her leaky boat afloat in heavy seas. She couldn't look at them, didn't have the strength.

"If I order officers of the CIA to attend your *interrogatoires* do I not require them to betray their sworn oath of secrecy? Do they not thus commit a federal felony?"

"An oath of secrecy," she said, "cannot be used by a law-breaker as a shield. *Regina versus MacHenry*."

"And how do you answer this: Operation Artichoke, or MK-ULTRA, or whatever you call it, these events ended twenty-five, twenty-six years ago; defendants say there are no witnesses – "

She cut in. "Witnesses? Sure there are witnesses, my Lord. The CIA's own agents. But they won't give us the names . . . "

"You concede they have no documents."

"My Lord, everything went through their shredder in 1973." This was just too exasperating. "They *admit* it."

"I'm bound by the laws of state privilege. I can't force former CIA personnel to appear on commission evidence, and I can't force them to answer your questions."

She let loose her anger now. "These people scream state privilege every time we make an application to discover their case. They've indulged in a most blatant form of stonewalling. We've been at this three years and we can't even set a trial date!"

"Miss Paradis, this is hardly proper reply. You've made your case."

"Well, quite *obviously* I haven't made it very well." She took a deep breath, and let it go in a rush of words. "My Lord, I have a client who suffers acute depressions almost every day, terrible black holes she can't escape from, attacks of anxiety that come out of nowhere, nightmares so horrid she fears falling asleep. She's limped through the last twenty-five years of her life like a cripple maimed in a terrible accident."

Her angry emanations filled the courtroom. She'd at least make the transcript good reading for the appellate court. She directed an open hand toward the gallery, toward her clients.

"I have another client who has regressed to the behavior of a teenager. I have a client who has suffered clinical brain damage and can't recognize his children. I have a client who says he spends every day feeling like a squirrel climbing a cage and thinks the police are tapping his phone. The CIA funded Coldhaven – they paid *that man* to play with people's brains."

She stung a fierce index finger at Dr. Gregor Satorius, seated behind his lawyers. His eyes flashed back at her.

"Now I protest," said his lawyer, rising, flushed.

She turned to him, furious. "Oh, protest away." She ignored him, left him standing, turned back to the judge. "Isn't it obvious? They're manipulating the courts because they're afraid of a trial. Gregor Satorius and the CIA. They're *afraid.* Ever since we started this action, they've been trying to hide behind the cloak of secrecy. A cloak . . . call it what it is – a judicial gown."

"Miss Paradis!" the judge warned.

"I'm sorry, I put it badly, my Lord."

"I ought to ask you to show cause for contempt."

"I was not disparaging the courts. I was disparaging the defendants for hiding behind the skirts of the courts." She looked straight into his eyes with a cool smile. "Figuratively, of course."

The judge seemed to be considering courses of action. The courtroom was silent.

"Is that all?" he said finally.

9

"It's all I'll be saying in *this* court, thank you." She sat. You *morviat*.

"Judgment," intoned the Justice. "The plaintiffs seek firstly for an order from this court for a rogatory commission to receive the testimony of certain persons residing outside the province . . ."

As he delivered judgment, Sarah doodled black circles, then filled them in, little dark assholes on her writing pad. She thought: This cabal of foreign spies with their Montreal brainwashing clinic, an absolute insult to Canadian sovereignty, let alone individual dignity. And the courts say this spy agency has a right to its secrets.

Can't fight the system from inside a courtroom, Marcel used to tell her that. The courts are integral to the class system, they're the grease that keeps it wheeling.

Marcel. Who on Wednesday packed his bags and skulked off after a three-hour screaming match, leaving her in a silent, limp rage, and putting her back on Halcion.

Marcel. Three stormy years. Now Sarah was alone and feeling empty and going on thirty-six.

She wished her day could be over, that she could escape into the weekend. But there were clients all afternoon and the Brotherhood executive at five – the Brotherhood, they've *got* to change that name – then dinner at her parents. She wouldn't have time to change out of her too-too-severe business suit. Well, she'd make it a short night, then curl up with a hot rum and a cool blue pill.

And try to tranquilize her way through the weekend, alone, Marcel-less, and seek strength for Monday. Satorius again that afternoon, his examination for discovery continuing. And she'll probably be in Labour Court that day, too. Busy practice, the judge was right about *that*.

And next week, demonstrations to be organized. The NATO defense ministers at the Bonaventure. The alternative peace rally at the Claude-Robillard. *Sans bon sens*. Too much.

After court recessed, Sarah walked out and into the hall and found Dr. Gregor Satorius standing in front of her, bow tie and black suit, seventy-five and white-haired, but with a back straight as a rake, and with clear blue eyes behind his rimless spectacles. His face was rosy with anger.

"I appreciate that my reputation means nothing to you, Miss Paradis, when matched against your overveening need for media attention." Overveening – after forty years in North America he still made phonetic errors. "But do you wish to destroy everything that I have done? My out-patient program, my clinic for the children?"

"We'll see you on Monday, Dr. Satorius. Please remember to bring my clients' records. Excuse me, I have to talk to my clients."

He moved to block her way. "When those poor people came to me they were damaged, neurotic. You know this. I tried to help them."

"My clients are waiting for me, Doctor." They were huddled in the corridor, watching.

"Your clients . . . you take your instructions from elsewhere, yes?"

"I beg your pardon?"

"I read in a magazine about you. Left-leaning civil rights lawyer. One who regularly visits the shrines of Moscow and Havana. Also *séparatiste*."

"Why is any of that your business?"

"And why is my business yours, mademoiselle?" He turned and walked away.

The self-important, self-justifying former president of the Canadian and American Psychiatric Associations with his guilt-born children's clinic. He will have brought on his own destruction.

Sarah went to her clients and hugged them each in turn, and they hugged her.

The Russian, Yasiliev, picked up a blue line pass, did a deke on Barry Beck, moved in on Lemelin alone, and scored high on the short side. Wally Mandelbaum screamed, "Beck, you flat-footed ox!"

The phone rang three times. Wally, a short man with curly hair and a drooping belly, and a small, knobby, barely goateed chin, didn't move from his easy chair. His recorded voice answered the phone.

"It's Mrs. Juringa. Billy has been pooping in his bed again. When I come in for my Tuesday, can I bring him up?" End of message.

"No, Mrs. Juringa," Wally said, eyes locked onto the TV screen. "It has become obvious you can't bring him up." She had done a lousy job of it so far. Shitting Willie.

Russkies two, NHL zero, midway in the second. If the NHL overpaid so-called all-stars don't at least tie they'll be down three-zip for the series. A close-up of some applauding Muscovite fans, probably Party brass, sitting rinkside. A McDonald's commercial.

Someone buzzed from the front door downstairs. Wally tightened up, gripped the arms of the chair. A couple of more buzzes, impatient. Mrs. Lavoie. Here for her Friday appointment. The men were outside her bedroom window again last night, watching her undress.

He'll phone her later with an excuse. There was this emergency. Psychotic had to be coaxed down from the trusses of the Cartier Bridge.

Beck took aim at a Russian forward bringing the puck over the line. "Nail him!" Wally called. "Way to hit!" The Soviet player took a swipe back at Beck with his stick. "Slashing!" Wally screamed. The referee agreed.

Three rings of the phone. Mrs. Cohen told his machine that Mr. Cohen realizes he needs help. "He's willing to see you, Doctor, at long last."

12

Gretsky, left alone behind the net, hit Loob on the move, and Savard got the rebound and tucked it in. Wally rose to his feet and roared.

Again the phone. Wally would unplug it, the calls were interrupting the flow of the game, its fluid, intricate dance.

"Hi, Wally, it's Kellen. I was just sitting here missing your ugly face. Well, just give me a call. Or I'll call you."

Wally made it to the phone before Kellen hung up.

"Whoa, hey, I'm here. Kellen?"

"Yeah."

"Savard just scored. It's two-one, Soviets."

"Wally, you're alone in your office?"

"Yeah."

"You're watching a hockey game?"

"It's not just a hockey game."

"You need help. Why don't you go home and watch it?"

Lemelin got a piece of it, a slap-shot high.

"Because I don't like messy divorces. What's up, Kel?"

"Thought I'd look in on you this weekend. I . . . ah, just had a couple of flashbacks."

Oh boy, Wally thought. He wrenched himself away from the game.

"Flashbacks? You're sure?"

"Yep."

Wally felt a heaviness, a distress. He'd thought Kellen had beaten them long ago and forever.

For many months after his release from Coldhaven, Kellen's flashbacks – or whatever they were – had come almost daily, unwilled, as if someone were working electrical switches in his head. Over the years they had diminished in frequency and intensity. The last one had been ten years ago.

"They were awfully damn vivid. Two in a row."

"You want to come up?"

"I've got a union meeting. How's tomorrow?"

"I'll free up for you. But brief me, Kel."

"I don't know, I've been feeling really odd. Pressure of work, I guess. Union stuff. Whatever. Then this morning,

Margot came by to tell me she got knocked up by her boyfriend. Must've figured out how to undo his jockstrap. They're getting married. Do I sound bitter? Guess I do."

Wally thought: Margot remarrying – sure, that could have triggered something. After the divorce they'd clung to each other, the friendship of the newly alone. Something strong had always been between them, still was.

But Kellen had been compulsive, controlling; and he hadn't shared, wouldn't talk to her of the wounding events of his life, his father's death, Coldhaven; taboos killed the marriage.

"I went into a deep funk and the flashbacks hit. The man flying apart in the padded room. That was one of them."

Wally could never figure that one out. Kellen had often described this recurring vision; it had the sense of a flashback to a real event but an event of which Kellen had no conscious memory. A young man walking toward him, roughly dressed, a malevolent smile on his scarred face, the man suddenly blowing apart into fragments.

Patients at Coldhaven Manor had been confronted with many curious images as part of the MK-ULTRA program – but what, Wally wondered, was that all about, the smiling scar-faced man disintegrating? A simulation? Perhaps Gregor Satorius had not published all the exotic experiments he was so proud of.

Or was Kellen's image no flashback at all but some terrible, allegorical nightmare?

To Wally, Kellen O'Reilly was still an enigma. Despite all their hard work together, Kellen still denied, denied, denied. To avoid shattering, he'd built from resources deep within him a shield of immense strength, but one Wally feared could crack abruptly under stress.

"The other one was Satorius at the ECT button. I'm strapped down chomping on my rubber mouthpiece and that's the end of the flashback except I think I smelled the odor of deep-fried brain."

"So, ah, why do you think these flashbacks are returning, Kel?"

14

"I don't know. Maybe Margot set them off. But even before she showed up, since yesterday in fact, I'd been having this weird feeling . . . like a sense of danger? It's as if my antennae have been picking up warning signals . . . " His words trailed away. "I'm having a hard time explaining."

"Come on over, watch the rest of the game."

"Listen, I'm fine now. I think. I just wanted to make contact. Tomorrow. I'll phone first."

He rang off. And for a while the game was spoiled for Wally as he fretted about Kellen. Too much a friend to be a good patient, a bright and tough and heroic man with a ravaged mind.

They'd been playground pals in Notre-Dame-de-Grâce, after the O'Reilly family moved there from the Irish quarter, Point St. Charles. They'd remained close through their separate Catholic and Jewish schoolings, and had roomed together as college students at McGill. Wally spent seven years there. Kellen never completed.

He'd been nineteen when he volunteered for Coldhaven; Satorius was offering three hundred bucks per head for a three-month stint in residence there. A little experimental therapy – quite safe – for folks having trouble adjusting to life. Your neurosis been bothering you lately? Come in, we'll fix you right up, and *we* pay *you*.

Wally had tried to dissuade Kellen from signing himself in to Coldhaven, but his young friend claimed he needed the money for tuition – and maybe the good doctor could do something about those bouts of depression. Wally had had no trouble divining their cause: eight years earlier, when Kellen was still in latency, eleven years old, he had locked within himself the pain of his father's violent death, refused to accept it. As he reached his late teens what had been blocked began to erupt in the form of headaches and depressions that affected his schooling.

A kid, he'd trusted the great Satorius to heal his wounds. But Satorius decided to cure Kellen not by working him through his father's death, not by working him through the denial and the anger – but by making him amnesic about

15

the event, by literally wiping his mind of that traumatic time.

In papers later published, Satorius disclosed to the scientific world the true nature of his experiments. He'd devised a means of eradicating patients' memories of the childhood traumas that grow into adult neuroses. A differential amnesia was induced by electroshock – jolts forty times more intense than later came to be acceptable by even the loudest proponents of that perilous therapy. He'd experimented with curare, too, to immobilize patients' bodies, and imposed on them weeks of drugged sleep and sensory deprivation.

Depatterning, Satorius called the process. Followed by repatterning – psychic driving – injecting patients with massive doses of lysergic acid, then bombarding them with recorded messages repeated endlessly on a looped tape through pillow speakers. Messages intended to implant, supposedly, a new and healthier self-image.

Depatterning produced the blank mind and psychic driving implanted the desired new pattern. Born-again narcotherapy.

Wally remembered people – professionals – saying Satorius should get the Nobel. Dr. Gregor Satorius, M.D. and Ph.D., Universities of Budapest and Paris, the father of psychic driving. The Mengele of the mind.

It was years later that the world discovered that his experiments in brainwashing had been funded by the CIA. Many of the human guinea pigs who were his ex-patients were now suing him and his secret sponsor. But not Kellen O'Reilly, who, stubborn and perhaps ashamed, had kept his anguished past even from Margot. Only with Wally Mandelbaum had he shared it.

But although Kellen had talked to Wally about Coldhaven, never had he spoken of his father. Still, to this day, he invariably retreated in anguish when Wally brought up the subject, and complained of headaches. And no one else dared test the topic in his presence. Massive denial syndrome, complicated significantly by the brainwashing at Coldhaven.

The problem in treating Kellen was not that he would not

16

talk about his father's death. He *could* not; it was gone from memory, and Kellen was confused about that, and ashamed.

Kellen made Wally feel helpless, inadequate. One doesn't work with a close friend. It's a rule.

Mario Lemieux swooped in front of the Russian net and tied the game on a tip-in. Wally remained slumped in his chair.

Friday, five p.m.

Outside the windows, the February sun was dying low in the acrid haze of the southwestern sky. Art Salazar, half of Sloukos and Salazar, looked down upon busy Boulevard Saint-Laurent, Montreal's ethnic stewpot, at the shoppers pouring out of Weissenstein Variety, at the lines waiting for the 55 bus, at the cars jammed impatiently on the street.

Standing there in his quilted jacket, as if waiting for the means of propulsion to arrive, Salazar felt a hard week lift from him, and thought of pork chops and ice cream with his family in front of the TV. In the next office, Leo Sloukos, his partner, was tap-tap-tapping at his adding machine.

All day Art Salazar had been getting from Sloukos – as his kids would say – bad energy.

He did not like to leave Sloukos alone in the office. After twenty years the little Greek chiseler had yet to earn his partner's trust.

"Time to call the sheet balanced, eh, Leo?" he called.

No response. Salazar came to Sloukos's open door and saw him at his desk, protectively hunched over some figures, his squeezed face looking like a big hustle was afoot.

"It ain't like you to work late on Friday," Salazar said.

"One of us is gotta pay the rent," Sloukos said without looking up, pecking out numbers.

17

Salazar strolled casually to his partner's desk. "Aren't you scared you'll die of overwork, Leo?"

"Say, ain't you got your AA meeting or something?" Sloukos grumbled, looking up, covering the figures with his arms. When Salazar tried to peek over his shoulder, Sloukos turned the paper over.

"Don't get close," Sloukos said. "I don't know what you got."

"I been your partner what seems like a dog's life, twenty years, and you keep secrets from me?"

"Because for twenty years you been stealing my clients. I forever rue the day."

"You're cooking up something," Salazar said. "A client's books. I don't wanna know about it, just don't drag the good name of the firm into it."

He gruffly walked from Sloukos's inner office, to the front door. "It's five o'clock, I don't wanna miss the traffic rush."

Sloukos, a slight but paunchy man, obstinate in manner, stared resolutely at the frosted glass of the front door while Salazar's footsteps retreated down the stairs to the street. He looked at the backsides of the letters painted there. WE SPEAK ENGLISH, they said. ICI PARLONS FRANÇAIS, HABLA ESPAGNOL, PARLIAMO ITALIANO, FALAMOS PORTUGUES, Μιλαμε αγγλικα.

He checked his watch, five-o-eight. He'd worried that Salazar would never leave, this snoop who should have his own business to mind.

He turned his paper face up. Twenty years at twenty-five thousand a year, plus a fair interest of median prime less two percent compounded annually, and something off for good will, and you round it out to an even, easy two million dollars – U.S. dollars – that's what they owe. And of course an equal amount for Bob the lawyer.

So the figure at the bottom of the page was a four and six zeros. Bob Champlain and he would have to kick back a third to their silent partner. But Rudy and the boys wouldn't have to know about that part of the business.

Sloukos noticed he was beginning to smell a little of his sweat, but kept reminding himself he held all the trumps, aces, and face cards – not to worry.

He heard the sounds of many shoes coming up the stairs, and took several deep breaths before getting up and opening the front door. He saw them advancing in single file, chortling at one of Alabama Bill's jokes.

"And the doctor says, 'Nurse, you got it all wrong, I told you to slip off his spectacles.' " Hoots of laughter.

Bill waved at Sloukos. "There he is, Leo the Lion."

Alabama Bill he didn't know so well, or Chip. Rudy Meyers he knew better, along with Mick Crowder, who was basically Meyers' asshole buddy, his guru-worshipper. Mystical Rudy, life is theater.

Sloukos grabbed Meyers' hand, the one not holding that expensive-looking attaché case, and pulled him in. "Rudy, how are you?"

Meyers' wispy Ronald Coleman mustache seemed pasted onto his upper lip. A wide, friendly moon-face. He took off his toque and swept a hand over his bald scalp.

"Good, Leo, good. I am aces."

Years before they had been young and handsome, but now baldness and beer bellies were the general rule – they looked like average business guys, officers of the local Rotary just back from holidays with their tans. In their shiny new padded ski jackets they could be on their way to Mont-Tremblant, or somewhere, except for their street shoes.

"It's f-f-frigging cold up here," said Mick Crowder, a stutterer, a smaller man than the others, only five-ten.

Chip said cheerfully, "You and Bob should of come to Florida, talked to us there. Where it's friendly."

"Yeah, and warm," said Alabama Bill. A lineman in his college days, he, too, looked jovial, and gave off an odor of maybe too many airline drinks. His red ski jacket didn't quite fit, it was tight across the shoulders like he bought it too fast off the rack.

Last through the door, Eddie the Cube Comacho beamed with affection at Sloukos, they had always got along fine.

"Eddie, business has been good," Sloukos said, patting him on the belly.

"How's yours been, Leo?" Eddie said.

Sloukos closed and locked the door and motioned the five men to seats in his office.

"Tough, Eddie, like I said in the communication." He turned to Meyers, glancing down to the attaché case on his lap, and took a deep breath. No more rehearsing, this was live.

His words came rushing out. "As friends we gotta be blunt. Bob and me, we got stiffed on the deal, the payments weren't supposed to quit only after five years. We did the paper, handled all the accounts, did everything like we was asked to."

He paused, looked from face to face. "We been patient. But we had to set a deadline, wasn't fair to either you nor us letting things slide."

Sloukos picked up the sheet of paper, the bill for unpaid services, and handed it to Meyers.

"I worked up some numbers here."

Meyers stared at those numbers without speaking for a long thirty seconds, then looked up, silent and angelic.

"One way to see it," Sloukos said, "is it's like you boys built up some good investments off our unpaid accounts. It's like a loan, money owed and not remitted, it should be paid back with interest."

Silence. Sloukos became effusive. "Eddie, that marina in Orlando, it's worth more than ten times this. Bill, you own a hotel or two. And I *heard* what you been up to, Rudy. Two million for Bob and me each is all we're talking."

In response, just smiles. Smiles which didn't make him feel relaxed.

"We'd make more than that, Bob and me, we wrote a book about what we found out, eh? Okay, you say nobody's gonna believe, but we got the evidence." He issued a stale, dry laugh. "Hell, we figured it was something weird but nothin' like *that*." He tried to laugh and his voice cracked.

"Where is the merchandise your, ah, communication alluded to?" Meyers asked.

"Bob has, ah . . . Let's say we can access it when we have to."

Another silence.

"Access what, exactly?" Meyers asked.

"Well, this item . . . remember, you called, wanted us to help get rid of everything? Well, we took all the files and shit out to the incinerator. Except for this particular item. Which we found." His voice trailed away into a hush, then he added, "The thing is, we have to hang onto it so as to avoid any feeling of insecurity."

Sloukos felt his strength draining under the warmth of their smiles. "The thing is, also, if anything happens to Bob or me it follows like the night and day the goodies will get in the wrong hands."

"How have you got that f-figured?" said Mick Crowder.

Meyers held up a hand to silence him.

"I'm a little loath to go into details," Sloukos said.

"You're a little loath." Meyers reached up abruptly, and with a muscled right arm grabbed Sloukos by the knot of his red-striped tie, and jerked the little man forward to within inches of his smile. "Yes, that is a well-chosen word. You are a little loath, Sloukos."

Sloukos found his arms pinned by Alabama Bill behind him. He choked, tried to cough, his eyes bulging from the pressure of Meyers' middle knuckle on his Adam's apple. Meyers pulled him roughly down to his knees, then placed the thumb of his left hand against the side of one of the accountant's eyes.

Sloukos, short of breath and red of face, tried to urge pleas from his throat, but they escaped only as throttled grunts.

"Do you know what the ancient masters teach?" Meyers said, with his cheery smile. "Do you know what they say to do with greedy little loaths?"

Sloukos saw fireworks from the pressure on his eyeball.

"They teach that greedy men must be illuminated by bold action, forcing them to look inward." With an expert tug of his thumb Meyers scooped out the eyeball, and blood gushed

21

from the socket, the accountant's face compacting into a little ball of pain. Meyers loosened the grip on his throat.

"Talk to us, Leo."

Thirteen people on the negotiating committee, to Kellen O'Reilly an unlucky number to be in the boardroom in so ugly a mood. Thirteen jean jackets, sweaters, and parkas, the nine men unshaven and unshorn, the four women lank-haired and pale, no makeup. And then there's Ms. Sarah Paradis, in her Italian black twill suit with the slit skirt, and the black silk blouse. Lady in black, impeccable, poised, little Ms. Go-for-broke, lawyer for the Brotherhood.

"I know it's not my place to advise about tactics," she said.

"But you're going to anyway," Kellen said. He got a frosty smile from her.

Kellen was in a foul mood and his fuse was short. His vodka headache was down to a low, rhythmic pounding. The news from his ex-wife still festered; the hallucinations still clawed at the back of his mind.

Sarah Paradis looked coolly about the room with piercing eyes that mismatched her pouting Gallic mouth. "The point is we made the threat, and we have to make it good. They'll come at us with fangs bared if they smell the slightest scent of weakness."

Two shop stewards shouted their agreement.

"Order," yelled Fernand Ouimet, the president, a hairy bear with a rich bass voice. "Brother Taillefeur, Brother O'Reilly, then me."

Taillefeur was O'Reilly's unlikely ally here, anti-strike, but for different reasons. Kellen suspected him of kiting messages to management. A racist to boot, who liked to get

22

loaded with the boys in the local tavern, then go out and find black kids to beat on.

"I don't want any part of something that's illegal," he said, his expression pained and pious. "If we're not careful – "

"We're not talking about an illegal strike," Sarah Paradis said sharply. "Officially, we're talking about a very long, extraordinary general meeting. All members can attend, and it's permitted under the contract."

"They'll try to break the union if we all try to walk out, Miss Paradis," Kellen said. "Work to rule, sure, as long as it takes, but – "

Ouimet broke in. "Kellen, she's right," he boomed in his rough, country *joual*. "You can't fight them by offering up our backsides like beaten dogs. Three more suspensions! I say we call the members out Monday night. I say we ask the members, let's show we got balls."

"Oh, let's please not," said one of the women, and there was strained laughter. Not shared in by Sarah, a serious type, Kellen thought, your typical strident humorless feminist.

"We walk off, we lose public support," Kellen said. "What little we have left."

Sarah said crisply, "If we don't go out we lose credibility, and we lose the struggle."

Kellen could feel himself losing his self-possession. "Who's *we*, Miss Paradis? I haven't heard you offering to carry any picket signs."

Her eyes flashed at him: "I've been working twenty hours a day!"

"I'm not interested in having some rich, elitist, lady lawyer with her leftover Marxist dogmas telling me when to go on strike."

She stood up, leaned forward on her hands, thrust an angry chin at him, and said in English, as if better to make him understand:

"Listen, *Brother* O'Reilly, neither my financial worth nor my politics are any of your goddamn business, and you can keep the sexist crap to yourself!"

A silence closed in.

"Sorry, I lost my head," Kellen said. "I didn't mean to call you a lady."

Sarah Paradis slammed her briefcase shut and pulled her coat from the hanger behind her.

"I don't come here to – "

Kellen lost four seconds of this.

You run down the hallway, you run, you run, men behind, terror within, you force your way out the door, greenness and sunshine and trees' distorted shapes . . .

" – while some total *drip* of an arrogant, macho bigot tries to smear me . . . "

Something put her into a mid-air stall, maybe his sudden look of confusion and shock. He became aware of Ouimet talking to her gently, pulling her back to her seat.

"Question," said someone.

"Brother Picard has called the question," said Ouimet.

Friday, five-thirty p.m.

After the meeting, Sarah Paradis hurried to her car, embarrassed: that had been a ghastly scene, she'd found herself almost frothing at the mouth. A bad day. A bad week. Nervous exhaustion was the phrase her doctor kindly used.

Marcel's fault. It was gall enough that he'd gone off with another, but into the arms of that faithless Guatemalan bitch? If Rosia were so fierce in her love of the FAR, why wasn't she in the mountains fighting for them? Instead of selling revolution in safe old Montreal, passing the hat, not to mention the cunt.

She'd never trusted Marcel. But she'd trusted Rosia, had confided to her all her thoughts.

God, what must her clients have thought of her in there? Flailing away at that *pissette* Kellen O'Reilly – but what had

24

she said that so deflated him? She remembered the shock on his face when she shouted at him. Shock . . . and something else.

He had spent the rest of the meeting in what seemed a frightened daze. Because she called him a total drip? It was probably the ultimate insult to a man.

Dinner with her parents tonight, one of their rare winter visits from the Bahamas. Senator Paradis will have his daggers ready, honed sharp with sarcasm. "I can't help it, my dear, but when you speak of the movement, I always associate that with the bowels."

She unlocked her car and sat, dug into her purse for the Halcions her doctor gave her, and found their little plastic container. It was empty. Popping these little blue ovals like Cheezies. She found the prescription and put it on the dashboard with the empty container.

The engine wouldn't turn over. All she got was a rasp and a grunt.

How could her little Yugo do this to her? A product of socialism that her father derided and made jokes about, it had never let her down before.

"This is Houston," she said. "Do we have ignition?"

Nothing.

She saw Kellen O'Reilly walk past, bundled into his old military coat, little blond ponytail stuck out from under his toque.

She tried the engine again. Grind, clunk.

He turned around and looked at her for a few seconds, contemplatively, then came to her window.

"Can I ask you a question?" he said.

Here it comes. Are you really a Communist?

"Okay."

"How long have your headlights been on?"

"Oh my God."

"You got jumpers?"

"No." She added, "I'll call a garage."

But O'Reilly was already out on the street, whistling for a cab.

"I can look after it," she called.

He ignored that, and she sat there like an accident victim while Kellen calmly directed a competent little movie, bringing a taxi alongside and buying a jump from the driver.

After: "Can I drive you somewhere?"

"I want the walk."

She studied him. Sad-eyed, distant, a long bony face that would be handsome were it not so ravaged. "I'm sorry I blew up," she said. "That was a terrible scene. I really feel very stupid."

"It's okay."

He was an ingrate not to have apologized himself, like a, well, a man. She shouldn't have pandered to him.

"How'd your court case work out?"

"Today?"

"The Coldhaven case. Your motion to examine the CIA."

"I lost it. It's been an off-day."

"Tell me about it."

She misconstrued that. "It would take a week."

He smiled.

"Come on. Get in."

He said in French, "North Outremont. It's probably out of your way."

It was out of her way. Chauffeuring this chauvinist home meant setting herself up to be late for dinner with her parents.

"Not at all."

Friday, five-fifty-five p.m.

R.W. (Bob) Champlain, *avocat*, maintained an office on Fairmount, east of Outremont, under the north slope of the mountain. Once he'd had a clientele of spenders – many of the big boys used him for minor things like bail – but lately it's been down to little old ladies phoning up to get their wills changed, or you're suing for bad debts you never collect and never get paid for on the contingency, or you get unemployed guys with their wife problems and landlord problems.

It got so bad, last week he laid off his full-time girl and hired a cheap young do-everything just for the afternoons.

He was watching her at the work counter. She seemed like a nice little *pouponne*, but an ice cube, he thought.

Jeanne-Marie, nineteen, a month out of business school, felt Champlain's awful presence and looked up to see him watching her from his inner office doorway, standing there in his beaver coat.

She quickly returned her gaze to the counter, and continued to seal and stamp the day's envelopes. *Un gros jambon*, she thought. The lawyer's lard and his red, upraised snout gave him a Porky-Piglike look. In her view, however, he lacked Porky's endearing qualities.

Champlain sneezed, and Jeanne-Marie flinched as a spray of bacteria shot from his snout. He applied a large handkerchief to his nostrils, and moved toward her, making muffled talk.

"I'm expecting a large fee this weekend." He stood over her shoulder, lowered his voice. "Maybe I could give you a raise."

His hand brushed down her backside, and she shriveled into herself.

"You'd like that, eh? A big raise from me?"

She moved away, began piling the envelopes neatly, bundling them.

Enfant de chienne, she mouthed to herself.

Champlain thought, a cold little popsicle.

Stepping outside his little street-front, he entered the early night of winter, buried his ears into his fur collar, and turned into the wind to walk to his car. Soon he must call Leo Sloukos – from the anonymous safety of a coin telephone – and ask him how everything went.

Bob Champlain had devised the strategy. He was the keeper of the key. Leo had the more dangerous role – talking

27

turkey with the Americans. Those are tough guys. But what can they do? The story would go right into the homes of the world.

He wiped his nose and trudged down the salt-wet sidewalk. His car was at the curb, fifty feet up the street. Behind it was parked a brown GMC Safari van, its engine running, its lights out. In the back of the van were five pairs of skis and ski boots. Alabama Bill pulled an automatic pistol from inside one of the ski boots, and passed it to Crowder. He pulled out a second gun from another boot, and ejected a clip. He could tell by its weight that it was full, and he shoved it back in.

The sliding side door of the van was narrowly open, and Chip held the handle of the door, tensing himself to throw it open. Beirut-style snatch and grab, interrogations to follow.

In the front passenger seat, Meyers was twisted around, slunk into his seat, watching Champlain approach. But the lawyer stopped. He let forth a powerful sneeze. He turned in his tracks and went the opposite way.

"Where's he goin'?" said Eddie Comacho, at the wheel.

"Don't lose him," Meyers said softly, urgently.

Comacho groaned. Okay, Rudy, what did the ancient masters say we gotta do now? Lay out your next brilliant plan, Rude. He waited until a car passed, then backed up in a half-circle, a bootlegger's turn, trying to keep one eye on the traffic and one on Champlain, who disappeared into the swirl of people at Fairmount and Park.

Friday, six p.m.

He hadn't uttered a peep since he snapped his seat belt shut. Hadn't said, for instance, Thanks.

In fact, he hardly seemed aware of her. He seemed distracted, edgy, *en démanche*.

28

Sarah listened to the hum of the hot-air fan.

"Is your car out of commission?" she said.

"I don't have a car."

All right. Now ask me a question.

Sure is cold out.

Yep.

He stared away from her at the balconied apartments and the snow-gray parks and churchyards on Boulevard Saint-Joseph.

Who was the gloomy specter she'd seen peering from his eyes at the meeting?

"Why do you not have a car?"

"I don't like to drive."

He picked up the empty plastic container on her dashboard, looked at the label, and put it back. The snoop. She was embarrassed.

"Thanks for reminding me," she said. "There's a little drugstore up here on Park. I'll be just a minute."

She caught the light and maneuvered past some road repair machinery and parked twenty meters from the drugstore. She picked up the prescription and the empty container.

"You hooked on those things?" he said.

She stopped the engine and sat quietly for several seconds. A fat man in a beaver coat walked by them honking into a big, caked handkerchief, and went into the pharmacy.

She said, finally, "I've been under a little stress."

"Tell me about it." He smiled.

Tell him. An almost nervous breakdown. Yes, tell him about Marcel and Rosia, comrades who betrayed her.

"I won't bore you with it," she said.

He smiled again as if they were sharing a secret. He really must think he's ravishing with his ponytail and sad-puppy blue eyes.

She got out clumsily, her black slit skirt riding up, and saw he was looking at her stockinged thigh, and she felt herself blushing.

Tranquillity will be dispensed to her from this little store, La Pharmacie Lagasse.

Kellen watched her swish toward it with a thin-legged, fluid stride. The very untouchable daughter of Senator Emile-Roth-burn Paradis. Amusing herself by being a socialist labor lawyer before she retires to her estate and marries a Molson. Nervous breakdown was his guess. It's why she exploded at the meeting.

He fished with his fingers through the silver paper in his pack of Player's, came up empty, crumpled the box. Patting his pockets, he found another cigarette pack but it was exhausted, too, and he muttered a soft profanity. He opened the window and leaned his head out, and called to a couple of beat patrolmen about to jaywalk Park Avenue.

"One of you gentlemen have a cigarette?"

They watched for a break in the traffic. "*Dans le cul*," said one. "Call operator for room service, *tchomme*."

"Give me your number, you dumb clod," Kellen said, but they were halfway across the street.

Kellen fumbled through the ashtray, dredging up two old, wrinkled butts smoked to the cork.

Bending down, squinting into the glove compartment, he missed seeing four men in ski masks jump from a slowing van and race into the drugstore.

He pulled out a small, bent cigarette from under one of her cassette tapes.

"Bingo," he said softly.

Hand-rolled and limp, it's better than nothing, but he's got to start cutting back, his throat is like a smoldering log in the morning.

He held it closer to his eyes: a joint.

He grunted an oath and got out of the car.

In the drugstore, Sarah was handing up her prescription when she saw Monsieur Lagasse's face go from pink and smiling to white and astounded, then heard a loud voice behind her: "On the floor! All of you!"

She felt puzzled, sensed incongruity. She heard sounds of shuffling and scraping, saw the pharmacist's hands go up.

"You, out from behind there."

She turned to see, waving a large automatic pistol at them, a man wearing a happy-face ski mask.

30

Monsieur Lagasse came from behind the counter, and went down on his stomach, and Sarah got down beside him. A robbery, my God, while fighting a nervous breakdown and waiting for the Halcion, she's in the middle of a robbery.

There were other armed men here, at least two; a purple ski mask and a Canadian-flag ski mask moving around, and behind the counters, someone guarding the door. Bright eyes and hard mouths through the ski-mask holes. Bulky, shiny new jackets, but, oddly, ordinary leather street shoes.

Despite her fear she knew that as a lawyer she must be a good witness, must remember the details. There were five other customers: two middle-aged women near the prescription counter; an elderly man, and with him, a seven-year-old girl, doe-eyed and panicky, possibly his granddaughter, lying near the checkout; another man, portly, lying between aisles. The cashier, a young woman, was somewhere out of view. Shelves against the front windows prevented passersby outside from looking in.

The portable radio near the cash register was on. Sarah could hear the disk jockey – a traffic report. The Laurentian Autoroute was getting back to normal.

"Everyone take it easy," said the happy face in a calm, controlled voice. No French accent, perhaps the slightest American drawl.

The man between the aisles was Bob Champlain, who was on his stomach beside some cold and allergy remedies, and was clutching a white bottle with a pump, Drixoral nose spray. He looked anxiously up at the man in the smiling mask.

"We will all take it easy," he said. "Don't worry, I'm a lawyer, I know how these things work. If everyone does what they say, no one gets hurt, eh?"

"You have it right, counselor," Happy Face said.

Peering to her left, Sarah could see that the monster wearing the red maple leaf – he was at least two hundred and fifty pounds – was waving a gun at the cashier. "I said, on the *floor!*"

"Don't hurt me," she said, in French, repeating it.

31

Champlain howled to her in French: "*Mautadit!* Get your *pantoufle* on the floor, you stupid bitch!"

Happy Face swung his gun at Champlain.

"I'm trying to help," he said in English, frantically.

From the radio: "Only two lanes open south on the Cartier, looks like a bad one; what passes for a police force in this town is trying to clear it."

"There's only a couple of grand here," came a man's voice from the area of the till.

Happy Face said, "Go through the lawyer's pockets."

"I never carry more than fifty." Champlain already had his wallet out, and he tossed it to Happy Face, who removed the fifty, and threw the wallet away, then kneeled down and banged Champlain in the back with the barrel of his gun. The large lawyer issued a small shriek.

Maple Leaf knelt and went through Champlain's pockets, and pulled out a set of keys on a ring, flipped through them, tossed them back at him.

That is the scene which instantly described itself to Kellen as he stepped into the store, a view between two rows of shelves: a man on his belly, two men in masks bending over him with automatics.

His scope shot wide open: others on the floor, more guns.

At the same instant, from the corner of his eye: a black ski mask.

"This is a holdup!" the man said. "Get your face on the floor!"

Kellen slowed to a stop and turned to look at the man, then down at his sidearm – a semiautomatic.

"I said get down!"

A moment passed.

"You folks sitting in your cars and cursing, keep the faith and love your fellow man – this is Henry Highbeam Jones looking after you with some olden goldies."

"I'll get down. Just say where."

"On the goddamn floor!"

Four in their team. He couldn't help thinking that was a lot of manpower for a little drugstore. Kellen could see Sarah's feet near the counter, her high leather boots. Druggist, six others.

"Let's go back to when life was simple. Here's the King with 'Devil in Disguise.'"

Kellen was moving slowly down to his knees. It was as if the voice of Elvis sent him away.

"Remember that he killed your father." Words soft and insinuating. The man's scarred face comes toward you, the gun bucks in your hand and his cruel smile disintegrates in an explosion of glass, a swirl of dust, you're hot under spotlights, melting . . .

As Kellen returned to the Pharmacie Lagasse he was diving into a shelf laden with hygienic sprays and roll-ons, toppling it over, then taking down a whole row of shelves, twisting, rolling, and Black Mask was firing, once, twice. And Kellen thought he was hit, felt a wetness beneath him, and was assailed by a dense, sweet perfume, not his blood, a broken bottle, and he was somersaulting in his old army coat into an open aisle.

There, the black-masked man was neatly framed between the tampons and the shampoo. Kellen shot him three times through the heart with his Smith and Wesson special.

And was moving again as the man in the happy-face mask fired, sending bottles spinning in the air behind Kellen, who dove again, getting off one shot while airborne – and, with ninety percent blind luck and ten percent marksmanship, his bullet shattered the man's gun hand.

No screaming in pain from Happy Face, only an expletive as his pistol was swept from his hand.

Sarah, her head bubbling with fright, pried her eyelids open and turned her head and saw Kellen's eyes peering from behind the overturned rack of perfumes and lotions.

"Montreal police. Drop the guns, you're under arrest."

A voice said from above her, "I'll kill her."

She looked up: the behemoth in the red maple leaf mask. His huge gun pointing at her head.

She felt the blood rushing away, dizziness.

"We'll kill them all," said Happy Face, holding his injured hand.

33

"Let these guys go!" Champlain shouted to Kellen, hysterical, lying prone, his face wet and white. "For the sake of Jesus, mother of God, let them go!"

Kellen's mind sped like a runaway train. Three guns: one on Sarah, one on the fat man, one on him.

"We'll execute them," Happy Face said steadily. "In turn. Starting in five seconds." Through the mouth hole, Kellen could make out a thin smile. An unnatural, unhealthy smile.

Kellen looked at Sarah, at the seven-year-old girl. Two long seconds.

"One hostage," he said. "Leave him at the front door."

Happy Face, still holding his bloodied hand, searched the floor with his eyes, which settled on his gun, a few feet away.

"Touch it and I'll take you out for keeps," Kellen said.

Happy Face froze, slowly straightened up. "Take the man with the nose spray, and take the little lady in black." Still the smile.

Maple Leaf reached down for Sarah's arm.

"Get your fucking hand off her!" Kellen spat. Lower, controlled, careful, "One hostage, that's all."

Sarah shivered as Maple Leaf took his gun from her. The other customer, the poor, runny-nosed lawyer, squealed a torrent of words as two of the masked men pulled him to his feet.

"Hey, why me? Take her, someone else." Then, with unction, "Listen, I'm on your side, I defend guys like you, my name is Bob, Bob Champlain, everyone settle down, nobody go crazy, I'll just escort them outside."

"We have a vehicle," Happy Face said calmly. "We hold him until we're in it. We kill him if you move toward the door."

They led Champlain quickly toward it, a gun at the lawyer's head, two others pointing at what they could see of Kellen: he had crouched his way to a safer position by the prescription counter.

"I'm a little guy with a little practice, they don't want to hurt me."

In his panic, Champlain felt he was still dealing with a

simple hit on a drugstore, and didn't get the big picture until Happy Face said softly, as they were out the doorway, "Okay, Bob, where's the key?"

"Rudy . . . " Champlain gasped. "That you?"

"After we gouged his eye out, Leo just couldn't stop talking," Meyers said.

The GMC Safari van, Eddie Comacho at the wheel, raced toward them, the big side door sliding open. Pedestrians were backing away, starting to run.

Champlain tried to bolt, and skidded doing so, his feet coming up from under him on a slick of ice, causing him to cascade to the sidewalk, pulling Mick Crowder over him, his purple mask twisting about, covering his eyes.

"Get him in here!" Comacho shouted from the wheel. "We're minus twenty-seven already! Now!"

But the vast bulk of Alabama Bill, in the maple leaf mask, collapsed onto the tangle as Champlain screamed for someone to help him.

"Let's go! Now!" Comacho urged. Distant sirens wailing.

"Shoot him in the mouth, Mick," said Meyers.

As Meyers and Alabama Bill scrambled into the van, Crowder, on top of Champlain, jammed his pistol barrel under the lawyer's chin. "Want to l-l-live, where's the key?"

"In my safe!" Champlain croaked. "I'm the only one knows the comb – "

Crowder's bullet tore through throat and brain and he got up, and leaped into the van as it accelerated, spinning, catching pavement.

Kellen was halfway to the front door, and fired one dangerous shot through it, splintering glass; he may have hit the back panel of the van, he wasn't sure, but the vehicle was around a corner before he reached the street. Quebec plates, blue on white, but he didn't get the numbers.

From the other direction Kellen saw, running toward him, guns in nervous hands, the two patrolmen who had earlier walked by him in the darkness.

They stopped, looked at Champlain's body, at Kellen holding his service revolver which was pointed at the stars.

"Detective Lieutenant, sir, ah, what happened?"

"Cordon it off and call in."

A squad car screamed braking to a halt.

In the store, Sarah had climbed wobbly legged to her feet, and was steadying herself against the prescription counter and staring with horror at the carnage of drugs, cosmetics, chocolate bars, and bodies.

"And I'll be calling *you*, so stick by your phone because Henry Highbeam Jones has got records to give away all evening long."

She was aware of the others rising, slowly, silently like ghosts, more policemen coming in, Kellen O'Reilly with them, slipping his gun into the holster under his armpit, strolling up to her.

"You all right?" he said.

"Yes." Lying.

"Well, thanks for the ride home."

She abruptly felt a surge of relief from fear, and hysterically began to laugh. He reeked of the most vulgar perfume. What are you wearing, my dear? Evening in Tijuana, Tropical Nights in the Sultan's Garden. Bullets and bodies and blood, she heard her voice pealing like cathedral bells and became dimly but terribly aware that she was out of control, in hysteria, laughing, weeping, cracking up, the mad scene from Lammermoor in La Pharmacie Lagasse.

Kellen watched a female constable walk her slowly to a chair. He went up to the empty cash register, where the druggist and his girl were standing, staring at Sarah.

"Can someone sell me a pack of cigarettes?" he asked.

Alphonse Bague, owner-operator of the number eight car of Le Top Dog Taxi Cie, warned Kellen: "Mr. Weatherman say he fallin' all way down to twenty below tonight."

That's Celsius. Multiply by five, divide by nine, and add thirty-two. What the hell does that come to? Kellen couldn't work it out. The world was once a simpler place, yards, feet, and Fahrenheit.

Alphonse grimly recalled Mr. Weatherman's forecast: "He say worse tomorrow, a pow'ful Ar'tic mass from Bafflin' Island." He held Canadian winters in ghoulish awe and continually switched dials to get more weather reports. In Haiti it had been warm.

"Some years you get calls about frozen taxi drivers," Kellen said. "In stalled cars. They say it's not a bad way to go."

Alphonse stopped at the corner near Station Twenty-six, and Kellen signed a chit.

He got out, felt the bitter icy air and smelled the acid in it, the winter smell of Montreal when winds don't blow. Chemicals from Lachine sitting in poisonous suspension in the air.

There was something else tingling in the air, crawling into Kellen's skin, something that was causing all these prickles of anxiety, maybe causing those ominous, baleful returns to a blank, black past, messages flashing back from Coldhaven. And during his tense and nearly sleepless night, there had come sounds as well, sounds just under hearing's threshold, vague whispers, coded messages. Were these signs of a nervous breakdown . . . or, worse, a creeping psychosis?

He had to see Wally.

He sought inner resources; he had to pull himself together, get into a working mind-set, become a cop again, investigate deaths.

Remember that he killed your father . . .

He willed the voice away.

Brittle and pale was the morning sun, sending angled shadows around the buildings and utility poles of Boulevard Saint-

Laurent, the north-south spine of Montreal, Kellen's street. He breathed it and ate it: his seigniory, from the Place de la Justice in the Old City through the neon glitter of Chinatown and up the Tenderloin, french fries and steamies, and into the ethnic helter-skelter of markets and restaurants of the upper Main; the schmatta, the garment district, the smell of hot bagels in the cold winter air; north to the swish Franco boutiques of Laurier.

Boul Saint-Laurent. His murder beat for the last nineteen years, most of them spent working out of here, Station Twenty-six, this ponderous, pollution-blackened stone structure of a century's age: originally – proud then – a fire hall.

Cold out here, but it will be hot inside.

Off-duty men and women of the Montreal Urban Community Police Brotherhood were giving leaflets to passersby. Others carried signs: POLICE DEATHS UP, FAMILY BENEFITS DOWN. WE KEEP YOUR STREETS SAFE, HELP KEEP OUR FAMILIES SECURE. To warm themselves, they'd lit an oil-drum stove by the alley behind the station – offending a city ordinance; Borko must be having a rabbit.

One of them, a young constable, said, "Great work, sir."

A kid. Freezing his butt for better pensions for veterans and a restructured welfare plan for families. The issues weren't just bread and butter; the Brotherhood was happy to take a simple cost-of-living raise. They sought to cut down on overtime in return for more family time. The executive committee of the Montreal Urban Community administration was as unbudging as a stone Buddha. Hold the line. Cut back. Pare down. Less government is good government. The mayors of Greater Montreal were prepared to stand firm on behalf of the beleaguered taxpayer. In this, an election year.

Kellen had been born in Point St. Charles, the P'int, the working-class Irish quarter where unions were bigger than the church. He knew his trade union activism had ruined his chances for promotion. He wasn't going to make captain. His militant dad never did either, it's no big deal.

Remember that he killed your father.

Shut it from your mind.

He went inside and got clenched fists from the long-haired, whiskered cops, and thumbs up tight to the chest, congratulations, good luck.

The old fire hall's garage doors had many years ago been bricked shut, and the fifty-foot-high interior served as the working guts of Station Twenty-six. Most of the main floor was open space, but the homicide office had been endowed with the partial privacy afforded by a new, ugly, and doorless drywall renovation. However, to the unceasing distress of its staff, the office lacked a ceiling.

Just outside the homicide area were a spiral iron staircase and a fire pole, both climbing to a balustrade and several offices behind it. In front of the open door of one of those offices, at the railing and just above the roofless homicide area, a uniformed Captain Borko, the station commander, was lurking vulture-like, waiting for Kellen's arrival. He tried to catch his eye, and waved, but Kellen didn't look up.

In the homicide section were several detectives, and assorted crooks, witnesses, suspects, finks, and other civilian gentry, complaining, being interviewed, being led in handcuffs, sipping out of plastic cups the watery coffee dispensed by a rusting, battered drink machine. Kellen sat down at his desk, upon which crouched the Monster, his ARC 386 computer terminal, its cursor blinking, anxious, hungry to begin the daily humiliation.

Raolo Basutti, in blue jeans and gray denim jacket, was at the next desk taking statements from Monsieur Lagasse, the pharmacist, and from his cashier. He excused himself and rode his swivel chair close to Kellen. He was thirty-eight, seven years Kellen's junior, compact, energetic, cheerful, a burly old-country mustache sprouting from below his sharp Italian nose like a gesture of defiance.

He sniffed with it. "You smell nice," he said.

"Eau de drugstore." Kellen had showered well and long. The perfume clung to him yet, sweet, mucous. "I see Borko's in full battle gear today. Who does he want to declare war on?"

39

"You. Feelin' all right?"

"I'm okay."

He'd been two hours longer at the drugstore, orchestrating things for the technical people. He'd been too busy to attend to Sarah, who finally settled down. After signing her statement, she'd been fetched away abruptly in her father's limousine. Kellen had seen the senator's shadowy figure in the backseat. Old resource-based money, pulp and iron and asbestos.

Sarah Paradis and her tranqs and her causes, an enigmatic and interesting lady. Correction. Woman.

Raolo said, "Kel, why'd you take that chance?"

Kellen licked dry lips. "I don't know."

Raolo didn't pursue the matter of his partner's well-being. With Kellen, he never pursued such things. Sunday, tomorrow, was a day off for both of them; a morning sled-and-toboggan outing was planned, up the mountain – him and Kel and the missus and Mario, Kellen's eleven-year-old godson. It would get Kel's mind off things; he loved Mario, loved to horseplay with him. Mario made him happier and younger.

Kellen looked at the unkempt pile of papers and pictures on his desk. "What was the take?"

"Just under three grand."

"Only junkies hit drugstores. This was the kind of operation you mount for a bank."

He spread out the photographs. Various angles of a dead man on a morgue slab. About fifty, fifty-five. A fair bit of muscle gone to fat. If it weren't for the three ugly holes in his chest, he'd look like somebody's Uncle George.

"Nice tan."

Borko called from above, "Lieutenant O'Reilly, can you drop up for sixty seconds?"

Kellen murmured, "Drop up." He didn't look up, but called, "Yeah, Eugene, I'll drop right up." To Raolo: "Any bumf on this guy?"

"Nothing. All the clothing tags snipped."

"His prints aren't in the IPS? Raolo, they've all got to have sheets. 7.62 Czech semiautomatics, where do amateurs get those?"

"Can't get a successful trace on the hardware, either – the guns aren't registered here or in the States. We don't know about Europe yet."

"Kellen," Borko called.

"It might've been a rented van," Kellen said to Raolo.

"I'm on it, Kel. We're calling the list."

Kellen passed one of the pictures to Lagasse and his cashier. She covered her face, couldn't look at the gunman's body.

"Ever see him?"

"Robbers usually case a score a few times before they go in," Raolo said, and seeing the blanks on their faces, he reworked that into a plausible French version.

"No," Lagasse said, "he wasn't a customer I knew."

Borko materialized beside Kellen, was suddenly breathing over his shoulder.

"If it's not inconvenient, Kellen, I wonder if we can join our heads together."

Kellen stood. "As long as it doesn't involve surgery, Eugene."

Kellen, at six-one, had to look up. Eugene Borko liked to stretch to his full six-and-six. Resplendent in blue, stiff as a pine tree, incorruptible Eugene Borko, born to the force. He checked his watch and bent to Kellen's ear.

"The Director is coming by in . . . precisely five-and-a-half minutes. We have to decide how to handle this with the press. I wasn't expecting you to finally show up at o-nine-hundred hours."

"Eugene, I killed a guy last night. I didn't sleep. I'll be with you in precisely three-and-a-half seconds." He turned to Raolo. "Champlain's office?"

"I put a man outside all night, like you said, the lawyer's office *and* his house. Nobody came by."

"Call his secretary and let's look at his appointments for the week."

"Detective Lieutenant O'Reilly," Borko commanded angrily.

41

"You'll excuse me," Kellen said to Raolo.

"He should get a goddamn medal, Captain, you want my humble opinion," Raolo said.

Kellen wearily followed the nagging Borko up the steel grill staircase.

"Your heroics of last night leave me cold. An innocent hostage was killed. You literally handed him over to his murderers, and I don't see how we can avoid an inquiry."

"I observe that you are uniformed, Eugene. That seems to be an omen of press conferences to come."

"There's going to be a great howl from the bar association about reckless police work. One of their precious own was killed." He sniffed. "You know, it's odd, I keep smelling perfume."

As they reached the balustrade, Kellen entertained the thought of going back down on the fire pole. Once, just once, he'd like to try that. They stopped at the railing in front of Borko's office, the captain peering anxiously at the main doors below, watching for the director.

"It started as a holdup. Before you made it a murder. A *lawyer*, Lieutenant."

"I am acquainted with this lawyer," Kellen said. "He was a small-jobber for the Mafia. Used to see him, years ago, defending speeding tickets for the Roncerelli family. Those guys were there to button him. The holdup was a cover to throw us off."

Borko looked taken aback at this. He pondered, then shook his head.

"O'Reilly, you have this fatal obsession about sinister Sicilian conspiracies. You better not go off half-cocked again. Johnny Ronce still has friends at city hall."

"Probably more than I've got."

"Your scenario doesn't compute. Czech 7.62s, Kellen. Roncerelli's boys don't carry those. Unusual for around here. Only seen a few, chambered for 7.65 Browning cartridges. Red Brigades favored them, did you know that? When they assassinated Genoa's chief prosecutor – "

Kellen wearily interrupted. "They were looking for something on this person, Eugene. A key."

"A key, what . . . Oh, hell, here comes the Director."

Police Director Emile Lachance walked in, looked up, and headed for the stairs. Sixties, spare and grizzled, he was as tough as he looked, but fair; he had rank-and-file respect, a street veteran. A police boss on a balancing act between a rebellious force and the MUC budget-cutters.

"Listen, don't use my first name in front of him. It's Captain."

"Hey, aren't you being a little precious? We used to team together. I remember when you still had acne and pissed in your pants every time I turned on the siren."

"And you're still in a car turning on sirens, chum. When you're not on job action. Ever wonder why you're still a detective?"

The chief bounded briskly up the steps, newspapers clutched in his hand, copies of *La Presse, The Gazette, Le Journal de Montréal, 'Allo Police,* all screaming their headlines about the shoot-out.

"In here," said Lachance, opening the door to Borko's office.

They walked in and he closed the door.

Borko's office always made Kellen jittery, something to do with all the equalizers on the wall. The captain's priceless collection of guns-used-in-action. He subscribed to all the collectors' magazines, was secretary-treasurer of Montreal's Old Gun Club.

"What is this about a work stoppage Monday night?" Lachance said. "You guys know that's illegal."

Kellen didn't respond right away, caught off-guard; this was the wrong agenda.

He found himself echoing Sarah Paradis. "It isn't a strike. Extraordinary membership meeting. All members can attend. Permitted under the contract."

" '*Cré maudit!* NATO defense ministers at the Place Bonaventure, some kind of alternative peacenik forum at Centre

Claude-Robillard. No police protection. We'll be an international laughing stock. *Saint-christ.*"

"Maybe the executive committee should agree to reopen talks, Chief."

"Also, some of the men in traffic section aren't giving speeding tickets," Lachance said. "They're handing out union pamphlets instead. If it doesn't stop, there'll be more suspensions. You're forcing me. I have to take the shit from both sides."

Kellen just shrugged.

Lachance sighed. "Unions. Your father would turn over in his grave. He was a loyal cop, whatever else they say about him."

Kellen felt a stabbing head pain. He turned away, shut his eyes until it left.

Lachance contemplated Kellen, and said finally, "Well, Lieutenant, I have to make a statement about this business of last night."

Kellen waited. He looked behind Lachance, at a glass case with the long-barreled Colt used at the battle of Chickamauga Valley and the Beretta Model 12 submachine gun with folding butt and silencer, abandoned at the OPEC headquarters in Vienna by the one and only Carlos the Jackal. Strung over it were two belts of live cartridges. He could bust Borko under the firearms regulations.

"Senator Paradis phoned me," Lachance said after the long pause. "He wanted me to thank you for saving his daughter's life."

Kellen needed a nic hit, and he pulled a cigarette out and probed his pockets for his lighter – but it was in his coat downstairs.

Lachance spread the newspapers onto a table: TWO DEAD IN DRUGSTORE; OFF-DUTY COP SLAYS ARMED ROBBER.

"The press thinks you're a hero. Senator Paradis thinks you're a hero. I have some doubt. I think you were trigger-happy; I think you endangered lives, your own included. But I'm going to go with hero, too. No inquiry this time."

Kellen lifted the unlit cigarette toward Borko, who stared at it for a few seconds, then brought out a lighter and thumbed it on for him.

"Thanks, Captain," Kellen said.

Saturday, ten-fifteen a.m.

Raolo Basutti straddled a chair in the reception area. R.W. (Bob) Champlain's part-time secretary, Jeanne-Marie, sat trim and timid at her steno's chair. Kellen browsed – nobody was asking to see a search warrant.

Champlain's files were all in a metal cabinet behind her desk. Single-shareholder companies, conveyances of land, a few wills and collections.

Jeanne-Marie handed Raolo back the head-and-shoulders morgue shot of the man Kellen shot. "No, I've never seen him."

"Any reason to believe Champlain had a large sum of money on him?" Raolo said.

"He said he was expecting a big fee."

"Did he say how much?"

"No. But this weekend."

Kellen found poor pickings among the active files. The appointment book likewise offered little of interest except for some notations penciled in for three different mornings in the last two weeks: "Meet L at McD's." "Meet L at Moishe's." "Meet L at Wilensky's." Restaurants, but who was L? Jeanne-Marie said she had no idea.

"Did he have enemies?" Raolo asked.

"Maybe. He was a shyster." She used the word *détoureux*.

In the card index – thankfully Champlain had not succumbed to the computer age – Kellen found the names of a

45

few companies he recognized. Medallion Imports Ltee. Bleury Contracting. They were old Roncerelli fronts. But the files were closed, the firms inactive.

"How's his wife?" Jeanne-Marie asked.

"She took it very well," Raolo said.

"I'm not surprised."

Okay, it seems poor old Bob was generally unloved. But what motive? And why the elaborate staging in the drugstore? And who were they? Yanks, big men who moved like they'd lost their springs.

He walked to the doorway of Champlain's office and knelt to the big floor safe just inside.

"What's the combination?" he asked.

"I was never told. I've never seen inside."

Big square 1940s Chubb, there'd be hell to pay if he drilled it without a warrant.

As he lightly spun the lock, the door wiggled on its hinges, and slowly, incredibly, teetered forward off those hinges and fell on Kellen's boot.

He swore in English several times, then in French, and hopped for a few seconds on one foot. The little round door had just missed his toe joints.

"They don't call you a flatfoot for nothing, Kel." Raolo knelt beside him and peered at the drill holes.

No back door to the office, or even a window. And no signs of forced entry. "We had a man out front?" Kellen said. "What time did he get here?"

"I don't know, there was a little confusion last night. Maybe seven-fifteen."

"They must've come straight back from the drugstore," Kellen said. "That's ballsy. Couldn't have had more than twenty minutes. What did they have, some kind of portable laser unit?"

Using a cloth, Kellen picked out objects from the safe and laid them on the carpet. Files, savings bonds, papers, an old brass jewelry box, unlocked. It contained a few small cut diamonds folded into a cloth, a braided gold chain, a woman's pendant necklace bearing a fat ruby.

"We therefore must deduce, employing our fine analytical minds, that they weren't professional jewel thieves," Kellen said.

The safe was empty now except for a plastic grocery bag, which Kellen withdrew. He opened it and pulled out a pair of red lace panties cut away at the crotch. Also inside were some loose condoms, black, labeled "Buck Brand," and three video cassettes: *Swap Meat, I Hear America Coming, Sally's Bachelor Party.* Rented from Le Marché Beaver, according to the stickers on their plastic boxes.

Also in the bag was a rolled-up, flesh-colored rubbery item. Kellen stood and let it fall open into the form of a deflated inflatable woman whose lipstick-bright mouth opened into a deep cavity.

Jeanne-Marie hadn't seen the other items, but she turned and looked at this. "*Oh, mon dieu,*" she said, looking away, blushing flames.

Kellen, then Raolo, peered carefully inside the little round entranceway to the safe. Empty now. All that had been stored here were a few jewels – hot ones, doubtless – and personal papers, and the various tools of Champlain's vigorous, lonely sex life.

"Thérèse never lets me look at these." Raolo opened one of the magazines to a beaver and whistled, a high arc, up and down.

Bing-bing-bing.

Chimes from somewhere. Music in the form of a single note repeated twice.

Raolo looked at Kellen. He whistled again. Nothing. He tried once more, higher.

Bing-bing-bing.

Kellen whistled at about the same pitch near the round open door of the safe, and the chimes beckoned him in.

He reached up and found, just above the open porthole, an object clinging by a little magnet to the interior wall.

He brought it out and whistled, and it answered him cheerily. A magnetic key chain with battery-driven chimes. A key locator. You whistle when you've mislaid it in the debris of your house or office. Kellen knew a hardware store on Van Horne that used to give these away.

But this one came from Juley LeGiusti's sex shop, Le Marché Beaver, advertised in bold print on a small plastic bubble that, when wiggled back and forth, displayed a naked girl dancing.

Kellen examined the brass key closely. Small, an inch long, flat, intricately cut.

"It has a number," he said. Three numerals, one-seven-three, were etched into its face.

"Haven't the faintest idea," Raolo said. "Some kind of strongbox?"

"Bank deposit, I think."

Raolo looked at the ad on the plastic bubble. "Le Marché Beaver." He looked at Kellen. "Juley the Juice's joint."

"Mafia," said Kellen.

Saturday, eleven-thirty a.m.

Cars filled all spaces legal or illegal near Juley LeGiusti's, so Raolo went up Saint-Laurent to Big Al's. In front was a municipal works crew – digging up the pavement for the fifth time in ten years here – faulty sewer pipe all over town, a legacy of older times, the pre-Drapeau years of the Big Take.

They parked behind a noisy generator and got out.

The old worn sign outside said, defiantly, in the illegal language, English: BIG AL'S HOUSE OF SMOKED MEAT. WHERE THE ELITE MEET TO EAT.

Kellen and Raolo entered to a broadside from Al, aproned, behind the counter.

"Well, if it ain't the dumb Irish cop and his retarded Dago half-brother. I already paid you off once this week. Ain't there no end to your greed?"

48

"You got a fresh pot on, or you still serving last week's?" Raolo said.

"I want mine to go, Al," Kellen said.

"You don't eat? You can arrest innocent people all day on an empty stomach?"

Kellen said, "We'll be back. We're going to check this joint out under the Health Act."

"Ruthie, coffee for the pigs."

Kellen walked out slowly, sipping from a styrofoam cup, into the cold front from Bafflin' Island. The sun skulked across the southern horizon, over the downtown spires.

Six months ago he was cursing the clammy, intolerable heat of summer. Montreal, and its yin-yang climate.

He bunched himself small in his thick khaki coat and, sore-footed still from the adventure with the safe door, walked the Tenderloin, past L'Exquise Klaussenfaus where strippers shop for pasties and mesh pantyhose, and La Restaurant Rosnikov's, pig's knuckles for four dollars; La Maison de Tattoo de Angel Smith, Frères Gonzales Tabacerie. Provincial statute required the signs to be in French, to protect the sanctity of the mother tongue against Franglish bastardization: Kellen enjoyed this oddball law, its capricious results.

He was keeping himself together, he seemed more clear-headed and focused now. The anxiety level had ebbed. But from the station he had phoned Wally Mandelbaum, an appointment at four.

Remember that he killed your father. But the man who killed Kellen's dad had never been arrested, never seen again. He was, for all Kellen knew, still alive and walking the streets.

Large, black marquee letters above Le Marché Beaver: *SEXE, SEXE, SEXE, FILMS ET EROTICA.*

Already, before noon, Juley had customers, old men like browsing goats, the Juice at the cash watching they don't touch the merchandise with their grimy hands. Sex aids and cellophane-wrapped magazines and cassettes. Four curtained-off back rooms offering private video viewings and other indulgences. For the less-affluent pervert, cheap tickets

49

were available for *Roxanne Goes to the Rodeo* in the small, thirty-seat movie auditorium.

Kellen headed, coffee in hand, for one of the curtained-off rooms.

"Hey!" Juley yelled.

A woman past her professional prime was buckling on her miniskirt, and she looked up sharply as Kellen whipped the curtain open. An obese man in a sports jacket, standing sideways to Kellen, suddenly froze in the act of doing up his tie.

Kellen took a sip from his plastic cup. "What did we tell you about no girls, Juley?" he said.

The Juice came running up. "Hey, lady, get out, this is a respectful establishment."

She indignantly swept the curtain shut.

Juley, a wispy, jittery man in flouncy Italian mods, said: "They sneak in here with their tricks. Detective Lieutenant O'Reilly, I just seen your picture in the news – I'm honored, any friend of Senator Paradis."

"That's one of Johnny Ronce's girls, isn't it?"

Juley drew him to the cash register, away from other ears. He frowned, serious.

"When Johnny insists, what can I do? Like, I'm between a rock and a hard place."

"I've got a hard place reserved for you, Juley. Complete with rocks."

They stopped talking as the fat man hurried outside, the *popaille* haughtily marching out behind. Kellen finished the cooling dregs of his coffee, then lit a cigarette.

"Come on, Lieutenant," Juley said, "what's this shit. I help you guys; it's a shakedown, donation to the strike fund, or what? Want you to know I'm on your guys' side."

"Customer of yours got blown away."

"Yeah, I read. Bob the lawyer – who did business here is all. Rented tapes. Bought what I call one of my blow dolls, matter of fact. Used to be close to some of the boys, but he dicked too many jobs. Lately he's been like hustlin' clients at bus stops. Had some down days at the horse an' buggy track last season. You check his clients' trust account, it'll be like a untuned car engine – missing a lot."

He paused. "That's the book on Bob Champlain. That, and last night he died holding a bottle of nose spray."

"I think it was an assassination."

Juley just shrugged.

"The only personal dealings you had with him was selling him this sick shit?"

"It's all. A good customer. I gave him one of these." Juley pulled from beneath the counter a box of key locators, the same ones, with the dancer in the plastic bubble. "Fifty bucks of stuff, you get one free. See, it's got like my little commercial announcement on it. Hide it some place, under the fridge, say, and if you're stupid, you forget, all you gotta do is whistle."

He whistled. Bing-bing-bing, they sang in unison.

"Have a couple."

Kellen shook his head and pulled Champlain's key holder from his pocket and dangled it. "You remember him putting this key on it?"

"Never seen no key."

Kellen turned – a man in a big overcoat was watching them, but went back to his magazines. The man was late fifties, healthy-looking, and swarthy, Mediterranean or Latin-American. Smoked glasses. Kellen felt an internal thrumming again, seemed to hear those subliminal voices, whispering, warning.

He lowered his voice. "It smells of family business to me, Juley. Boundary dispute? We got visitors from out of town?"

"Why out of town?"

"They couldn't speak French. They were Yanks, potbellies."

"Maybe the Gambinos from the Apple. They been busy."

But it didn't seem right. The elaborate cover-up, a staged robbery. Those guys usually take you out heads up, over a plate of prosciutti.

The Juice turned away to a customer at the cash, the

Latino type, who paid for a bottle of something called "Pro-Longing" with a twenty-dollar bill.

"Don't get sore muscles," Kellen said to him in French.

The man didn't turn his head. He got his change and walked out.

Kellen told Juley, "I got off a cowboy movie shot, hit one guy in the gun hand. He needed surgery. Who's looking after Johnny Ronce's girls?"

"I don't know. His last doctor just died in a alcohol clinic."

Kellen took a couple of paces, lifted another curtain. A pair of slim bare legs with canker sores. Another pair of legs, hairy and thick, trousers around the ankles.

"Section 193: operating a common bawdy house. You're looking at a deuce less a day."

"Jeez, *okay*, I'll find out what I can," Juley said.

"I want you to find out more than that. How's your cousin, Sal?" Sal LeGiusti, administrative secretary to Mr. Roncerelli.

"See him on family occasions."

"Tomorrow's Sunday. Make it a family occasion."

Raolo came running in. "Kel, dispatch says we got a body in an office, Saint-Laurent and Rachel. Took a bullet to the brain. Accountant. Name of Leo Sloukos."

"Leo . . . " said Juley. "Jeez."

"You know the guy?" Kellen said.

"He, ah, does some of Johnny's numbers."

"Call me, Juley." Kellen quickly followed Raolo out.

Saturday, twelve-thirty p.m.

The cleaning lady sobbed softly on a chair in the waiting room of Sloukos and Salazar, near the open front door which listed all the languages spoken here. Cross off Greek, thought Kellen.

The offices had been tossed, torn apart messily: papers thrown everywhere. Filing cabinets and desk drawers were open; books lay on the floor.

The photographer was finishing the body. The morgue techs waited to take over.

"How long ago?" Raolo asked one of them, Bertrand.

"Ten hours anyway. He's well into rigor, losing heat. Body's still warm enough for some rectals, but meantime I'd guess early last night."

Kellen had one good last look at Sloukos as the stretcher was brought in. Sitting with an expression of forlorn hope in his big tilt chair, behind his desk. Eyes open. A bullet hole between them. One of those eyes sitting in a socket that seemed nothing more than a red welt.

Sloukos's right arm extended across his desk and the fingers held a Mitchell .41-caliber derringer.

An ID man pried the accountant's fingers from the grip, and picked up the gun with a pencil and began to dust it. Two morgue techs folded Sloukos's arms over his chest and lowered him to the stretcher.

Raolo said, "He comes back to the office last night to clean up some accounts, surprises a B and E artist, maybe a couple of them. He goes for his gun and one of them plugs him between the eyes."

"Why does the right one look like jelly?" Kellen looked around. "The good ones leave things tidy. It's like a stage set."

Art Salazar came huffing up the stairs and into the office, and started when he saw his partner going out past him.

Kellen got a last hit from his cigarette and squeezed the butt and put it in his pocket. "Mr. Salazar?"

"My God, I had nothin' to do with this."

"When did you last see your partner?"

His gaze mesmerized by the stretcher-bearers' cargo, he spoke rapidly, "He's working late on some numbers. I say,

'Good, work late, it's five o'clock, I don't want to miss the traffic rush.' A joke. I leave him with a joke on my lips."

"Was he planning to see anyone last night?" Raolo asked.

Salazar slumped down on a chair near the cleaning lady. "He mentioned nobody. He was a loner. Not me. I got a family. Ask the kids, I was with them all night."

An officer handed Kellen the derringer, dusted now, and in a plastic envelope. "Can't find any cartridges, sir. No sign of more than one bullet being fired."

"Know where this was found?" Kellen asked Salazar.

"It's nothin' to do with me."

"In Mr. Sloukos's hand."

The accountant looked surprised. "Never told me he had a gun."

"You guys do any work for Johnny Ronce?"

"Who?"

Kellen went to a card index, found the tag he had placed there. "Napolitani Old-Style Spices Inc. Please don't fuck with us."

"It's Leo's client, nothin' to do with me. We each had our own."

"Any reason to think your partner was holding a lot of cash Friday?" Raolo asked.

"Honest, he kept things from me. Guns, money, Mafia, I don't know from nothin'."

Kellen looked at Sloukos's appointment calendar. "Meet Bob at McDonald's, Saint-Denis," said one entry two weeks old. "Bob at Moishe's," said another. Bob Champlain. It had to be, the dates and places coincided.

"Eureka," he said, and whistled.

He heard the chimes faintly from his pants pocket. Bing-bing-bing.

He felt the walls collapsing on him.

His hand moves on the dial and a surge of power rips through your brain, and you scream silently into oblivion.

Then he heard Raolo ask, "You all right, Kel?"

Saturday, four p.m.

Kellen talked and paced and filled an ashtray. Wally Mandelbaum drank coffee and made notes and worried.

"Okay, I want to get back to the drugstore in a minute, but let's deal with the last flashback, the one this afternoon. That's twice, two days in a row, you had an image of being strapped to the bed and zapped by Satorius."

This had been one of Kellen's most common recurring images before the flashbacks, about a decade ago, waned and desisted.

"I've never had a flashback so clear," Kellen said. "I had a sense of *being* there, as if I'd been sent back in time for five or six seconds. I felt drugged, Wally, on acid, a heavy hit of it; Satorius looked like something out of *Fantasia.*"

"Mickey Mouse, apprentice to the sorcerer," Wally said. "Okay, drugged – what else?"

"Scared. Plain fucking terrified. I wasn't on that bed of my free will."

Wally had often thought it odd: those electroshock treatments had been intended to erase memory. And clinically it had been proven that ECT had a reverse chronological effect: the stronger the shock, the further back in time was memory erased. Yet Kellen had, well, a *kind* of memory of the moments immediately preceding this particular shock. Had some significant event – tied somehow to that exploding scarfaced man – become imprinted so deeply in Kellen's mind that even electroshock couldn't erase it?

Clearly, Wally knew, Kellen was haunted by something he had been induced to forget. He had tried to escape from Coldhaven at some point – an attempt to run to freedom was also an oft-recurring mental image. The attempted escape, the scar-faced man disintegrating, Satorius at the ECT button – they seemed like fragments of a larger, important memory.

"The flashback in the drugstore – you think it was precipitated by the man holding a gun on you?"

"I don't know. The last thing I remember before it hit was a song on the radio, an old Presley tune."

Wally had checked Kellen's file: this particular flashback – the man exploding – had recurred more than a hundred times during the years it had taken his friend to recover from Coldhaven; but until yesterday he'd never reported seeing a gun in his hand, a gun that he fired at Scarface. New, significant information.

"Run through it again," Wally said.

"It was confusing. This bozo had a gun on me, zap, flashback, and I'm nineteen and *I'm* holding a gun, and I fired it, I guess, and the man blew up. Then I was back in the pharmacy, jumping around and shooting. For real. And, ah . . . nothing."

"There was something else?" Wally asked. Kellen seemed to be struggling, holding back.

"What do you mean?"

"Any other new details you remember from the flashback in the pharmacy?"

Kellen hesitated, and fought off Wally's unrelenting gaze, retreated from it.

Remember that he killed your father.

He hadn't heard Satorius speak those words, of course he hadn't, he'd imagined them. And it would set Wally off, he'd want to talk about the death of Kellen's dad, his feelings about his father's murder, and he didn't need the pain.

"No, nothing else."

Wally sensed that Kellen had just rolled up into a ball, an emotional fetus position.

"So I ask you again: Why do you think these things are coming back, Kellen? And why so strongly?"

"I don't know."

"Well, something buried is coming to the surface. Why? What's triggering them? Margot? Your job? The strike? All those things, maybe?"

"I don't know. You're the shrink."

"What shrinks do is try to ask the right questions, Kel. I don't hear you trying to answer them."

Wally guessed that although the trigger was a combination of all those stressful elements, the gunpowder was something Kellen was repressing, some work problem. His friend was a brilliant cop and – despite his union activism – harbored unspoken ambitions, had probably set his cap for captain and for the job his former partner, Eugene Borko, recently won. And maybe his labor militancy was his way of denying these aspirations, deflecting a sense of failure.

But behind it all, Wally believed, the wellspring of all anxiety: the specter of Sergeant Brian O'Reilly, Kellen's father, glimmering through the fog of repressed memory. Sergeant O'Reilly, who went to a tragic grave.

"Wally, last night when I went crashing into that display counter, I . . . ah, hard to explain . . . it was like I was forced to act, to . . . kill that guy. Something inside seemed to be impelling me."

"What do you mean 'something inside'? Describe that feeling."

Kellen strolled to the window over the street and stared out. "The sensible thing for me to have done was to hit the floor, wait out the robbery, and not endanger lives. I had a . . . kind of . . . "

Wally waited.

"Urge to kill."

Wally didn't believe it. It wasn't Kellen, wasn't part of his makeup. Maybe his actions had been more suicidal than homicidal. Kellen had sometimes, years ago, during the worst period, talked about taking his own life.

"You say that before these flashbacks started up again you'd been feeling a little odd," Wally said.

"Yeah, like I've been picking up signals." Tingles in the cold air of Montreal. "And sometimes, almost, well . . . I almost hear voices." He smiled dourly. "I sound a little psychotic, right?"

"Psychotic you're not. Neurotic I can buy. But that's okay. Everyone's neurotic. I'm neurotic. It's hip. You're basically healthy." Wally heard himself fudging, tinting the truth for a friend. Don't be so goddamn reassuring. Kellen O'Reilly needs help. What he also needs is a different psychiatrist: neutral, uninvolved.

"Neurotic," Kellen said. "A neurotic who flashes back to things he can't remember."

Through the curling smoke of his cigarette Kellen looked up Metcalfe and McTavish Streets, past buildings shimmering in the late afternoon sun, to Royal Victoria Hospital on the flanks of Parc Mont-Royal. He looked beyond, up into the glowering mass of this city's stone-hearted mountain king. Mount Royal. On his island in his river.

Only a few blocks away, between the canyon walls of the former mansions, nineteenth-century Scots' affluence on the mountain slopes, stood the house of Coldhaven. It sent him messages of hopelessness.

"I heard he's still working," Kellen said. "When he's not in court."

"Yeah, he runs some kind of out-patient program through the university, teaches a class or two. Coldhaven's closed but he keeps his old office up in the tower. I think he's got the joint up for sale to pay his legal bills."

Coldhaven, a mansion turned private clinic, was said to have been donated to Satorius by a thankful, wealthy client, who everyone suspected was a funnel for the CIA's brainwash-funding front, the Society for the Investigation of Human Ecology.

Wally watched Kellen staring bleakly out at the old, gray-stone manor house. A good man, proud, intense, emotionally scarred. The problem: he was a friend. Good friends make bad patients. Old adage among shrinks. But Kellen adamantly refused to see another psychiatrist; he trusted Wally, no one else. Even in Margot he hadn't shared. A therapist's most agonizing dilemma: the curse of friendship.

Wally got up from his chair and went to Kellen and put an arm around him, his hand on his shoulder, and looked out at Coldhaven with him, and there it was – that little tower window, Satorius's office, a light burning. Is he there now, churning out his self-serving papers?

How could the medical faculty let him keep his honorary

chair? Wally wondered. How could some people still think he was God? He'd *played* God – with men's and women's psyches, and it was only now coming out, in court depositions, the stories of the shattered minds, his evil purposes.

"Wally, I can't function like this."

"It's probably a little last burst of activity, Kel. A few final firecrackers on the string." No, Wally thought, that's false reassurance; *deal* with him. "Listen, Kel, I told you years ago, and it's still true: part of your past is in a locked box; you have to free it."

He took a deep breath; time to bite the bullet. "You sentenced yourself to three months' hard time in Coldhaven because of the trauma over your father's death – "

"I went there because they paid my tuition."

Defense mechanisms were up. "You were depressed, too."

"Yeah, okay."

"And ever since Coldhaven you've had this goddamn amnesia. About your father and his shooting – "

Kellen had a sudden blinding headache. Pain that drowned Wally's words. "It's not a problem," he said fiercely.

"Shouldn't we try to open the locked box, Kellen? Isn't it time we talked about your dad?"

"It's not a problem!"

Wally took Kellen's hand and held it tight. "Kellen. Relax." Wally could feel himself losing it, the will to punch through the pain.

"Okay, Kel, I want to tell you this: we're going to talk about it, maybe not today. Let's get this strike business over, and let's let that stuff with Margot decay for a few days. You've been going through a lot, and you almost got killed. Take a few days off. Watch some junk on TV. Read some escape fiction. Next week, we'll take a day. Let's find a way into your past. There's a key somewhere and we're going to find it."

Kellen felt himself loosening, the pain abating. After a long silence, with Wally still holding his hand, he managed to smile.

"A key I have found," he said. "I don't know what it

unlocks. I turned it over to forensics. Maybe I should turn *myself* over to forensics."

He turned back to the window and looked down to the sidewalk.

"There's someone watching your place," he said.

Directly beneath Kellen was a man in a parka. Standing in front of Wally's stairs, by the building directory. Now starting to walk away, around the corner.

When Wally got there, he saw no one.

"He's gone," Kellen said.

Wally examined Kellen's face, weary, jaundiced from the rays of the dipping sun.

"You want to take a break, Kel?" he said with false heartiness. "Listen, I taped today's game. The last period you won't believe. Five goals in twenty minutes. Why don't we have a beer, maybe we can watch the highlights, then we'll go at it some more."

"I have a meeting," Kellen said. "You're right, Wally – let me get through the scramble of the next few days. I'll work hard with you after that, I promise."

Saturday, five-thirty p.m.

The session with Wally had relieved some of Kellen's anxiety, but he still felt like he'd been run over by a truck. He didn't know if he had the strength to carry this fight. Fernand Ouimet's angry, scattered speech was like a jackhammer in his ears.

"Every year more cops killed," Ouimet roared to his twelve-member executive. "All we ask is to help the families,

60

and now they suspend our members. Are we going to let them pick us off one by one? Not Fernand Ouimet, no, by God! *Je m'en contre-crisse!* We let them have a lawless city Monday night; we give them a taste of that!"

The Montreal Urban Community administration had just suspended six officers for passing out union leaflets on duty. The action had been calculated to put the union in a rage, Kellen realized. The Montreal Urban Executive Committee was daring them to walk out, wanted them to.

"They'll send the army in," said Constable Taillefeur. "Even worse, the fucking RCMP." He was an east-end precinct shop steward; he had lots of rank-and-file redneck support, and was assumed by some to be management's fink. "Then Bourassa sends an emergency bill to the Assembly, and we're stuck with some stingy Jew arbitrator's decision. I'm with the union, don't get me wrong, but Brother O'Reilly speaks for me."

It galled to be doing so. "They *want* us to go off the job, Fernand," Kellen told the chairman. "They want us to abandon our best tool – work to rule."

"Which doesn't work," said Sarah Paradis. "At least I haven't seen *you* work to any rule." She smiled at him from down the table.

Someone laughed. "Yeah, he was supposed to be off duty last night and he busts up a robbery."

Kellen looked down the long table at Sarah, unruffled after last evening's events. She must have got her prescription filled.

"It's too late to turn back, Kellen," she said. "The whole city is watching us. If we back down now everyone will know we can be broken."

Kellen knew he had the respect of some of the fence-sitters. Maybe he could swing it, he'd suddenly become a local hero. The debate was whether to accept or reject the negotiating committee's recommendation for Monday's twelve-hour walkout: an all-night meeting, eight at night until eight in the morning.

"If they apply for an injunction – " Kellen started.

"I'll fight it," Sarah said. "I'll win it. The collective agree-

61

ment says *all*, all members are entitled to be at an extraordinary meeting. It's a loophole, sure, but it's there, in print."

Corporal Bertrand, one of the directors – and a man who had just seen his twelve-year-old marriage collapse – said impatiently: "*Tabernac*, Kellen, remember what we are fighting for. A welfare plan that's half-assed decent. Shorter days so the guys can get home once in a while to see their kids. We're not asking for a hell of a lot and they're giving us a hell of a lot of nothing."

Taillefeur said, "Well, I say we're asking for trouble. Sure the fuck Monday night we'll get some juiced-up spook with a knife banging some white girl out in the middle of Côte-des-Neiges Street with no one able to call a cop, and, man, we're shit. Forget getting *any* contract."

Taillefeur had once shot a black teenager, a thief who'd tried to run. The constable had been acquitted of manslaughter on his evidence that the gun had fired accidentally.

Kellen sat for a moment, studying Taillefeur, then said, "What the hell, okay, I move we go ahead with the strike . . . ah, the extraordinary meeting."

Ouimet slammed the table with delight. "A convert to the noble cause!"

"Second the motion," came a voice.

"Move the question," came another.

"All in favor?" said Ouimet.

"I want my vote recorded," said Taillefeur. He was in a minority of three.

Afterwards, as they let themselves out of the union building into the knife-cold night, Sarah approached Kellen.

"How are you getting to wherever you're going?"

"Taxi."

"I want to take you."

It was said as a demand, get in my car. He followed her to the little Yugo, in the lot behind the Brotherhood offices on Gilford Street. Inside, they sat quietly. She let the engine purr.

He studied her carefully drawn, almost-tailored oval face. She looked at him with cool, tranquil eyes. Tranquilize.

62

"I think you may have saved my life," she said. "I haven't thanked you."

"Any time."

She took them onto Saint-Denis, and south.

"This isn't taking me home," Kellen said.

She was still smiling. "It's Saturday night, Lieutenant."

He sighed. "Yeah. It's Saturday night."

Saturday, seven p.m.

She took him to L'Express, bright and brassy, haunt of the arts-and-pop crowd. She looked chic, designer black leather jacket and multi-hued scarf. Kellen felt odd-man-out here, a long-haired, gray-grizzled sixties leftover in his denim jeans and jacket. But he was enjoying Sarah's company; she was taking him away from himself.

"You were very brave to follow those men into the drugstore," she said.

"Actually I was out of cigarettes. I didn't see them."

"Please don't spoil it for me. Anyway, Father thanks you for saving my life. However, he says I'm not to see you until he gets a full report on whether you're some kind of dangerous rogue cop."

Sarah was as bubbly as the champagne she sipped. She was showing her alternate self: not the earnest political lawyer, but a woman teasingly friendly, offering him easy smiles.

She talked about herself and her family, flipping from French to English in the unselfconscious way of a born Montrealer. She'd been raised in an estate house in Sault-au-Récollet, near the North River, had studied at the Sorbonne and McGill and Laval, where she'd earned a master's in labor law at the age of twenty-three. After that she'd been a hippie, a bit of a druggie, a ski bum, and a spoiled brat until her conscience caught up with her a few years ago. As a result of meeting a poet, a major *séparatiste* – supposedly well-known but Kellen had never heard of him. Marcel something.

And with the coming of political consciousness her law practice drastically changed. Before, she had worked as a labor lawyer for a big politically linked firm, but after Marcel came into her life she started her own office, and was suddenly in the newspapers fighting the deportation of a plane-load of Central American refugees, and winning.

She took on more celebrity civil rights cases, and last year sued the Montreal Urban Community in a test case involving discrimination against pregnant women employees. She won, dazzling the Brotherhood, an intervener, who hired her on a retainer.

Kellen was caught aback by her, by her frankness and her vanity. But he found that refreshing, her undisguised self-esteem. She seemed real, no false pride, no Yuppie affectations.

And so far she hadn't asked him prying questions.

Later, she took him to a little Chilean bring-your-own-wine restaurant run by, Kellen suspected, Communists, a married couple who loved Sarah, and fussed over them. The other diners – Sarah knew many of them by name – seemed to be drawn from the revolutionary chic community. Anti-imperialist political posters on the wall.

They ate *pollo escabechado* and drank good Bordeaux, and Sarah talked about her friendship with a revolutionary named Rosia and about the stormy years with Marcel. Over cognacs – supplied illegally by the management – Sarah gave him the latest chapter.

"Anyway, I got in from New York a day early. They were in bed. *My* bed. I went to a hotel and waited for the breakdown to come. A few days later I woke up in the psych ward of the General Hospital." She sighed. "I found out she's taking him to Guatemala; he wants to teach in the *campo*. They're going to get married."

She fingered a little blue oval Halcion from her bottle, and looked up at him.

He shook his head sadly.

She said, lightly, "They anti-depress."

"They're drugs." Severe expression.

"Let's hear the speech. Do you give it at schools?"

She boldly popped the pill, washed it down with Bordeaux.

Kellen remained impassive. "I've seen kids cut those little blue ovals with toot and mainline it."

She closed one eye, studied him harder with the other. "Why'd you become a cop?"

A question in cross-examination, sudden, he wasn't expecting it.

Senora Bonilla fluttered by with the cognac bottle, pouring them doubles, on the house, for Companera Paradis and her friend, and dropped the bill for dinner on the table between them.

They both reached for it.

"I'll get it," Kellen said.

"I'll get it."

"I'll . . . make it up another time." He surrendered the bill to her.

She asked again, "Why'd you become a cop?"

Kellen said, "It's, ah, kind of personal."

Immediately he felt badly. She'd opened herself to him; he hadn't repaid in kind. He struggled, feeling an unease, and said, "I thought I would carry on the tradition."

"Your father was on the force?"

"Yeah." He wanted to derail her; he didn't know how.

"He's retired now?"

"Dead."

She looked at him as if expecting a fuller account. He felt the headache coming. But he felt impelled to add something, to explain.

"My dad was murdered, shot on duty." His words came in a rush, incredibly, unwilled.

"Oh, I'm sorry. I didn't know that. What happened?"

"I . . . don't like to talk about it. It's history." The headache started to build.

And what could he say? The facts were buried below his

memory. As a boy he'd refused to believe, to hear details. He kept no clippings, no reminders to this day. Sergeant Brian O'Reilly had taken a bullet to the brain, delivered by the driver of a car he pulled over. Assailant unknown. That's all there was to know.

He felt the whip of her silence, and added, "It screwed me up for a while. I was eleven, a critical time I guess, for a kid. I was a smart kid, though, straight A's, and a scholarship to McGill, modern French literature, believe it or not. But I lost interest in school. Became what you see."

He hated this, being unable to share the other, secret, terrible part of him. Why couldn't he? The holding within, he knew, had already destroyed a marriage.

"Your mother?" she asked.

"She's gone, too. Stroke, a few years ago."

"Brothers, sisters?"

"Grew up alone." He didn't mention Margot, wasn't sure why.

Sarah wondered what the strange ingredients were that comprised this man. He gave little, just those blue, distant stares. She felt foolish; she'd rattled on inanely about herself, and when she asked a few questions he became so miserly with himself.

She'd found herself, unbelievably, *interested* in him. A brave man who won't drive a car; attractive, but doesn't seem to have a female relationship. Something odd about Lieutenant O'Reilly.

Not like the other police, those beef-and-boiled-potatoes guys. He was softer, more sensitive than a cop should be. And let's face it, she was a romantic, and he'd saved her life; there was a sense of Arthurian fairy tale about it all. Strong, silent, troubled man rescues virtuous maiden. She wanted him to like her, to return to her a confidence about herself that Marcel had stolen.

He was studying a poster, a bald eagle with a long, thin country in its claws. LA CIA MATO A CHILE. SU PAIS SERA EL PROXIMO.

His eyes were so melancholy. Sarah felt an urge to touch him, to plunge her hand through those impregnable walls, to make contact, and did so now, quickly, her fingertips settling on the back of his wrist.

He jerked his arm away reflexively, and looked at her with a startled expression, then just as quickly, with an embarrassed one.

"Sorry," she said, "you were deep in thought." She translated the poster for him: " 'The CIA murdered Chile. Your country could be next.' I guess you don't believe that."

"Why wouldn't I?"

"I'm sure you think it's all a disinformation plot engineered by Moscow."

"I do? Why?"

"Most cops are right-wing *pepsis*."

"Maybe you can re-educate me."

She felt spurned, his withdrawing his hand from her like that.

" 'Your country could be next,' " she repeated. "Chile, Iran, Guatemala – why not Canada? Canada's just another banana republic to them. Hire trained killers and call them Contras. Trade coke for arms. Keep the world safe for democracy by washing brains and controlling minds. Shoot folks up with LSD and curare."

She heard herself shrilly lecturing, nervous, filling the empty space between them.

"That's what Satorius was doing for them. Right here in Montreal. He ran a CIA amnesia project. Operation MK-ULTRA, sub-project forty-seven." She felt her anger. "I'm going to drag him through the courts backwards if I have to." Another pause; he wouldn't look at her. "Know how it all started?"

No answer. Where had he gone? She rattled desperately on.

"The fifties, Korea? All those POW's coming back as honest-to-God Communists – they'd probably learned some real history for the first time in their lives, but of course the Pentagon couldn't accept *that*, so someone decided they'd been brainwashed."

Just staring at the wall from behind a veil of cigarette smoke.

"Anyway, total paranoia in the Pentagon, obviously the Red Menace had mastered the tools of mind control. The CIA had absolutely *massive* funding for MK-ULTRA. Hundreds of projects: clinics, colleges, hospitals, prisons."

Another Halcion would be good, Sarah decided.

"Maybe we're just guessing, but we think the experiment Satorius ran for the CIA here had to do with erasing the memory of enemy agents – or maybe their own agents – so they couldn't talk if they were caught. None of my clients remember much about Coldhaven, maybe just the first few days there, but all the rest's a blur. Some of them weathered it better than others. Some of them are a mental mess.

"I mean, all that acid and electroshock. Psychic driving, Satorius called it. It's where they strap you to a bed, pump LSD into your veins, and you hear Satorius's voice over and over – "

She stopped talking abruptly as Kellen covered his eyes with his hands, his head bowed. What the hell was going on with him? She fished another pill out.

He took an unhealthy, deep breath of smoke and looked up and saw the pill in her hand. "Tranqs." He smiled wanly. "For the memories."

As she guiltily popped the pill, she saw tears in his eyes.

"I was at Coldhaven," he said.

She felt a violent, cold shiver of shock with the sudden awareness of the intense and awful truth about this man, but after several seconds she recovered, and felt herself flowing to him, and slowly reached for his hand. He didn't withdraw it this time.

Alabama Bill squatted tensely in the black shadows of a second-floor balcony. The nearby window was closed, but a
night-light glowed dimly red from within, where a man emit-
ted raspy snores that rattled the windowpane.

Normally, Bill would've wanted to be across the street, but
all you had there was a park: trees and kids' swings, no shelter.

So he was up on the balcony of the second-floor duplex
that was next door to the second-floor duplex of Detective
Lieutenant Kellen O'Reilly. He had a gun and a radio, and
was colder than shit.

"Try the sill," he whispered loudly to Eddie the Cube
Comacho, who was squatting at Kellen's balcony, at the front
door, looking under the mat. You always look for a key before
you start fucking around with the lock. Basic training.

The door key is not so important; Eddie knows ways to
open doors. The safety-deposit key – that's important. Then
they've got to con their way into the trust company vaults.

This was a long chance, searching O'Reilly's home. He
probably still had the key on him. He'd pulled it out of his
pants pocket in the store where Eddie bought a bottle of that
stuff that's supposed to keep you hard, Pro-Longing, it was
called. He and Eddie put it onto the soap tray in Rudy's
shower at the hotel before they came down here. Give him
a little extra longevity the next time he tries to make out with
Five-Finger Mary. But old Rude's got no sense of humor;
he'll just come out with some speech about people not taking
this holy mission serious enough.

Eddie found the door key all right, on top of the sill. He
waved it at Bill, then tried it; it worked. Alabama Bill wondered how Canadians could be so innocent – even the cops
are trusting. Maybe it's the cold winters; robbers don't like
the working conditions. He massaged his freezing feet with
his gloved hands. He could say adios to some toes if he had
to stay out here much longer.

Meyers and Crowder were in that nice heated van a couple

69

of blocks away. Meyers with his arm sling. The doc did a good job on the hand. But no doctor was gonna bring Chip back. O'Reilly ought to pay for that one. Anyway, whether he left that deposit key in the house or still had it on his person, they were going to get a hold of it tonight. Even if they had to get messy.

Eddie Comacho stepped inside, and clicked the lock shut from within.

Sunday, twelve-fifteen a.m.

Long after the Bonillas had locked up and turned the lights down and left them a burning candle and more cognac at their corner table, Kellen was still talking to her about Coldhaven: his depatterning, the psychic driving, his memory loss, the flashbacks now returning, his fears that they would always haunt him, his detestation of Satorius and his former sponsors.

Words poured as if from a breached dam. And he exulted in it, felt released. The headaches were gone.

He had someone to talk to. An odd someone, from a world so apart from his. Could he have believed yesterday that tonight he would be so revealing to this woman, so vulnerable, naked? Yesterday – was it only yesterday? – she had been an aristocratic snob. Tonight she was full of caring, listening as if spellbound.

"Some things I remember, some I don't. I remember the sleeping room, and a portable ECT unit. I remember a tape-recorded message repeating over and over again under the pillow, but I've absolutely no memory of what the words were. I remember hypodermic needles. I don't remember any faces, even the medical staff, even Satorius – except at

70

the beginning, when I was in his office, being interviewed, signing the release."

"You signed it without informed consent, it's absolutely worthless. Why aren't you suing them?"

"There's a policy in the police department," Kellen said softly. "No psychotic cops on the homicide squad. I didn't mention Coldhaven when I applied to the Police Academy. Only you and Wally know."

"Wally?"

"He's a shrink. Mandelbaum."

"And you . . . you've told this to no one else?" Were there no women who loved him? she was wondering.

"Margot . . . I guess she knew something. We never discussed it."

"Margot?"

"My ex-wife."

"You didn't mention a Margot."

"It never came up."

"Why me? Why now?"

"I don't know. I trust you."

"I feel honored."

There was a period of quiet during which she studied his lined face, reflecting candlelight from its planes.

Then he said, "They've done something evil to me. Yesterday it was as if some other man was in my skin, the murderer in me." And grimly, he added, "Maybe Satorius put him there. The CIA have a man inside." He chuckled at that, low, sardonic.

"That's . . . crazy talk," she said, taking his hand again. She looked into his haunted eyes, feeling awed and scared, unsure about him – and then she had a frightening thought: could this crazy talk be coming from a crazy man? How unfeeling of her. He was damaged, repairable.

"Drive you home?" she said.

"Don't stop at any drugstores."

She was a little giddy with Halcion and drink as she maneuvered the car up to Outremont North, but she concentrated, and performed without error until she put a wheel on the pavement in front of Kellen's duplex, clipping an empty garbage tin with a clang.

From a darkened upper window came a shout. *"Taboire! Y'a du monde qui dort icitte!"*

Kellen, feeling limp after his unburdening, thought: Old Saint-Yves, my sour neighbor, good morning to you. He turned to Sarah and permitted himself a smile.

Would she be insulted if he asked her up? She was a woman of pedigree, and might get the wrong idea. All he had in mind, frankly, was talk. More talk, more truth-telling: sweeter than sex.

Flat on his stomach on the balcony, Alabama Bill could feel warm air rush from the open window, and hear the old man grumbling from behind it. Go back to bed, you old goat, he prayed. He was almost rigid with cold.

He heard the Yugo's engine idling. The car of Sarah Paradis, the lawyer, the lady who'd been in the drugstore, daughter of a powerful Canadian senator, it turns out. Rudy said don't touch her if you don't have to. Complications.

The window slammed shut above him. Bill's muscles were like frozen slabs of meat; he could barely move his arms. He plucked the radio from his belt and blew into it hard three times.

In Kellen's kitchen, Eddie the Cube Comacho blew into his radio once and clicked it off, and said softly to himself, "Yeah, I read you. Really on the alert there, Bill." He'd heard the clanging noise outside, and was now standing by a window and looking down at them in the car.

They used to call him Eddie the Cuban, but it got shortened. The last time he was in Cuba was the Bay of Pigs. Rudy signed him on for that fiasco, too. Put some of that Pro-Longing on your joint, Rudy. Go for the permanent hard-on. To match the rest of your personality.

Yeah, Rudy said this was going to be like all downriver on a sternwheeler. The old master mariner, leading them on another magical mystery ride. Downriver, hell. They could all of them end *up* the river. Or worse. What did they do in Canada – gas you or behead you, or what?

He'd already done the bedroom and living room, using surgical gloves, whistling nervously while he worked, like Snow White, but no ding-ding-ding, the three little musical notes he'd heard in Le Marché Beaver.

They'd lost O'Reilly after he finished talking to that little weasel running the sex shop. The other cop came rushing in, Basutti, and they went sirening off. Assuming the lieutenant never came back home or to his precinct office, he's still got the key with him.

Eddie figured what's taking them so long; they're necking in the front seat, and he's trying to coax her up. The lady was brought up good, she'll probably go through the proper etiquette before she spreads them and serves dessert.

In the car, Sarah turned off the ignition and headlights, and the silence was as penetrating as the encroaching cold. Why did she do that, turn the motor off, the heater? As if she assumed he'd ask her up. And he hasn't.

He wasn't getting out. Just sitting there, dragging on his Player's. Looking at her, smiling.

Their voices joined in mixed chorus.

"Well, I had better be . . . " over something he was saying about a cup of coffee.

Another pause.

"I grind my own beans. I have to tell you, they're from Guatemala."

Eddie Comacho watched them come up the spiral stairway and went back to the bedroom, where he'd locked the cat in, and as he opened the door the cat shot out from behind it, and disappeared somewhere. Comacho slid into a deep closet, around a corner into a nook, behind the suits and sports jackets.

On the neighbor's balcony, Alabama Bill saw the lights go on in O'Reilly's apartment, and knew he couldn't leave; he was backup. What was Comacho up to? As he waited for the pop of a pistol he felt a sharp pain in his prick. Do they sometimes freeze and snap off? Frostbite, he could be damaged for life.

In the living room, Kellen took Sarah's coat, and hung it by the door with his own. Under his jacket, strapped to his shirt, a holster showed. Mao mewed at his feet, anxiously, making demands.

She thought: lonely man with a cigarette, a cat, and a gun. *The murderer in me* . . . There had been tears in his eyes as he talked, and he'd tried to control them, and couldn't. Marcel, a poet, had never cried.

She wanted Marcel to see her now. In the home of *un boeuf*, a cop. A form of incorrect behavior. He'd derided her work for the MUC Police Brotherhood, the sale of her services to fascist, albeit unionized, pigs.

He didn't ask her to sit. Just looked at her, as if puzzling about what to do with her. He wasn't used to this, obviously, a woman in his house.

"Would you rather have something else?" He would have to wash some mugs. He felt unprepared for her, was embarrassed about his old, worn furniture.

"No, fine, coffee, I should."

She decided she would be polite, have her coffee, they would exchange busses on the cheeks like good friends and she'd go.

He'd make an incredible witness. For her clients. A police detective – how could a jury not believe him? Maybe, if she talked to his psychiatrist, this Mandelbaum . . .

"What's the hassle, Mao, you hungry?" The cat dogged his heels into the kitchen.

Sarah poked around the living room while she waited: desk, typewriter, some manuals. Telephone and answering machine. Map on the wall. Workaholic on work to rule. He'd told her: Between job, union, and computer seminars, I don't get out much.

One of the manuals on his desk was by Microsoft, software programs. On the table by the TV chair: a Proust and a Camus, *The Plague*.

The rest of the room was more comfortable, some prints

on the wall: Manet's portrait of Zola, Cézanne's *Déjeuner sur l'Herbe*, an El Greco. And books, nearly a wall of them, fiction from Flaubert to Updike; some texts, forensic, medical. Something called *The LSD Papers* caught her eye. The furniture was old: a soft chair in front of a TV set, several magazines and newspapers on a rack nearby. His maid could come more often, empty his ashtrays.

Had Margot lived here? There was little sign of a woman's touch.

The coffee grinder growled in the kitchen. *Yesterday it was as if some other man was in my skin* . . . Dread had been in his eyes.

He returned with two mugs, a bowl of sugar, and a measuring cup filled with milk, and set them on the desk. He turned on his machine. "Hope you don't mind, sometimes the station calls."

The first call was from Raolo. Kellen turned the sound up and returned to the kitchen.

"It's Saturday, three-thirty. The pathologist says Sloukos's eye has gotta've been gouged out, then stuck back in."

Kellen, waiting for the kettle, heard her say, "Oh, my God."

In the closet, Eddie Comacho could just make out Raolo's words. He fidgeted with his Browning 9-millimeter, checked to see he had a spare clip in his pocket, along with the silencer.

The next call was also from Raolo.

"Saturday, four-fifteen. Budget agent in Iberville rented a brown Safari to a couple of guys said they were going skiing, gave him a deposit of five hundred U.S. instead of a credit card impression. Two hefty guys, both over fifty. One signed himself as Roy Salvador, address in Key West, Florida. Apparently valid driver's license. Theory: Iberville's toward the U.S. border, no international airport there, so they drove up, parked their car somewhere near the Budget office. The Québec Sûreté there are looking for a vehicle with U.S. plates. The U-Drive man is coming to the station tomorrow."

Eddie Comacho, listening, thought: Have to get rid of that Safari van, all right. Using that old Roy Salvador ID was a fudge-up rush job on Rudy's part. They hadn't had time to get good papers or do a run-through. Two days, they'd thought, then out of here.

Raolo again. "Oh, I forgot, we got some tobogganing tomorrow with Mario. You still on for it? I'll schedule the rent-a-car guy for the afternoon."

The next call was from Margot. "Oh, *God*, darling, I just heard about it. I'm calling from Tremblant, just got down the hill and turned the radio on. Are you all right? Do you need me?"

She gave a number, Brad's condo in the Laurentians.

The final call was also from her. "It's Margot at Tremblant, it's twenty-two-thirty fucking p.m. and I'm sitting by this lonely phone while everyone's getting mulled on mulled wine at a party two doors down. Goddamnit, call me!"

Kellen returned to his living room with the pot of Guatemalan drip coffee.

Sarah was sitting at his desk chair with her legs crossed. She looked at him curiously: *Do you need me?* What was that?

"An actress who played lead against me for several years. Margot, the ex."

"She doesn't seem very ex."

"We're pals. She invites me to her weddings."

"When did it end? Your marriage."

"Formally, four years ago. Finally, yesterday, Friday. She's getting married to a doughnut mogul."

She took the mug of coffee from him, still looking at him oddly, wondering about this ex-marriage.

"I'll be just a minute," he said. "She's stubborn enough to sit up all night, waiting."

"It's okay, call her." She found the whole thing funny.

Kellen went to the bedroom, to phone from his extension.

Eddie stiffened in the closet, his hand tensing on the grip of the gun. This O'Reilly was like a fucking gremlin. All their plans began to foul up when he joined the cast. Chip blown away. Rudy's hand in splints.

And now Rudy was losing his edge and his cool; everyone was picking that up but of course no one was saying. Senor

76

Comacho should sprout wings and fly to some winter nesting ground, but there was no country so distant and no hideout so hidden that Rudy wouldn't find him. He was scared more of Rudy than the law.

Kellen sat on his bed and dialed. The phone rang once and Brad answered, sleepily. Kellen thought about hanging up. But he asked for Margot.

"No, no, I'm awake," she said. "I was just reading the audition script for the kazillianth time."

He reassured her as to his well-being. He told her he'd found the divorce papers in one of his attic storage boxes; he'd arrange to get them to her. They talked for a few minutes, but the thought of Brad beside her, pretending not to listen, depressed him. Margot in one bedroom, Kellen in another, Sarah in the living room – he guessed he wasn't making much of a hit with that one.

But when they rejoined over their coffee, she said, "I like the way you still love her."

"It's funny, after the divorce, we got closer in a way. Once the pressure was off."

"So why the divorce?"

"I shut her out too much. I was controlling."

"And she, I assume, was faultless." Here's your opening, detective, put the lash to your ex.

"Pretty much so. Except she used to hide my cigarettes."

"How cruel. No wonder you divorced her."

Sarah was perched on the arm of an easy chair, waiting, smiling nervously. She wanted him to do something, touch her.

"There were lots of reasons it ended. She wanted children. I . . . ah, that never happened." He took a gulp of coffee. "Doctor told me I'm the last of my line. She's pregnant now. I'm happy for her."

He paused, thought. "Basically, I guess, it fell apart because I couldn't let her get inside me. I couldn't seem to tell her about Coldhaven. She said there were too many dark rooms."

"Maybe she was afraid to explore them." She added softly, "I'm not."

77

He looked at her uncertainly. She held his eyes, telling him it's okay, unable to say it in words.

He put down his coffee mug and bent to her and kissed her. She got up and raised herself on her toes and pressed herself to him, and they kissed again.

She drew back and read his question and told him yes with her eyes. She wanted him. She felt it urgently, shamelessly. She pressed her head to his trembling shoulder, and said:

"Don't think I usually do this." She felt foolish and laughed. "I want some respect."

They came together again in a tender twining of lips, and she felt the hardness of him – and the crueler hardness of his service revolver moving against her right breast.

"I want you to take the holster off," she said huskily. "It's spoiling the moment."

He stood back and looked at her and shook his head and laughed. He kissed her again, long and soft, until their lips and tongues seemed to fuse in the heat. Then he took her hand and they walked to the bedroom.

There, in the dimness, she undressed, shyly, sensing him looking at her, sensing his uncertainty, feeling her own. She watched him place his change and his house keys on a dresser near the closet door, and slip his gun harness over the doorknob.

As Kellen hung his pants in the closet he heard a whining alarm in his head. He felt a strange, unbalancing sensation, and heard distant, unintelligible voices calling, and thought: Oh, no, God, no.

"Remember that he killed your father." You must kill, you can kill, you must kill, he killed your father, and the gun barks and jumps, and the killer is a thousand images of broken glass.

He came back into darkness and the bedroom, and heard his own strangled gasp. He saw Sarah looking at him, bent forward, hands behind her at the bra fasteners.

"Kellen?"

You scream. "It's not real! Nothing is real! What are you doing to me?" You hurl the gun at the wall and the wall billows

and becomes a curtain, and you run past it, you run, you run,
a door, a hall, walls shrinking toward you, and the men are
coming behind, the men in white . . .

He saw her naked form moving toward him.

Another lurch.

Stairs, a final door to freedom, and you burst from darkness
into sudden blinding sunlight, and the leafy arms of trees reach
out for you, and you hear grunts and oaths, and they're gaining,
gaining . . .

And it was over.

She pressed her body to his, and felt the trembling in his
chest and the sticky hot sweat on it.

"What is it?"

He waited for a few seconds, then said, "I thought they'd
never stop. I was flashing back to Coldhaven."

"Are you all right now?"

"Yeah."

Sarah clung to him, fearful of the powerful demon that
seemed locked in Kellen's soul.

"Okay?" she said.

"Yes." He stroked her hair slowly, still shaking. "I heard
my voice screaming," he whispered. "Why is it coming back?
Why now?"

"Do you want a cigarette?"

"Just be with me."

They clung to each other for a few more moments, then
she took his hand and led him to the bed and pulled him
gently onto it.

She would send her heat to him. It would melt his pain.

She laid him back on the bed and held him and kissed his
face, and ran her hands over his body, and kissed his neck,
his chest, his stomach, his hips, and she felt his body shudder
and soften and move. She took him in her mouth until he
was alive with her. Then she slowly journeyed back up his
trembling body, and they joined in a hunger of tongues,
turning, turning, his hands on her, caressing. She felt lush
and wet, felt her loins melting against his, and wanted more
of him, all of him.

She was astonished at herself, her need to give was urgent, and within was an organic mix of lust, loving, healing, and revenge – the revenge against Marcel, a lover far distant and different, more cold and powerful in bed.

She was shocked at Kellen's gentleness.

She had expected the alleged controlling. A fleeting query: What kind of lover had Margot been to him?

Sarah raised herself above Kellen's supine form. In sudden astonishing ripeness, she wanted completion, and gasped as she brought him inside her. She closed her eyes and kissed him deeply and shuddered as the explosions came. She clutched him and whispered, "Oh, please come now."

Eddie Comacho moved slowly out of the closet, low, with his gun up. He crouched almost mesmerized at the closet doorway, feeling his armpits sweat, his tongue ragged and dry. He held his gun on the lust-blinded, undulating forms on the bed, and with his other hand fingered the keys that Kellen had placed on the dresser.

He rejected them and, bending low, stepped carefully to the door, watching them writhe.

As Eddie slipped through the narrowly open doorway, Kellen cried out, a profanity of release.

Sunday, ten a.m.

Church bells pealed, sharp and high in the cold air, awakening him. Sunlight teased him through the icy window. Sarah's hair was splayed over his shoulder, her sleeping head there, her breath warm on his chest. His mouth tasted like a newly tarred road, cigarettes all evening, cigarettes and love-making and coffee, and after that, cigarettes and love-making and a bottle of wine until four in the morning.

He'd talked to her about his childhood dreams, of being

80

something important to his father, a son to make him proud. *Don't ever become a cop,* his dad said a year before his death. No life insurance. The city had left his widow and son a miserly gratuity in death benefits.

Yes, he'd talked to Sarah about his father. Without pain. The only hero figure of his life. He told of how the agony of his loss carried into his teens, how he'd heard of Satorius, everyone at college talking about him, the miracle-maker.

Said he'd fix Kellen right up. And now Kellen couldn't remember the facts of his father's death. Electrical lobotomy.

Kellen and Sarah had tried to analyze those three quick, clicking snapshots of last night: more clues to the past; Kellen had tried to escape from the padded room, from Satorius and the men in white.

The young Kellen had screamed: *Nothing is real! What are you doing to me?*

Something very important had happened on that summer day, and was trying to leak out, seeking escape from the buried mind.

Before they'd fallen asleep, Sarah had importuned him. *You have to give evidence. Please. For those poor people. For yourself . . .*

Could he ever bring himself to do that? Expose himself to the whips and pillories of public scorn? No, he couldn't endure that . . .

He slipped his arm out from under Sarah – she didn't stir – and got up to answer the knocking on the door, grabbing his terrycloth robe. Mao yawned at him from the easy chair in the living room, and stretched.

When he opened the front door, it came back to him: Sunday. Plans had been made.

Raolo Basutti, in a parka and mittens and toque, was standing there with shy eleven-year-old Mario, similarly clothed. On the street was their family Ford, a toboggan strapped to the roof. Thérèse was in the front seat. The motor was running.

"You don't look ready," Raolo said.

"Gee, is it that time?"

81

He thought of Sarah in the bedroom, felt perplexed, awkward. This was a social dilemma for which he was little armed by experience.

"Maybe you should, ah, invite us in, Kel. It's kinda cold out here." Raolo beckoned to his wife, who got out of the car.

"Yeah, yeah, sure," Kellen said, standing aside, waving them in.

If she awakes, she'll hear the voices; she'll stay hidden in the bedroom. He wasn't ashamed, but he didn't want to embarrass her.

Thérèse kicked her boots off at the mat and kissed Kellen on the mouth. "Whew. Where'd *you* celebrate last night? Got coffee on?" She spoke French; English was to her an unwieldy, awkward tongue. She'd been an east-end welfare worker, and before that a farmer's daughter from Beaupré, near Quebec City. She was full of verve and bounce, still in love with Raolo after thirteen years of brick-solid marriage. But she was out of love with his job. One avoided talking cop-shop around her; the subject tended to ignite her short fuse.

"Coffee, it's on its way," Kellen said. Guatemalan drip. He'd have to come up with an excuse for not joining them. But he'd promised the day to Mario.

He pulled the boy's toque off and tousled his sandy hair.

"Did they really shoot at you?" Mario said.

"Yeah, but I caught the bullets with my teeth and spit them out."

"Oh, sure." He laughed.

Kellen liked to spoil Mario, bestowing on him a parental affection he would never have a chance to give to his own; he'd wanted children, it wasn't just Margot. He blamed Satorius, without proof, for his sterility.

"These guys treating you all right?" Kellen took the role of godfather seriously.

"Yeah, I guess."

"Hear you aced your grammar test."

Raolo said, proudly, "Ninety percent ain't bad. Listen, Kellen, if you want to do this some other day – "

"It'll be good for him." Sarah's voice. Kellen had just

82

turned to go to the kitchen, and saw her standing at the bedroom doorway, covered to mid-thigh in one of his white dress shirts.

She came toward the Basuttis, smiling, offering her hand. "Hi, you're Raolo Basutti, aren't you, the partner in crime. I'm Sarah Paradis."

Raolo uneasily took her hand.

"Ah, and that's Thérèse," Kellen said. "Raolo's wife. And Mario."

Sarah shook each hand in turn, and said she was delighted to meet them all. To Mario she said, in French, "Did you bring your sleigh?"

"Yeah, we're going to Beaver Lake." Mario picked up Mao, petted him. The cat lay limp in his arms, feigning indifference.

"I'd join you if I didn't have to work," Sarah said.

The phone rang. Kellen darted for it, a digression.

"H'lo."

"That you?" Juley LeGiusti.

"Yeah, it's me."

"Wanna come to the store?"

"You open already? It's Sunday morning."

"So? *You* been to mass?"

He heard the bells outside scolding him. He put his hand over the mouthpiece, and said to Raolo, "It's Juley the Juice."

"What's he got?"

Thérèse slowly shook her head. "Oh, God, here we go."

Sunday, eleven-fifteen p.m.

Thérèse was a woman unafraid to speak her mind, and her silence in the car as they drove to Juley's was foreboding and oppressive. Kellen could sense her barometer falling. They'd

83

promised her that after this little side-trip, they'd head up the mountain, get in at least a couple of hours on the toboggan run.

They pulled up in front of Le Marché Beaver, and Thérèse and Mario waited in the car while Kellen and Raolo went inside.

Juley took them into his main theater, safe from prying ears. Thirty plastic chairs and a screen. They walked up a small flight of stairs to the projection area, behind a curtain. Reels of film were arrayed on a table. The place smelled musty, rancid.

The setting didn't bother Kellen. He felt clean and whole and well. Cleansed somehow by Sarah, purified by her. No inner tremors so far today. She'd urged the four of them out of his house; she would shower and go to work from there, and – she whispered this to him as the coffee dripped – in case he was free this evening, so was she.

They'd decided on dinner. Kellen would prepare it. He wasn't bad in the kitchen, he'd immodestly announced.

Raolo had chuckled salaciously as they walked into Le Marché Beaver. "She's the lawyer, right? You dirty hound dog." Kellen had smiled smugly.

"Sit," said Juley.

"Prefer to stand," Kellen said. "What couldn't you talk about on the phone?"

"I hope I'm appreciated for this."

"Yeah, Juley. Give."

"Okay, a stripper says two guys in ski jackets, one of them had his arm kind of bandaged, showed up Friday night at the Club S'Extasie."

"One of Johnny Ronce's joints," Raolo said.

"They were met there by a Dr. Tom Luk. Ex-Saigon, whom Johnny's helping him with his papers. Checks Johnny's girls for, like, the clap. The stripper's name is Linda, don't know where she lives, but she goes on duty at one this afternoon. Linda as in Lovelace."

Kellen nodded. "Where do we find this Tom Luk on a Sunday?"

"I dunno. He's, like, a illegal alien."

"Did you see your brother-in-law like I asked?"

Juley lowered his voice, although the door was closed. "I mighta seen him at a get-together last night at my uncle's."

"You might have talked to him?"

"The impression I get is, like, they're friends of the Family, but they ain't in the Gambino organization. These gentlemen are, like, from the South, New Orleans, Atlanta, like around there."

"That's, like, all?"

"What am I, gonna tell Johnny and the boys I help the bulls out, I give them the total dope on everyone because I got a friend on the force I like?"

"Think of it as a license to pimp, Juley."

As they walked back through the shop, Raolo said, "Jeez, I forgot, we got no one to fill on Sundays. I have that Budget guy coming all the way up from Iberville in half an hour."

"Well, we have to catch that dancer, too. Linda."

"Okay, let me handle this," Raolo said.

When they returned outside, Thérèse was standing outside the car, glaring at them, arms folded. Mario was strolling around, sneaking looks at the partially curtained windows of the sex shop.

Kellen stayed back beside Mario, away from possible shrapnel, as Raolo explained to his wife that they may have to stop by the office for about half an hour first. Hour at most. Then just one other quick stop, and they're away.

Thérèse said, "I thought this was your day off."

Kellen couldn't hear what Raolo said next, something apologetic. But Thérèse was suddenly walking away toward Mario. "No, that's too late. He has hockey practice this afternoon. I don't suppose you'll be at that, either." She grasped Mario by the arm and dragged him away from the windows. Angrily, "Get away from that filth."

"Okay, look, drop me off at the station," Kellen said. "And I'll – "

"Oh, no, I wouldn't want to split up the two loyal partners." She pulled Mario to the Ford. "Get in, we're going sledding." She went to the driver's side. Raolo tried to follow her.

"Jesus Christ, just go to the goddamn station," she said, and as she sat behind the wheel, a final shot, her voice quavering: "You're supposed to be his father. When the hell do you ever see him?"

Mario looked at his dad from inside the car, struggling to smile, as if to say: It's okay, I understand.

Raolo and Kellen speechlessly watched the car pull abruptly from the curb and speed away, toboggan on roof, sleigh in the backseat.

"Roses tonight, pal," Kellen said.

Sunday, eleven-forty a.m.

From his desk at the station he tried to phone Sarah at her office – for no reason, really, just to hear her voice, a form of pinching oneself, seeking proof of the reality of her, and of the long fervent night. He got her answering service. He tried her home; her recorded greeting was businesslike, her other voice, reserved for strangers and clients. But it was enough.

He was truly feeling better. No shakes, no inaudible voices so far today. He had allowed himself a vulnerability and, in doing so, found new resources, strength. He felt emotionally scrubbed and scoured.

Thoughts of her intruded fitfully as he listened to Raolo debrief the car rental agent from Iberville.

"How much was this weekend rate?" Raolo said.

"Seventy-four dollars a day plus insurance, no mileage. They didn't have no credit card, I t'ought that was strange. For those type of guy. Looked like businessmen."

"This man who called himself Roy Salvador, he say when he'd return it?"

86

"After the weekend."

Raolo looked at Kellen. "His office is staked out. But these, ah, businessmen will probably abandon the van. Think they're still here?"

"I think they want that key."

Forensics had it. They'd identified it is an old-fashioned, hand-cut safety-deposit key, a type most banks no longer use.

"That's him, that's one of them." The Budget clerk was looking at a picture of the man Kellen shot.

"Salvador? The man who signed the papers?"

"No, the ot'er man. This one he never said nothing. The ot'er, wit' the big round face, he did all the talk for bot'."

The Budget agent said the picture he saw on the license was of the same round-faced man. With a little smile and a little mustache.

"Kellen," Borko called from above.

Kellen looked up. Borko smiling over the balustrade in his striped gray formal suit. He liked to stop at the station after church on Sundays, the Christian Reformed Baptist or something like that.

"Yeah, Eugene?"

"Turn on your computer." He came down the stairs, a long-legged, two-step-at-a-time stride.

Kellen flicked the switch and the Monster's screen glowed amber. An FBI sheet. Name: Rudy Meyers, aka Roy Salvador. Thousand-dollar fine for illegal weapons, 1978. That was the only conviction, but he'd been found not guilty of another charge: narcotics trafficking three years ago in Florida.

"I was just on the line to the FBI," Borko said, appearing like an archangel at Kellen's shoulder. "Our boy was bagged a few years ago with fifty, count 'em, fifty tons of Colombian *punta roja* in his living room. Must've had a hell of a lawyer."

"Can't quit working homicide, can you, Eugene?"

"I wasn't sure you'd be, ah, in attendance on your day off. I'm not interfering? It's your file, Kellen. I don't like the tools to get rusty, that's all. And I owe you an apology."

"Why is that?"

"The murders are indeed, as you deduced, the work of the

Cosa Nostra. Meyers is connected into a family that runs Miami, New Orleans, and Houston. The d'Ambrozzios. It's dope, Kellen. Big dope, in amounts people murder for. I leave you with that." Borko marched triumphantly out.

The officer at switchboard – Station Twenty-six had no civilian employees – rang his line. "A lawyer just phoned," she said. "He didn't want to speak to you now, asked if you could see him Monday morning, nine o'clock at his office. J.C. Beaulieu. From Charles, Saint-Etienne, and Montague."

Big law firm. "What about?"

"He says he wants to show you a couple of last wills and testaments."

"In connection with?"

"That's all he said."

"Okay. Any other calls?"

Her voice went low, conspiratorial. "I'm supposed to pass the word from the union. Everyone at the Hélène de Champlain banquet room, tomorrow night, all night. They say to bring a sleeping bag if you want."

"Anyone else phone?"

"Nope."

Maybe she tried to reach him at home. He dialed the access number of his answering machine:

"Allo?" Sarah's voice.

"Excuse me, I think I have the wrong number." Margot in her clumsy French.

"No, no, it's for Kellen?"

"Who's this?"

"I'm Sarah Paradis. I . . . well, I just happen to be here. Kellen went out tobogganing."

A long pause at Margot's end. Kellen sighed.

"Oh, I see. Okay, ah, tell him Margot called."

88

Satin and chintz and skin in the Club S'Extasie, three girls to a customer, and only fifteen of those. Four of them were at the bar, surrounding a stage above which a naked woman was swinging on a trapeze to soft rock. Two other women were on stools in front of tables, doing close-up strips for unhappy men with leaden eyes.

Another stripper approached Kellen and Raolo's table. She was stringy and tired-looking, topless with small slack tits.

"You asked for me?" she said in poor French. "You want me to dance?"

"Just to talk," Kellen said, switching her to English. "You're Linda?"

"Maybe. You horsemen?"

"City. Understand you worked here Friday night."

"I work every night, eh? I have two kids, and an old man in the can."

"Let us make life easier." Kellen put a fifty on the table.

"I shouldn't be seen talking to you guys. Mr. Roncerelli sometimes comes in." But she liked the red-colored bill. She studied it: all the scarlet Mounties and the black horses' asses on the back.

"Couple men were here to see Dr. Luk. One was injured."

"Okay, yeah, he had his arm in a sling, kind of bandaged up. They were both big guys. Ski jackets. Sort of older."

"Talk to them?" Raolo asked.

"No. Dr. Luk came up, and then took them straight down to his room."

"Where is that?" said Raolo.

"Clinic downstairs. Never saw them come back up here, but I was doin' other things, eh?"

"Seen him around lately?" Kellen asked. "Luk?"

"No, and I wouldn't. He's too weird, a boat person. I use my own doctor."

"We'll be back," said Kellen.

She tucked the fifty into her bikini panties. Kellen and

Raolo walked past the stage as a dancer, or whatever she was – gymnast – bent over and honored them with a shimmering moon to the tune of "Private Dancer."

A door behind the stage led to a staircase, dimly lit. Below, a hallway with a musty smell, a low boom from upstairs, the sound of bass and Tina Turner.

Over a smoked-glass pane on one of the doors was a wooden sign: EMERGENCY ROOM. PLEASE COME IN.

Okay, but how? It was locked.

"Can we get a search warrant?" said Raolo.

"Maybe he takes Visa." Kellen snuck a credit card into the opening above the lock and fiddled a while before it sprung.

Raolo clicked the light on, careful, not smudging anything.

The room was bare and uninviting, three chairs with foam cushions, a curtained-off area serving, probably, as an examining room, and a door marked Private. A table with a *People* magazine and a *Reader's Digest*. A cabinet with medical supplies.

Kellen could hear the music from upstairs, the thrumming of a drum, a monotonous bass beat Kellen felt through his skin. He could make out the words of the song.

Raolo opened the curtain. The rumpled sheets on the examining table showed rusty stains of blood. A pair of medical scissors and a roll of tape. No cleanup after minor surgery.

He felt a draft, a cold prickle of wind, and looked up and saw a window to the alley, open on its hinges just a little, a crack. Half-a-meter high and one wide, caked with ice.

Tina Turner sang.

"Let's get a team down here," Kellen said. He took out a tissue paper and turned the doorknob of the room marked Private.

A chair was knocked over, partly jamming the door. Kellen pushed inside, and saw a pair of tan leather boots, baggy green slacks, white shirt, white medical jacket, a bowed head, the whole package dangling from a cord tied to a ceiling fixture. Oriental man, about thirty-five, his expression one of gentle dismay.

Raolo just said, "Oh, boy."

Kellen looked at the stuff on the desk. Newspapers, Vietnamese typeface. Framed snapshots. This is his wife, in a long silk dress, in a room decorated with bamboo, Oriental prints. Here are his kids, five of them. Three girls, two boys. Here he is in his graduating robe, standing with his wife and children outside a university building.

"Dr. Luk," he said.

Sunday, three-fifteen p.m.

The Lord Swinburne was class. You get the typical guy, a drink and a little poke before confronting the wife over dinner; she's pleased because he smells so clean, he must have stopped off at his health club. The Lord Swinburne – private spa for gentlemen. Johnny Roncerelli, proprietor.

He helps with his customers' marriages. He provides a service to the community.

Working hours, Johnny liked to work out of his office on the main floor, because sometimes not being near the exit door brings bad luck. His daily ritual was to head up to the spa at four; he'd peel off his clothes in his private elevator, rising nine storeys heavenward, feeling in fact like he's done God's own hard work, and he's owed this small favor in return.

Up here, the top floor, you're toweling off after the pool, you can look out the vista down Côte-des-Neiges, the Hill of Snows, you can see the Wax Museum and the Oratory from here, and the big phallic tower at the University of Montreal, and, naturally, the mountain.

Many of the good citizens of Montreal come here, respectable, you get city councilors, guys with big dealerships, brokers, stock promoters.

He knew most of the gentlemen in here now, not all. But they all knew him, Johnny Ronce.

Sunk to the second of his three chins in a bubbling whirl-pool, hot jets pounding tired flesh.

Nobody goes into the number-one swirlpool between four and four-thirty, it's Johnny Ronce's time. Seven days a week.

It's not that there's a sign up. Unless it's in the form of Joe Caporicci and Cut-'em-Up Hymie Zlotz, sitting in chairs behind him, against the wall, guns in their armpits.

Joe was reading a comic book, looking very serious, the Green Phantom was catching hell.

Hymie contentedly puffed on a cigar, watching one of the girls take some schlemiel into a massage room, two hundred potatoes and you get the "complete," they called it.

Hymie wondered what it was like, the complete. His old lady would cut his nuts off.

Johnny Ronce, breathing in the liquor of the rich, damp air, bubbles frothing at his nose, opened his eyes to see Kellen O'Reilly sliding naked beside him into the whirlpool.

"*Madonna puttana!*" he shouted.

Joe sprang to his feet, the comic book went fluttering to the tiles. His gun was out.

"Dis is private," he yelled.

"Easy, boys," Raolo said. He was beside them, wearing only a towel, which was knotted around his waist. A hand was beneath the towel, pushing the material out. Everybody could see what Raolo was holding was too big to be the kind of rod most guys come equipped with naturally.

Johnny Ronce started chuckling.

"Raolo, I like you, you got personality, a sense of humor." He swiveled his massive neck a half-turn to the two men behind him, both standing now. "What are you guys, jerkin' off back there? Coulda been a Iranian assassin. Order a girl over." His voice was a squeaky tenor.

He said to Kellen, "A pleasure to be your host on this tranquil Sunday."

"Man, do I need this," Kellen said. He raised both sets of toes from the water and wiggled them.

"Listen, it's like a reward. You bust ass all day, you don't lose hope, you got a relaxative at the end." He shouted,

"Désiree, ask these gentlemen what they want." He lowered himself to his first chin.

"Hear you have a new grandson."

"Clarissa, my second youngest, finally. Her first. He'll make the heavies, a Marciano, nine-and-a-half pounds."

"You'll give her and Vinnie my regards. Your health? No more problems with the back?"

"That's right, I remember – I was laid up with a bad disk on the occasion of your last unnecessary visit. It's better, I got some guy doin' chiropractice on me. Aches in the morning, but you learn to live with the various inconveniences. How's *your* health, O'Reilly? I heard you was in a gunfight."

"Which brings me to a question. Some pals from out of town come to you, one's been shot. Who do you send them to?"

"It's an emergency, I call an ambulance. Like any normal citizen." They were suddenly on business terms, Johnny was gruff, chary.

"I just came back from Dr. Luk's office."

"Dr. Luk? Can't say if he's a gentleman of my acquaintance."

"He couldn't practice in Canada. You helped him out, right? – a new refugee and his family."

Johnny quickly wearied of the subject. "Thirty below tonight, I hear. Winter, we should pass a law against it."

"Yeah, it's a bitch out there." Kellen worked his bottom up against a hot jet. "I could even stand it a little hotter in here. You like it a little hotter, Johnny? You like the heat?"

"You like your job?" It was Johnny who was suddenly hot, their masks abandoned, enmity out in the open. "You want I should call the complaint department? You recall maybe the incidents surrounding the last time you tried to hassle me?"

This was better, the politenesses out of the way. Kellen enjoyed getting Johnny Ronce going. He didn't give a *bien merde* about his friends at city hall.

A young woman squatted in front of the whirlpool, her black breasts mirrored on an empty tray-top.

93

"Hi, I'm Désiree. How you gents makin' out?"

"How old are you?" Kellen asked her.

"Eighteen."

"Bring me your ID."

Johnny went off like a steam whistle. "Okay, what's this shit?" Angrily, to Desy, "Get outa here!"

She backed away, eyes wide.

"You got a little problem with Dr. Luk."

"So he's a refugee a'ready," Johnny rasped. "It's a problem with his papers, we got a lawyer on it. It ain't a federal case."

"It's a federal case. Criminal Code, Revised Statutes of Canada, Section two-twelve, murder one."

Johnny's eyes became little seams.

"Give me this again?"

"They strung him up, tried to make it look like suicide. Your pals. From the States."

Johnny rose walrus-like from the tub.

"My new croaker? *Dio orete!*"

Raolo was leaning toward him now. "Who are they, Mr. Roncerelli?" he said in Italian.

"*I'd* like to know who they are."

He sputtered, sank heavily back into the pool. He wrenched his bulk around to Joe and Hymie. "I do a favor, this is the way I am treated? They hang my croaker? After I spend fifty grand on immigration? I want you gentlemen to, ah, escort Dirty Harry's comical relief man there, Raolo, outa earshot – walk him around the pool."

Raolo moved away, keeping an eye on things and his gun hidden.

Johnny was still seething as he brought his face close to Kellen's, talking quickly.

"Okay, even though you come into my athlete club and lay the threats on, even though I don't like you, I will say I respect you as a reputable person of integrity in this community."

"And even though I don't like you, Johnny, and I don't like anything you stand for, I want to do a service for you. I want to get those *porcos* who stiffed your doctor."

94

"Off the record. Nothin' comes back on me. No subpoenas."

Kellen thought about it and said, "Okay."

"I don't got to tell you nothin', you can't do shit to me, it's a favor. I'm doing my free will."

"I understand."

"Okay, let's say, figuratively, two unnamed individuals come up to see me Friday night. Possibly they know a acquaintance of mine, and this gets them through the door. Let's say they ask me to phone this acquaintance in Houston, who maybe I owe a favor. I phone. This is the favor: find a doctor for the individual with the bullet wound in his hand."

"These two individuals – do they maybe trace their roots to the old country?"

Johnny looked shocked. "If they're friends of the family you think I would waste breath talking to such as you, a civil servant? Such things are handled in the private sector."

"Who are they?"

"Nobody passed out no business cards. Whom the fuck these unnamed individuals are, I ain't got the faintest idea."

Sunday, five p.m.

After Kellen left in a cab, Raolo returned to Dr. Luk's office, to make sure ident had finished and a guard was posted, and generally to clean up the day's loose ends before heading home to save his marriage. Cold ham sandwiches tonight.

He kiddingly asked Kellen what's on for dinner at *his* place, maybe he could join him and his new lady friend this evening. Sarah Paradis, rich and pretty, not somebody you'd ever aspire to marry or nothing like that, but even temporary she'll be good for Kel, he's been lonely.

His partner looked better today, but generally he's seemed

pretty rocky lately. Raolo had hinted he should take a week or so off pretty soon. He should've been tougher, bluntly told him as a friend to take his collected holidays right now, forget the strike, forget these button men – it's just another gang war, don't let it weigh so much.

It's as if he has some personal thing about these American hitters. Well, maybe he has. They tried to off him in a drugstore. Kellen's at his best when he takes things personal, though he sometimes acts like the law only applies to the bad guys, not him.

But why is he so tense lately? He wished they could talk, Kellen and him.

The pathologist was still at Luk's office when Raolo got back there. Yes, it's conceivable Dr. Luk could have been strangled, he told Raolo. And after that the corpse was strung up. He couldn't rule it out. The autopsy probably wouldn't disclose anything conclusive one way or another.

A coroner's jury who didn't know the facts would say suicide. Main one being that Dr. Luk was a risky witness to leave alive.

But other people had caught glimpses of these guys – the stripper at the S'Extasie, some of the patrons. So killing Dr. Luk seemed a little desperate. Like they were running scared after that shoot-out, had lost their cool.

No fingerprints. Not even from the hand the doctor set and bandaged up.

Johnny Ronce had told Kellen they weren't *Famiglia*. Kellen said he believed him. A strong Mafia connection then, but not Mafia. Who are these cowboys anyway?

Sunday, six p.m.

Kellen had picked up some fresh whitefish on The Main – he'd do it poached, with his famous marinade – and some ripe avocados for his famous salad. He found his recipe and searched through his spice cabinet, checking off the list of ingredients. Thyme, okay; marjoram, okay; cloves and garlic, okay.

Mao followed him about the kitchen. He was expecting fish on the menu tonight; he could smell it.

Kellen took the Stolichnaya from the freezer compartment of the fridge, and a half-pared lemon from inside the fridge door and a bottle of soda, and fixed himself a drink, lit a cigarette, and started making dinner for two.

He had come home to find a note on a saucer in the middle of his kitchen table. "I feel wonderful," the note said. "I enjoyed the night. *C'étais extra*." She'd be here about six-thirty.

He wondered if it could possibly work out, the self-pitying cop and the senator's daughter. She had surprised him; he'd misread her badly. Not stuck-up at all. That came from his own blue-collar prejudice against the rich. She was open, unafraid, self-assured. The Jeanne d'Arc of the Quebec Left. Yet she had allowed him to know her softness and had spoken of the things that hurt her. And she had brought light into his dark rooms.

Margot – the aerobotic apolitical actor, concealer of cigarettes – suddenly seemed, in retrospect, always to have been more buddy than lover. More sister than wife. Too often disengaging quickly after intimacy, as if in guilt. Anglo. Handles pain with a stiff upper lip.

But he loved her, and she could still make him jealous. He would have enjoyed the vengeance of seeing her face when she phoned his house and Sarah answered.

Imagine her getting pregnant by that clod.

"No, Mao, that's incorrect thinking. We're happy for her, aren't we?" Mao would understand Kellen's jealousy; he'd been neutered, too. It was fundamental to all species, that repressive sense of one's own infertility.

His cat-mind on more important matters, Mao was on his hind legs, front paws on the oven door, stretching his nose closer to the fish on the counter.

"You know better," Kellen said. The cat went back down on all fours.

A rapping on the door. His brain switched quickly back to Sarah. She was early. He hurried to the door, drink and cigarette in hand.

But it was Margot – in an *après*-ski outfit.

"Hi. Can't stay long."

Brad was across the street in the Porsche, staring at them. Blond, muscular, handsome. Two pairs of skis on the roof rack.

"Just want to make sure you're all right."

"I'm good. Glowing with health. How was the ski weekend?"

"Beastly. I almost froze my face off."

"You, ah, want to warm up? Ask him to come in for a drink."

"He's shy; he says he'd feel awkward."

He looked down at Brad again. Brad looked away. Shy – it wasn't the picture of him Kellen had drawn from imagination.

"I told him I was just stopping by to pick up the divorce papers." She peered past him, inside the living room, as if looking for evidence of wrong-doing.

She waited as he went to his desk and got the papers. He'd gift-wrapped the envelope, tied a ribbon around it.

He handed them to her at the doorway. "My wedding present."

"Thanks," she said, and laughed. For a moment she just stood there. "So . . . what's new?"

"Oh, nothing."

Another pause. "Well, what's with this Sarah Paradis?"

"Sarah who?"

"You know who. Did you sleep with her?"

"A little bit."

"You bastard. You were with her all evening while I was worrying my insides *raw*. I hope she's prettier than in the photos I've seen."

Kellen smiled down at Brad, and waved. He seemed unsure how to respond, then vigorously returned the greeting.

"How was she?" Margot asked.

"What do you mean, 'How was she?' "

"In bed."

"Totally awesome. How's the part coming? The conniving ex-wife. Sounds like you're ready for it."

"I'll know tomorrow. Probably blow it. You've made me tense." She took her eyes off him, lowered them. "You could have got killed."

"I'm fine. I'm okay."

She put the divorce decree into her bag. "Thanks for this, Kellen. You're sweet."

She boldly kissed him on the mouth, holding the kiss for a few seconds. Then she hugged him, and he saw Brad pretending not to see this. She turned quickly and ran down the stairs to the car.

Sunday, nine p.m.

A bottle of wine helped but did not completely dissolve the shyness that seemed to enclose them at the table. She said the right things about his prowess in the kitchen – she could see he was proud of that. They talked food and books and pop psychology – neutral subjects; background jazz was by Oscar Peterson.

Sarah was timid, correct. There is something about going to bed with a man on the first night that makes the second night a little angst-ridden. In fact, she'd been mortified all day about getting so *dérangé* with drink and pills, and raping him – well, almost – in his own bed.

Guilt had embellished the making of love in that bed. The

night had been rich with a sense of adultery. The ghosts of Marcel and Margot lay alongside them, taunting them.

If they make love tonight, she'll try much harder to be alone with him.

But they shouldn't. She'll say no. Politely.

What if he doesn't ask?

No. She must leave after dinner, after an appropriate time. An attitude of friendly reserve was in order for this evening, a slight applying of the brakes. She knew she wanted a relationship with this man; his mystery dazzled her. But she was afraid of him, too. Fragile, he could break into splinters, like that terrible man in his flashbacks. Maybe, too, he was . . . dangerous.

She knew that was part of the attraction.

How deeply was that attraction shared? A section of him seemed cordoned off, Sarah being allowed to look but not touch. Margot's section. Sarah felt she was competing with the past. What would it take to win him away from his divorced wife?

She'd been disappointed at his greeting at the door. A brief touch of the lips, not holding. Maybe he felt awkward about last night, too.

She'd promised herself: no Halcions tonight. She didn't need them; Marcel was quickly receding into the misty haze of history. Anyway, it would be too uncomfortable popping pills in front of the preachy Lieutenant O'Reilly. He was right; the pills were wrong. If she wanted a tranq this badly, they couldn't be good for you. But, drugless, she felt edgy, moody, not sure how to recapture the closeness and the richness of that electric night.

Sarah had a secret agenda for this evening. But in the meantime she talked shop: the coming strike, the last-minute maneuverings by the MUC administration, her planned tactics in response. Tomorrow the employers were applying to Superior Court for an injunction to stop the police walkout. She'd worked all day in the courthouse library preparing for that.

Also tomorrow: a session with Satorius, his examination for discovery continuing. But she didn't mention his name, preferred to wait for Kellen to do so, maybe to continue his confessions of the night before. But he seemed to wish to avoid the subject.

Mao finished his dinner first, and returned from the kitchen licking the last flecks of fish from his whiskers.

They lingered at the table, joking, talking, finding common ground, learning about each other. After they put the dishes away, and were sitting in the living room with coffee, on the couch, at about arm's length, she began to make her case.

She started by talking about her clients, the amnesic, nightmare-haunted, phobia-consumed, twitching, pitiable wrecks she had collected together in her crusade for retribution against Satorius and the CIA. She talked about the iniquities that were performed on them, the pain they would always feel, and the pain she felt for them.

Kellen looked at her steadily through ten minutes of this, then interrupted calmly.

"I won't give evidence, Sarah."

She stalled, her speech unfinished.

"I don't just want you to give evidence. I want you to sue for damages."

"I'm a career policeman. I'm not going to resign in disgrace."

"Resign? Don't be ridiculous."

"Or be fired."

"That's why there's a union."

"There'd be a public inquiry. I don't think I can handle that. It's just the way I am." He looked at her with a firm, set expression. "What I told to you was in confidence, Sarah."

"I know," she said softly.

He slowly drained his coffee, in a manner suggesting the subject was closed.

"Is that what you want to be? Always? A policeman? You could easily start up a private investigator's office. I know lots of lawyers who would send business to you."

"I'm a city cop. It's all I'll ever be."

"I may have a losing case without you, Kellen."

"You may have a losing case anyway."

"Not with you on the stand. Please, Kellen, just listen to me."

"I'll get more coffee. Cognac? A liqueur?"

"No, I've got a full day tomorrow." She wasn't going to add this, but she did: "I have to be going soon."

He was on his way to the kitchen with their cups. He halted. "Yeah, I've got to slog through about a mile of shit tomorrow myself." He left.

She didn't like this, the sudden cooling breeze. She felt rejected. And now she knew she was going to be stubborn, and could see possibilities of the evening coming to a calamitous end.

But her attitude was firm. He had a responsibility. If he refused to help himself, he could at least help her people. If he didn't have a generous enough heart to go public and get behind this cause, maybe he wasn't the kind of man she wanted in her life.

Kellen put her refill on the table in front of her and sat beside her again. Too far away, she thought, too much space between them.

"They don't remember Coldhaven, Kellen. You do."

"I don't."

"The flashbacks are a form of memory. I'll get your psychiatrist to testify to that. You can tell the world about some of the terrible things that were done there."

He laughed softly. "Tell the world. It's a political thing with you, isn't it, Sarah? You can't win this case, you know that. You can't get judgment against the CIA, they're beyond the pale. And if you do win damages from Satorius, good luck collecting them – he's almost bankrupt; Coldhaven is sinking under the weight of its mortgages. I know you love your clients, but don't you think you're putting them through a lot of hell just because you want to make a statement?"

Sarah bristled. "No, I do *not* think that. Damn it, it will be good for you, Kellen. Healthy. Come out of the closet. Get free."

"Yeah, O'Reilly comes out of the closet. Captain Borko, sir, I need some time off because I've got to go to court to

102

tell the world I've been having flashbacks. I've been a nutcase all these years."

"God, what are you afraid of? You've given evidence hundreds of times. A homicide detective. They'd believe you, a jury would."

But her jury tonight was stone-faced, unbudging. "They'd crucify me on the witness stand. PSYCHO COP ADMITS URGE TO KILL."

She felt provoked by his selfishness, and couldn't help herself, heard her own aggressive words:

"Crucify you? You, you, that's all you care about? What about my clients? You're a cop, don't you believe in justice? They deserve a little of that, those poor men and women, just a little justice. They're good people, Kellen. And they're afraid; some of them are terrified at the prospect of facing their tormentors in court. But at least they have guts enough to stand up and be counted."

"Well, count me out."

She stood up, riled at his obstinacy.

"It might not be a matter of choice. I could have you subpoenaed."

She regretted that immediately; it came out of anger.

"Don't play with my life, Sarah."

She stood in silence, emotions bubbling: fury and disappointment. "Thanks for dinner." She turned and went toward the front vestibule. "This isn't working out too well, I'm sorry."

She sensed him behind her.

"It's me, I'm tired and cranky. Don't leave yet."

His fingers came lightly to rest on her arm. She stopped in the middle of removing her coat from a hanger, and she turned, downcast, but letting him see her tears.

"I wouldn't force you into court, that was a wrong thing to say."

He took her in his arms.

"I guess we're both a little tired," she said, and smiled. "We didn't get much sleep."

"Hey, we were doing fine until the coffee. Must be the

103

Guatemalan beans. Want to stay a little longer, repair the damage?"

"There's no damage." She backed away, held him at arm's length. "But I should go. I have that injunction application tomorrow."

"You're okay?"

"I'm okay. We're all okay." She kissed him fiercely. "If you think I'm becoming . . . *stoqué sur tu*, please stop me. I'm sure it would only cause problems for you."

She was out the door, struggling into her coat, heading down to the Yugo.

Kellen waited at the doorway until her engine started, and he waved, and she did, too, forcing a smile.

He was unsettled by the evening's abrupt ending, and not sure how to take her last words. *If you think I'm becoming stoqué sur tu . . .* Stuck on him, in Franglish. Was she warning him that she was falling in love? Was this becoming more than just a little affair on the rebound to mend their separate rendered hearts? He wondered if he could allow himself to love this passionate ideologue. Maybe he should ask Margot for permission. He laughed grimly to himself.

No, the only one stopping you from love is yourself, Kellen. But this evening he'd been afraid of love – of exposure, of being defenseless; he'd been shy, polite, hidden – maybe he'd not wanted her to think he was a crybaby, always too eager to pour his heart out.

Tonight's clumsy parting was just a little hiccup. He would phone her first thing in the morning, arrange to meet with her, explain. She would have to understand. How could he sit in court as their forensic experts confidently gave evidence he was suffering from a disease of the mind, undergoing hallucinations, delusions of persecution? Could he ever steel himself for that, to stand naked before the world? Not in his present condition.

Sarah said he'd been working too hard. Wally Mandelbaum told him to take a few days off. Raolo wanted him to grab a week or two of holidays. Okay. Soon. For sure. Even a weekend. Borrow Wally's cottage at Lac Echo. A fireplace, a couple of bottles of wine, and Sarah Paradis.

Much work to be done before he could rest. Murders to be solved.

He felt exhausted but tense, and feared he wouldn't sleep. He sat back in his easy chair and clicked on the television with his remote control. Images swam in front of him, beautiful people saying funny things in an unreal world. Mechanical laughter from the sound track.

Tomorrow: try to get that trace again on the derringer found in Sloukos's hand . . . key number 173, got to locate that safety deposit somehow . . . blackmail was the only likely scenario, Sloukos and Champlain had dirt on these men, pay dirt; they got paid out, all right.

An eye gouged, three murders, including a physician strangled and hanged for his services; these guys weren't your average Southern gentlemen.

But neither were they Mafia. Although Johnny Ronce implied they have a big connect inside it. Roy Salvador, alias Rudy Meyers. *Big dope, Kellen, in amounts people murder for.* Did they want to leave that trail so conspicuously blazed by the driver's license, or had they been in a hurry, grabbed what ID was at hand? If the latter, they must be desperate, prepared to be incautious, gamble that no one would see the GMC Safari. For what stakes were they gambling?

On the other hand, they had gone to particular trouble to stage the deaths – a B and E, a holdup, and a suicide. Maybe some creative mind on the opposite team suffered thwarted aspirations of being a set designer. Or maybe they were cleverer than he thought: the driver's license of Salvador-alias-Meyers, a man with a drug sheet, might have been forged as a deliberately false lead – if the staged robberies don't work, make it look like drug executions.

Lawyer J.C. Beaulieu wants to talk about wills and testaments; could be nothing, could be a breaker. Nine tomorrow.

He should have somebody draw a will for him. What was that awful rush that swept through him just before the action in the drugstore? Not just adrenaline – another ingredient added. An implanted desire to kill? Had he been subject to some bizarre experiment at Coldhaven intended to split the psyche, to break the inner savage free of the rational man? He had to talk to Wally tomorrow. But he was feeling better now, maybe the illness was over . . .

Later, several minutes into a Canadian television drama, he fell asleep.

Monday, nine a.m.

Charles, Saint-Etienne, and Montague's forty-five lawyers claimed two floors in Place du Canada on Boulevard Dorchester, the downtown power alley. J.C. Beaulieu was a Q.C., high up in the firm, one of their big hitters.

The elevator opened onto a hardwood forest, burnished oak floor-to-ceiling, thickets of *ficus benjamina* in pots. Two receptionists, both busy, a half dozen businessmen and women with briefcases waiting, tapping feet, jotting notes on pads, reading *The Financial Times*. Handsome lawyers and secretaries made up to look like department store mannequins drifting about in the background, as Kellen, in jeans and old military coat, waited at the receptionist's desk.

It seemed a long way from The Main, from murder.

Monsieur Beaulieu came out personally, dapper and ski-tanned, gray-templed in pin stripes, a man you'd confidently bring your contracts to. Kellen followed him to his office.

"I primarily work with wills and estates," Beaulieu said, "and therefore two varieties of clients. Those who contemplate their deaths, and those who are death's benefactors."

Kellen took a seat in front of the desk, which was polished and ordered, a single file on the varnished desktop. The view from the window was north; the awakening sun shone sallow and cold on the mountain. Alphonse Bague, who was waiting for him outside, the meter turned off for his best client, had translated Celsius into Fahrenheit for him this morning: twenty-six below.

Beaulieu sat, clasped his hands, looked at Kellen directly. He spoke accentless English.

"I knew Bob Champlain from law school. University of Montreal. Not well. He was, if I may be blunt, a slackass. I used to lend him my notes. He seemed on his way to becoming a fringe person, and I think he succeeded. Coffee, ah . . . Detective?"

"No thanks."

Beaulieu consulted his file. "He was here on an appointment a month ago. Seventh of January, eleven-fifteen. He was alone. I have never met Mr. Sloukos. He presented me with two sealed envelopes. Inside, he said, were wills which he had drawn himself. Wills which I was not invited to read, and which remained in these envelopes until yesterday."

He passed them to Kellen. Standard long envelopes, the name of Champlain's law firm stamped on the top left corner. Typed on the face of each: TO BE OPENED ONLY UPON THE DEATH OF . . . In the one case Robert Walter Champlain, and in the other, Leo Dimitry Sloukos.

"Mr. Champlain told me I had been appointed to administer their estates. We talked a little. Whatever happened to so and so. A bit of politics, horses, we both enjoy the track. He left."

The lawyer was good, Kellen thought, straightforward, economical, knew the value of time.

"I usually don't go into the office Sunday. But I was intrigued by the coincidence of these two violent deaths. The wills were inexpertly drawn, but sufficient, in standard form, witnessed, and notarized, gifting everything – *almost* everything – to their respective next of kin."

Beaulieu retrieved the envelopes and removed the wills, unfolded one, and opened it.

"Each will, however, contained a similarly odd bequest. I thought about where my duties lay before calling you. I wanted to do the right thing."

Kellen nodded. He liked him doing this. The right thing.

Beaulieu placed horn-rimmed spectacles on his nose, and read: " 'I bequeath the contents of a certain safety-deposit box, numbered 59, at the Essex and Edinburgh Trust, offices on Saint-François-Xavier St., etc., etc., to a certain Leo Dimitry Sloukos, his address, etc.' " He looked up over his glasses. "Sloukos directed a similar legacy in his will, making Monsieur Champlain *his* beneficiary of the contents of that same deposit box. But each named the same alternate legatee."

He read on. " 'In the event that the said Leo Dimitry Sloukos predeceases me, or dies within thirty days of my death, whichever event shall first occur' – rather tautologic, isn't that? – 'then I bequeath the said contents of the safety-deposit box jointly to the news editors of *La Presse* and *The Globe and Mail.*"

He raised his eyes above his glasses, inquiring what Kellen thought about that.

"I, as solicitor for the estate, am instructed forthwith to render jointly unto the said news editors a key to such deposit box, in the event such be found among the deceased's effects."

He looked Kellen square in the eye. "Of course if no key is produced, the box will have to be drilled open. That could take several weeks, several trips to court. I probably have an immediate responsibility to contact the newspapers, however. I can wait at most twenty-four hours."

Kellen didn't want the media tampering with this. The wrong headline – just mentioning these wills – and the bad guys will be back over the border, out of reach. J.C. Beaulieu seemed to share Kellen's wavelength, was hinting at courses of action.

"I, of course, don't know if you found such a key during your searches. Or how hard it would be to get a search warrant."

"For a company called Essex – "

"Essex and Edinburgh Trust. Saint-François-Xavier."

Kellen nodded. "Will you copy your file for us, Mr. Beaulieu?"

"My pleasure."

When Kellen walked outside onto the plaza and into the brittle cold, his eyes were pulled north, up the street, Cathédrale becoming Metcalfe, Metcalfe becoming McTavish, a narrow defile through the heart of the city, Coldhaven Manor perched high at the end of it, watching him, raptorial, predacious.

He climbed into Alphonse Bague's cab, and felt the heat pouring from the Chrysler's big, pumping fans. Alphonse was bundled small in a big jacket, listening to the weather report.

"Coldes' day of Feb'r'y since fifteen year. Tomorrow, he say world record for Montreal, 'nother cold front comin' from Bafflin' Island, it gonna sit *on top* the one we got a'ready here. Where to, Lieutenant?"

"Bafflin' Island."

Alphonse turned to look at him.

"Station Twenty-six, Phonse."

Monday, ten a.m.

Kellen fed some commands to the Monster, which ignored them and blinked its cursor, tauntingly.

Beside him, a young woman detective was taking statements from two of the dancers at the S'Extasie. She was putting everything right into the computer, fingers whizzing expertly over the keyboard.

"Wrong command or file name," Kellen's computer chided.

He gave up for a while, and phoned Sarah's office again. Still in court. He said he'd try later.

109

Raolo came in and dropped the little safety-deposit key on Kellen's desk. It was tagged. Separately tagged was the key locator, with its chimes and dancing girl.

"Talked to commercial crime. They say Essex and Edinburgh Trust is an absolutely straight *vieille compagnie* in *Vieux Montréal*. I phoned them, got the assistant manager. Thank you but no thank you. Return with a court order. Won't even confirm who signed for the safety deposit."

"Arrest him for obstruction," Kellen said.

"Yeah, and we'll beat the shit out of him in the wagon." He sat beside Kellen, stared at the key. "So what do we, get a search warrant?"

Borko, from above. "Hey, you guys, I want you to meet someone."

"A warrant will take fucking forever." He returned to his computer.

"Hey, Kellen, Raolo."

Kellen glanced up: the bad-news giraffe, wearing a crisp, ironed blazer. Beside him, a handsome black man in a three-piece suit, puffing on a big black pipe. Forties, gangly, loose, played wide receiver for Michigan State.

"Who's that guy up there with Captain Queeg?" Kellen said, banging several times at the Enter key. The Monster stubbornly withheld its secrets.

"I'd guess FBI," Raolo said. "Borko must've called the Yanks in."

"Wonder if he's brought some bumf on this Roy Salvador; hope he's got some mug art." He stared at a screenful of unintelligible figures. He was aware of Borko bounding down the stairs.

"Developments," Borko said as he entered the detective area.

"I wish you'd get off our case, Eugene. Like literally."

"I'm off your case. So are you. There are some matters of more local moment which have to be dealt with. I'd like you gentlemen to close some of your waste-of-taxes files before you go on strike tonight."

"Okay, what's up, Eugene?"

"They're no longer in Canada."

"We're grateful for your help, Raolo and me, we really are." He went back to his keyboard, rapped out another command. "However, I think we know what we're doing."

"It appears that you don't." Borko peered over his shoulder at the screen, examined Kellen's pathetic attempts to key into an information bank.

"The firearms registry won't let me in," he said, sullen, beaten.

Borko daintily tapped out some fresh commands. "You seem to have modemmed into the Chicago grains futures market. You know, a police officer who refuses to catch up with the times . . . I didn't see you gentlemen at the last data management seminar . . . There."

The screen told them the Mitchell derringer found in Leo Sloukos's stiffened hand had been stolen a year ago from a dentist's office in Miami.

"And lo," said Borko, "a hot gun. I know a man who carried one of these little fellows in his boot. Shot off his big toe with a hollow point. Hugh, come in here."

The black man was at the doorway, looking in, interested but not pushy. He padded softly toward them.

"Special Agent Hugh McVeigh, FBI. Detective Lieutenant Kellen O'Reilly. Detective Raolo Basutti."

"Hope you fellow porkers don't think I'm butting in." Gruff, friendly voice.

"Agent McVeigh's been tracking your killers, gentlemen."

Kellen studied McVeigh. A half-lidded stare, not soft, maybe deadly. Something about him. Perhaps not a receiver, a linebacker. His pipe had gone out, and he was holding it by the bowl like a gun held upside-down, his index finger where a trigger might be.

He said, "Rudy Meyers is ex-private eye with a heavy Mafia connect who's been using the Contra net to trade arms for toot."

"He got a face we can look at?" Kellen asked.

McVeigh showed him some head shots. Moon-faced man with a tight smile.

"Works with the family d'Ambrozzio," McVeigh said. "Miami. They hired a lawyer and an accountant here in Montreal – "

"Our deceased victims," said Borko.

" – to set up a dummy business importing South American jewelry. Nose jewelry."

"They have a man inside, Kellen," Borko said.

McVeigh looked sharply at Borko, a complaint, the captain talks too much.

"They had to get the green light from some capo here in Montreal," McVeigh said.

"Johnny Ronce," Borko said.

"Who turned them down, so the d'Ambrozzios never used the Company, and reneged on the fees to set it up. The lawyer and accountant came up with a real great idea: blackmail. They're now in the great eternal beyond. And here we are."

"In Station Twenty-six," Kellen said.

"Yeah." McVeigh looked around. "Odd kind of shop."

Thumbing more tobacco into the bowl of his pipe, his eyes drifted across the room, settling on the legs of one of the dancers from the S'Exastie. Kellen quickly slipped the bank deposit key into his pocket. He looked at Raolo, and saw his partner had caught the move.

"And where are these boys now?" Kellen said.

"Stateside. We have them in Lauderdale. They flew back last night, the four that are left."

"You have it, gentlemen," Borko said. "They're no longer in our jurisdiction. Matter goes over to the Feds: RCMP and the FBI. Agent McVeigh and I will work out the transfer of exhibits."

Kellen got up and went into the little bathroom adjoining the homicide offices. He splashed water on his face and listened to Borko, his tone effusive now.

"By the way, about tonight, Kel. We can't leave the station unmanned for your little strike. There'll be a skeleton crew?"

"No, Eugene."

"I'll drop back when you've completed your ablutions." He stalked off.

Kellen worked up some lather and began, carefully, shaving his grizzle of whiskers and his mustache. When he came out, toweling his face, Raolo was staring at him.

"Where are Champlain's effects?" Kellen asked.

"Kellen," Raolo warned.

"Get the car."

Monday, eleven a.m.

In the cruiser, driving to Kellen's, Raolo said, "So maybe Johnny Ronce lied about it's not Mafia. He's a cagey old bugger. He coulda been having us on."

"I don't think he lied. Neither do you."

"Okay, so the FBI guy has bad information?"

"Something to that effect."

"I don't like this, Kel."

"You don't have to stay in."

At home, Kellen showered and put on his most conservative suit, gray with a banker's stripe, mothballed for weddings and funerals. It felt good to be in a suit again; he felt substantial and solid. He slipped on his slate-green Piaget tie and rolled his ponytail up and pinned it, and set a felt porkpie hat on his head.

At his desk, he copied Champlain's signature about thirty times, Raolo watching, not saying anything. Dissatisfied, Kellen got his partner to rig up a professional-looking sling for his right arm.

From the station's exhibit locker Raolo had signed out Champlain's wallet and the jewelry box taken from his safe – first removing, on Kellen's instructions, the small cut diamonds and braided gold chain.

Brass, seven inches square, the box lay open now on Kellen's desk. In it, on a nest of cotton batting, was the ruby pendant necklace, which, assuming the bright red stone *was* a ruby, must be an item of considerable worth. Kellen presumed it had been stolen and fenced to the lawyer.

He stuffed the box into the big side pocket of his greatcoat.

Monday, eleven forty-five a.m.

Essex and Edinburgh Trust was in the old financial district, a British Empire leftover, early nineteenth century, uncomfortable with its neighbors, the new boutiques and artists' lofts and fast fooderies in the touristy, preserved old city.

Sooty concrete pillars outside, sedate within, an eerie hush sifting through the air like dust.

Kellen oriented himself as he stood at a wall counter, and watched a woman, apparently the safety-deposit clerk, open a massive steel door and admit an elderly couple to the vaults. She disappeared into it for a minute then re-emerged. Bifocal half-glasses were hanging by a strap from her neck. A spinster. The Essex and Edinburgh has been her only lover. Twenty years of toil and loyalty.

She'd probably know all the regulars. But try not, gain not. He swung boldly toward her desk, smiling.

"Champlain, R.W., I have a safety-deposit box," he said. A quiet, library voice, and a faked French accent. He was holding the brass jewelry box in his left hand, the one without a sling.

She looked at him severely.

"Do you have identification, Mr. Champlain?"

Fumbling with his good arm into his inner suit pocket, he dropped the jewelry case as he brought out a wallet. The case fell onto her desk, opening. The ruby pendant necklace spilled from it.

"Oh, dear," she said, starting.

"Clumsy with this damn shoulder." He stood there awkwardly, his wallet open. She picked up the necklace.

"My mother's," Kellen said. "Promised I'd keep it safe." He laughed.

She softened. "This is quite lovely."

"I bought it for her," he said. "She's . . . well, she has Alzheimer's. She . . . loses things. We wanted a secure place for this."

He opened the wallet in front of her, Champlain's wallet. Minus the driver's license with the picture. Law Society membership card prominent. He hoped she hadn't read the newspapers closely.

She glanced at the identification while placing the necklace back in the case, then pulled out Champlain's signature card from a file drawer.

She looked the card over, then put it in front of him and handed him a pen. He bent low, scribbling the signature with his sling arm, performing with difficulty.

He stole a quick glance at the notations on the card. Rented jointly by Champlain and Sloukos. Opened three years ago. Touched since only once, last November. They'd signed in together; maybe they didn't trust each other alone with whatever instrument of blackmail it held.

Kellen followed her through the metal jaws of the vault. It seemed homey inside, leather upholstered chairs, flexible-necked lamps pouring pools of gold on felt-covered tables.

At one of those tables, across from a long wall of safety deposits, the elderly couple – white-haired, stooped, maybe in their eighties – were examining papers, certificates, smiling, chatting softly.

The vaultkeeper inserted her key into one of the two locks, and turned it and withdrew it.

"You can assure your mother her valuables are safe at the Essex and Edinburgh."

She smiled, showing long teeth. Kellen smiled. She left.

He put the key in the second lock, and turned it and heard the deeply satisfying clunk of tumblers falling.

He slid the box from its long rectangular hole and carried it to a table, gently, almost lovingly, and raised the door.

Inside: one item. A five-inch-wide cylindrical film canister, taped shut. Has weight to it.

A little movie. Okay.

Raolo knew about this stuff, he did volunteer work for the force in local school auditoriums.

He placed the canister into the jewelry box with the necklace, a snug fit, and he replaced the empty deposit box.

He nodded to the nice old couple and walked from there. As he signed out, he talked with the vault clerk about the cold weather.

From Eddie Comacho's newly rented Land Cruiser – a four-wheel-drive because snow had been forecast – Eddie and Mick Crowder watched Kellen walk from the building toward Raolo's cruiser, removing the sling, transferring the brass box to his left hand.

"Now?" Eddie said.

"Rudy says don't take chances. Rudy says f-follow them."

"Rudy says, Rudy says. God speaks, Crowder jumps. Fuck Rudy, he's just sending us up sh-shit c-creek."

Crowder looked pained. Comacho thought: He really bends over and spreads them for old Reverend Moon. Meyers and his buttfuck buddy. Well, they're *all* going to be fucked in the end, the way this abortion's coming down.

He pulled out.

"Don't follow too close," Crowder said.

"Don't tell *me* how to drive." He had trophies.

Monday, noon

"The Attorney General of Quebec versus Tremblay," Sarah Paradis said. "It's compelling authority, Milady. Quebec Court of Appeal."

116

She walked to the adjoining table, where sat the lawyers for the Urban Community, and put in front of them the thick volume of case reports she had quoted from. "I'll lend this to my learned friends. They overlooked it in their brief."

She knew she was playing to her clients a little bit. Ouimet and some of his directors sat with hopeful smiles in the gallery behind her. Only Constable Taillefeur seemed unhappy. Probably wanted her to lose.

Guy Lamartine, the MUC's chief counsel, rose slowly to his feet while trying to do a fast read of the headnote, the case summary. He looked up hopefully to the judge. "We say it doesn't apply."

"In what way doesn't it apply?" asked Madame Justice Benoit.

"Totally different fact situation."

"Well," said the judge, "someone has to win these things, and someone has to lose. You lose this one, Mr. Lamartine. The Tremblay case is right on point."

Sarah slid relieved into her seat. Lamartine remained standing, white-faced. The MUC staff members and municipal politicians on the benches behind him looked downcast.

"I have to agree with Miss Paradis; the matter should not have come before this court. The *tribunal du travail* is the forum with jurisdiction. I don't have power to order anyone to report for work, and your application is denied."

"Your Ladyship has an over-riding power," Lamartine said.

"To do what?" said the judge.

Sarah packed her papers tidily into her briefcase. Outwardly she was calm. Inwardly she was clapping and cheering. She'd got lucky today, and drawn a half-decent judge.

"To prevent anarchy in the streets."

"That's not my department." Judge Benoit smiled, not pleasantly. "You're in the wrong court, *monsieur*."

Sarah walked triumphantly out with her clients. It would take hours for the MUC administration to get their tackle ready again for the *tribunal du travail*, the Labour Court. She doubted they'd do it in time to stop the walkout.

"Want to prevent anarchy in the streets?" she asked Lamartine. "Make us an offer."

He shook his head brusquely. "I'll see you in Labour Court."

She would have lunch on the fly. After that, Dr. Satorius, his examination for discovery at the *palais de justice*.

She found a telephone and called Station Twenty-six for Kellen. Not there. She said she'd try later.

Would he be furious with her? She'd made an appointment with Dr. Wallace Mandelbaum for late this afternoon. Dr. Mandelbaum had seemed pleasant on the phone, but turned hesitant when she mentioned Kellen. And then said, "No, come in, I'd like to meet you."

A psychiatrist and a friend, he must know that Kellen will never become whole until he lets go all his anger about Satorius and the CIA. Until he demands full compensation for what they stole from him.

Maybe Dr. Mandelbaum would agree to persuade him to go public. They would help him, together. The courtroom would be his therapy.

And Kellen had a duty to her people, damn it. She wasn't going to give up on that.

Monday, twelve-ten p.m.

As Raolo drove from Old Montreal Kellen packed away the sling and examined the canister for markings. Nothing. A taped tin cylinder. But, here, scratched with a knife, faintly, the numerals "47-02."

"Borko will have your nuts on the wall, hanging between his Beretta sub and his Boer War cavalry carbine."

Kellen stripped off the masking tape, which was dry, brittle.

"The RCMP – "

"Fuck the RCMP."

Raolo shut his mouth and drove west by the somber stone banks on St. Jacques, uneasy with events, with Kellen's mood, his blithe damn-the-torpedoes attitude. This wasn't just cutting corners, it was going straight across the neighbor's lot.

"If they ask, you didn't have anything to do with it." Kellen separated the two halves of the canister and popped the reel of film out.

Raolo glanced at it. "Sixteen-millimeter. Looks what they call a two-hundred-foot daylight spool. It's inadmissible evidence, Kel. Take it back. Let's get a warrant."

Kellen pulled out about twenty inches, and put an eye close to one of the tiny frames. Couldn't make out much, maybe it's a person.

"I'll put in my notes that I came by cab."

"Nail us with perjury, too."

"You don't have to stay in, Raolo."

"Oh, fuck off."

Kellen laughed and slapped Raolo on the shoulder.

On Saint-Laurent, Raolo parked behind the wooden barricade in front of Big Al's. The sewer repair crew was probably inside the deli; it was lunch, the poor guys warming their frozen buns over smoked meats and coffee.

They walked briskly up The Main. Zagreb Salle à Manger, Khan Super Marché, Slovenia Boucherie, *Cuisine Indien et Jazz dans le Café Tandor*. The air was moving now, flutters of wind snapping at their cheeks, wind from the north.

Agent McVeigh and I will work out the transfer of exhibits. Agent McVeigh, sure. Kellen really trusted him.

The alleged blackmailers were back in Lauderdale – bullshit. Leaving behind the film they came for? A movie for which men have died – an accountant, a lawyer, a doctor, and of what profession was the fourth, the man Kellen took out, the supposed associate of the d'Ambrozzio gang.

He and Raolo beat the cold out of their arms as they entered Juley's sex emporium. "You got anyone in the theater?" Kellen asked LeGiusti.

"Not yet." The Juice was dressed sharp, loose Italian moderno. He examined Kellen, conservative in stripes. "Where'd you find the suit, Catholic Aid?"

He attempted to follow them to the door of the theater. "Like where do you think you're goin'?"

Kellen turned to him and spoke low. "Your movie house is closed for sanitary inspection. Anyone comes in I'll confiscate your blow dolls."

Juley waved them on. "When do you guys go on strike? I can't wait."

Kellen followed Raolo into the theater and closed the door, found it didn't lock.

"Jam it with a chair," he said.

"Why me?" Raolo looked dubiously at the array of chairs he might choose from: twenty rows of them, reinforced plastic. Patches of newspaper were stuck to some of the seats.

"I have senior rank, Raolo."

"Can I borrow your gloves?"

Kellen threw them at him. He was charged up now, in good fettle after a ten-hour sleep. There'd been none of those uneasy feelings, harbingers of flashbacks, since the night he'd spent with Sarah.

The projection room was reached by a flight of stairs to a wooden platform, and only a curtain divided it from the seats below and from a screen too large for this small room. Nobody was going to have to squint to make out the details of *Trixie Gives a Treat*, the reel Raolo removed from the projector.

He threaded their film on. "Has to be rewound."

The reels whirred for a while, then there was a snap, and a ragged end of film clattered on the spool.

"Woops," Raolo said. "I don't know, Kel, it's real old, it could break again."

"Let's play what you've rewound."

Raolo worked it back onto the reel. "Lights," he said.

Kellen clicked them off.

"Camera." A big dark rectangle hit the screen.

"Action," said Raolo. He squinted but didn't see much, just an out-of-focus figure moving in the foreground. The film was black and white, the screen quartered by cross hairs, a divided rule along the bottom edge.

"Scientific film," Raolo said. He'd seen lab people work with it.

Sounds of clicks and scratches. Spotlights on the ceiling. The walls were of what – padding, soundproofing? Some kind of barrier . . . a curtained screen . . . dividing a room into left and right.

Against the far wall was a . . . window? A doorway? Raolo saw a figure enter from the foreground, to the right of the curtain, which screened him from the rest of the room: a potbellied middle-aged man in a T-shirt. He began walking toward the back, toward the doorway, if that's what it was. Then Raolo saw the man's reflection in it . . . Not a doorway, but a tall mirror, precisely angled, but disguised to a careless observer as an entranceway.

What is this? Raolo asked himself. Games with mirrors.

The image sharpened. The man stopped walking toward the mirror and scratched his belly.

To the left of the curtained room divider, the back of someone else's head now rose into the foreground. Scrawny, big ears, short hair. He was facing the T-shirted, potbellied man's reflected image in that mirror, but was screened from the man himself. It appeared to Raolo that the younger man was drugged – he couldn't see his face, but he was shaking.

From somewhere offscreen, a calm voice with a foreign accent. "Remember how he beat your mother. Do you hate him?"

Raolo heard his partner, a sound like he was sucking air.

Raolo saw the younger man's hand hesitantly raise a gun and point it at the mirror.

A sharp report, smoke.

The potbellied man's image swirled apart in chunks and chips.

Raolo heard a soft whisper of astonishment from Kellen, and looked at his face, haunted, spectral in the projector's glowing lights.

The man with the gun – still with his back to the camera

– seemed to duck beneath it, and disappeared. A third man, broad-shouldered in a lab coat, came into view behind the curtain divider, and he directed the potbellied man toward the side of the room and off the screen.

Kellen, staring at the screen open-mouthed, thought at first he'd endured an overpowering déjà vu, but now knew it was more than that – it was a version of his terrible flashback.

But different perspective, different man in the mirror. The same Hungarian-accented voice. Gregor Satorius. Who now entered the frame, a man of fifty, ramrod straight, crisp and square-chinned with a trim military mustache and deep-set eyes. He was writing with chalk on a small blackboard.

The mike picked up his voice faintly.

"Not, yet, Mick."

Another voice: "He walked in b-before I could stop him."

"All right, bring him here."

Two men in white were now in the background, adjusting another tall mirror into place. Someone's huge, blurred fingers holding a blackboard in front of the lens.

On it: "MK-ULTRA 47 / PHASE 02, FINAL TEST / SUBJECT O/13."

The fingers erased the figure "O/13" and chalked "O/14" in its place.

A stocky orderly entered the picture, urging forward a resisting Kellen O'Reilly, Subject O/14, nineteen years old, his eyes terrified, his pupils wide, dilated, drugged; he was trying to pull away from the orderly's hand on his arm.

"Holy God," Raolo said.

A young, roughly clothed man now entered the frame from the right, on the other side of the curtain, and this man bore a familiar mirrored image, the face of Kellen's thousand waking nightmares, the flashback man with the scarred face and the evil smile, pausing now, turning to face the mirror, waiting.

"Remember that he killed your father," said Satorius, handing the young Kellen a revolver.

Watching this, watching himself, Kellen seemed in almost a comatose state. But suddenly he felt his surroundings bend, go crooked, surrealistic, a trip on the Yellow Submarine, and he fought his way out of it, finally rejoining mind to body, but still sensing, caustic in his mouth, the taste of that fleeting interlude of insanity.

The gun fired; the mirror disintegrated: Kellen's vivid color-bright flashback in grainy black and white.

"It's not real!" the young Kellen screamed. "Nothing is real! What are you doing to me?"

He hurled the gun and ran to the curtain divider, and he threw it open . . .

The picture suddenly left the screen; it went blank . . . and then expanded, the picture returning, exploding into color.

You run past the curtain, you run, you run, through doorway and hall, from the men who control your mind . . .

And with the split-second flashback, Kellen felt a sharp, vicious headache and came spiraling back to his own time.

And the room was dark and shifting like the sea, and the screen was white and he was listening to a sound, snap-snap-snap, his mind snapping, audibly, over and over, and he closed his eyes and stepped back and braced himself hard against a post like a sailor in a gale at sea, and concentrated all the strength within him, concentrated it upon his mind, pulled in the flapping sails until he was steady and could open his eyes.

Snap. Snap. The sound decelerated. The film had broken once more, its frayed end slowly whipping around the reel. Kellen watched Raolo click off the projector. Then silence for a while.

"You all right, Kel?"

"I think so."

"You want a coffee or something?"

Rudy Meyers put more coins in the binoculars and spied to the west and spied to the south. Dressed in sparkling white, all Montreal was beneath him. He was on the observation deck of the world's longest inclined tower, above the Olympic Stadium. Below him, suspension cables webbed down to its retractable roof. He'd been carried up in a cable car. A recorded voice had boasted, "Five hundred and fifty-six feet above the ground, equivalent to the top of a fifty-storey building."

He liked the feeling, being up here, above the fray. He also liked the feeling of being almost alone – only a handful of people hanging around here, on a cold, cold Monday. And little activity on the Stadium grounds – it wasn't quite baseball season.

Somewhere down there in the gray jumble of streets and square roofs was Lieutenant O'Reilly, who now, according to latest report, had personal possession of the film. Meyers' associates had been instructed to obtain that film from him. And to kill him, though he was an officer of the law.

Meyers had left Crowder in charge, the only one of them he could entirely trust. He wasn't going to place too much reliance on the cowardly Comacho, with his snide innuendos that the master craftsman had lost his touch. There *had*, of course, been errors – he'd never known a clandestine op to wander so far off the rails as this one – but as he always told his clients: No task is impossible; some just take a little longer.

This is spycraft, the ultimate game, and the winning gambler is the ruthless gambler. When the prize is worthy, one is not afraid to raise the stakes by killing the innocent. Meyers had liked Dr. Luk. He had nothing against Kellen O'Reilly. Who had his respect, in fact.

Matters would resolve satisfactorily. It is a matter of will. Meyers had the will.

His bandaged hand was in his jacket pocket – he'd discarded the sling – and it gently throbbed. It wasn't pain. He had conquered the pain. His Korean master had taught him how to do that. One does it by centering, by focusing every part of one's self on the pain, becoming the pain. And then it fades away.

He heard the rumbling of the ascending cable car, heard it stop.

Meyers took one last tour of the city through the binoculars, the frozen Port of Montreal, still and vast, and the long, flat hills beyond. "Mont-Saint-Grégoir, renowned for its sugarbushes," his pamphlet read. He stared at Mont-Saint-Grégoir, perceiving symbolism, aware that Gregor Satorius was near him now, three feet away, standing stiffly at the rail, staring out. Meyers could see him reflected in the window.

Saint-Grégoir. Seventy-five now, thin and pale. For a quarter of a century Meyers had not had to endure the querulous company of this demanding, irascible scientist.

Meyers had been thirty-one at the time of that anxious summer in Montreal, perfervid in his many causes, his mind bloated with Nietzschean virtue, Superman before God, the individual before the slavish masses. How confused was young manhood, how fractured. How more composed he was now, since finding the path to his center.

Gregor Satorius, however, had the appearance of a man who had aged but not grown.

He was wearing a cape. A recent affectation, Meyers presumed, somewhat theatrical in effect – but Meyers liked theater. Observe life as theater, his teacher had said, and play your finest part in it.

"I wanted merely to talk to you," Satorius said in a low, tense voice. "To meet is not a good idea."

"Using the telephone is a worse one. You are well, Gregor?"

"I am not. A faulty heart valve. Too much stress. I have carried a burden alone. My lawyers are literally eating me out of house and home. I have listed even Coldhaven for sale."

Meyers wished he hadn't asked the question. "We will see about some financial aid."

"Don't just see about it. Honor your promises. I am in

desperate straits. Blackmailers attempting to bleed me from one end, a Communist lawyer from the other. Today again I have a session with her – the Witch of the East."

"We have, ah, retired the blackmailers, Gregor."

"How much were they asking?"

"Four million dollars."

"My God. For what?"

Meyers stood up from the binoculars, glanced around, and came a step closer to Satorius. "A film which Sloukos boosted when he and Champlain were helping you incinerate your records. I thought you were supposed to supervise."

"I saw them burn all the films, and the files, everything." He hesitated. "It was done in a hurry after you telephoned."

"It is a dangerous film, Gregor. It is from Phase Two."

"Who is in it?"

"The whole cast of characters. You are the star."

Satorius's eyes widened. "And do you have it?"

"Not yet."

"So, you have *botched* this?" Satorius said, incredulous.

Meyers could sense the fear in him. He smiled his unflappable smile. "I don't think so," he said. "We'll know in a few minutes."

Monday, one-twenty p.m.

Kellen entered Big Al's House of Smoked Meat in a state of psychic shock, sounds and smells coming at him from some kind of outer world, from which he felt detached. Behind the counter, pushing meat through a slicer, Big Al, his rasping, jocular voice. "The Gestapo's here, Ruthie, turn over the Jews."

Ruthie pointed to an empty booth near the back.

"The usuals, guys?"

126

"The usuals," said Raolo.

"No," said Kellen. "Just coffee. For me." He got those words out all right; he was okay, it was just the shock.

Raolo walked toward the back but Kellen's engine seemed to stall. He stood immobile, staring at a girl with her hair the thickness and color of a putting green, little scallops of it hanging over to the side. She was eating soup. Her boyfriend had a non-ethnic hamburger and chips. His hair was like the crest of a blue jay. Their leather was covered with sparkles.

Kellen couldn't fit those young people into his current reality. His eyes roved about around the glass display cases. It felt as if he'd been shot up with something, a disorienting drug.

Long, curled red peppers and thick, pimply pickles stared back at him from the jars on the high counter. Chopped egg and herring. Their perfume amid the odor of hot meat, dense and rich. And he could smell a cigar somewhere, and people's sweat and he heard voices buzzing everywhere: English, Yiddish, French, Polish.

And Big Al's raucous shouts.

"Three hots and a lox."

"Read the sign, you got eyes, no checks, we take the Queen's picture only unless you got plastic."

"Hey, O'Reilly, you forget where you left your head, or somethin'?"

Raolo stopped in front of six sewer workers stuffed into a four-man booth, taking courage from their third refills before going back out to the cold.

"We're cops. Car's in the way, we'll move it."

"Solidarity, *mon vieux*," one of them said.

Raolo turned, sensing Kellen wasn't with him. He saw him near the counter, now moving slowly up the aisle between the booths. He looked halfway to being a space case. Raolo was still trying to piece together Kellen's mumbled account of his Coldhaven history, pronounced in gasps of disconnected phrases between drags from his cigarette as they walked The Main to Big Al's.

Both Raolo's head and his heart were in turmoil. He didn't

127

know what to do, but his first instinct was to protect Kellen, somehow.

What *was* that weird experiment they did on Kellen and those other people? Some kind of psychological test is what it looked like.

As Kellen slid into his seat across from Raolo his eyes fixed upon a multi-chinned woman about to set to work on one of Big Al's famous Montreal smoked meats, too thick to fit into any standard mouth, dripping with mustard and threads of meat and fat.

Ruthie slid coffees in front of them. Kellen shakily lit a cigarette.

"Okay, let me follow this, Kel. When you were at this Coldhaven place, they, ah, wiped your memory."

At the booth opposite, two bearded elders were arguing fiercely in some unidentifiable Slavic tongue. Kellen tried to concentrate.

"He used a program of shock treatments. They erase memory. A skilled shock doctor can do it selectively."

His eyes were pulled back to the woman, and he watched her mouth begin to work, nibbling at the edges, watched her swallow, the throat muscles wobble.

"You can regress people to childhood," he said, "make them six year olds again."

"Yeah, uh . . . Okay. And so I don't understand these flashbacks. They're like – what acid is supposed to do to you?"

Her tongue flowed out, her mouth wide, a pickle going in slowly, sliding in. She looked at Kellen and he quickly looked away. Voices shouting. Slovenian or Slovakian or Serbian. Too many distractions here; he couldn't concentrate.

"They're not just flashbacks; they're messages. I've been hearing voices, too, Raolo, people shouting at me." Were they trying to explain to him what had happened at Coldhaven? "But I can't make their words out; they're too far away."

Raolo thought: Visions and voices. Normally he'd say these are your standard brand-name hallucinations. What they call signs of schizophrenia. It's temporary, he had a shock. He'll be okay.

128

"Messages," Raolo repeated. "You're getting messages."

"The other guy with the gun, Raolo, the one before me, Subject O/13, did you see his face?"

"No."

"It's like he's someone I know, a friend or something, an acquaintance. I'm sure I know him." He closed his eyes tight, reopened them, took a drag from his cigarette. "I seem to know all those people, Raolo. Those male nurses with Satorius. They're all in my head, waiting just outside my rim of vision."

"Drugged-up patients shooting at mirrors; it's weird – but are you going to kill people over this movie?"

"There's something else on it."

"Like for instance what?"

"I don't know."

The film was in bad shape, old celluloid; Raolo didn't want to chance running more of it through a projector. What were they going to do with it? he wondered. The film canister was still in Kellen's coat pocket, and he hadn't proposed any answers to that multi-million-dollar question.

"So, ah, aside from the flashbacks and stuff, how are you right now, Kel?"

Kellen looked Raolo directly in the face. He felt ashamed, he'd been unfair to Raolo; his partner had always had a right to know.

"I haven't been well, Raolo. Right now I think I'm having a little . . . maybe a little breakdown."

Kellen lit another cigarette, his other half-finished, burning in the ashtray.

Raolo's sandwich arrived, and he stared down at it. "It's okay. I figured you been feeling poor. It don't matter."

He raised his head, looked at him, reached across, and put his hand on Kellen's shoulder and squeezed it.

"It don't matter."

Kellen blew out a big sigh of smoke. He brought the brass jewel case from his coat pocket and removed the film canister.

"We'd better take this in before we damage it more. Get the lab to work on it, make some copies."

"Take it in . . . to the station?"

"To Borko. You better call in first, tell him to get the Chief down there for this one."

He sighed. He felt himself start to come together, to heal. No secrets. No secrets anymore.

"I'll be right beside you, Kel."

Kellen thanked him, and handed the canister to him, and put the jewelry box back in his coat pocket.

Monday, one-thirty p.m.

Sarah flipped through the skimpy pile of file folders. "That's all?"

"This is all I am able to find," said Satorius. "Just the patient admission forms. They weren't destroyed with the rest."

"When did all this destruction of evidence take place?"

"I object," said his lawyer. "Argumentive."

"When were the other documents destroyed?" Sarah said.

"A few years ago. *Before* your action was started, I should add. The medical records were of no use to anyone; they occupied space which I needed. I see you have my published papers. They are the only useful history."

"You're supposed to be a *scientist*, Dr. Satorius."

"I object to that," said his lawyer.

"And so you should, because he's obviously not much of one. Scientists don't destroy records."

"Don't answer the question, if that's what it was."

Sarah had no judge to appeal to. This was only discovery. The fourth person in the small *salle d'interrogatoire* was an official court reporter, impassive at her shorthand typewriter.

"*Where* were the medical records destroyed, Doctor?"

130

"There is an incinerator behind Coldhaven Manor." He shrugged. "Everything went into it."

"Who did the burning?"

"I can't remember, a maintenance worker, one of the cleaning ladies, someone like that."

"Did the CIA tell you to destroy the files?"

"Miss Paradis, again I will insist that I have done no business with the CIA. Not knowingly. I received funding from an organization called the Society for Investigation of Human Ecology."

"You knew that was a CIA front."

"I know it now."

She opened one of the files: Mrs. Vivian Sumner, coded Subject Number S/35. Seventy-one now: would she survive to see justice done? Or to see the inside of a courtroom? The defendants' labyrinthine strategies of delay had caused three trial postponements.

But if called to the stand, what could this woman say? A witness without memory.

She opened another file. "Okay, Mrs. Oberoff. You've provided her admission form. Her discharge form. A document entitled 'Release of Claims' which isn't worth two cents. A receipt for her clothing and personal items. Coded Subject Number O/33, she was just a letter and a couple of numbers to you."

"Yes, patients were given a code, so to protect them."

"This is Subject O/33 about whom you wrote in the *American Psychiatric Journal*?"

"Yes. You have read the article? A fascinating case history."

"Mrs. Oberoff, who underwent a program of fourteen ECT's, eight shocks per treatment, a hundred volts each."

"Subject O/33 was psychotic when she was brought in, Miss Paradis. Schizophrenic reaction chronic indifferent type, as I recall. She was much improved when she left the clinic. All these people were mentally ill to begin with. I felt sorry for them. I was no miracle maker – many of them I helped, many I could not."

Good luck when you put them on the stand, he was saying. Poor things. The defendants will try to portray them as disturbed persons who imagined their complaints, and who continue to display the symptoms of their original psychoses.

If she only had one witness with half a memory . . . Kellen was living a lie and it was tormenting him.

Monday, one-fifty p.m.

A sough of wind whistled down Boulevard Saint-Laurent and cut Kellen's eyes like a whip as he stepped from Big Al's, and he blinked, and saw that the world outside was grayer, the futile winter sun now a haloed ball behind sausages of cirrostratus. These were clouds that warned of storm – he'd heard that somewhere, Alphonse had explained it to him.

The sewer repair crew moved in eerie rhythm to the generator, which seemed alive, pulsing, growling. A five-ton utility truck rumbled on idle; a man standing on the stepboard was adjusting the timing.

Now a clangor of jackhammer, and Kellen held his gloved hands to his ears. He thought he smelled singed hair, an olfactory hallucination now.

He withdrew his left hand from his head. There, between the index and middle finger, where he always keeps it, a burning cigarette. From his yellow-stained fingers, the wind lifted a few strands of gray-blond hair.

MK-ULTRA 47 / PHASE 02, FINAL TEST / SUBJECT O/14.

Remember that he killed your father.

Was that some kind of cue statement Satorius had keyed into Kellen's psychic driving program? What in the name of God was the experiment about? A sick, sick therapy. Rid yourself of hatred for those who damaged you? Free yourself of neurosis through play-acting, satisfy a subconscious yearning for revenge?

Or maybe this was a Nazi experiment, a study of man's ability to murder.

Commissioned by the CIA?

"Kellen," Raolo called. He was by the patrol car, a Caravelle, which was wedged between the barricade and a pile of three-foot concrete pipe sections. Its front bumper was to the street; the car was ready to move out.

As Raolo unlocked and got in, Kellen walked slowly toward the cruiser, taking a last draw from his cigarette, looking at the traffic's busy flow around the construction area, cars, trucks, taxis blowing steam from their exhausts. Only a few hardy pedestrians out, flitting into the food shops.

He was slowly recovering from that brief break with reality he'd suffered, but still felt fifty degrees off balance. He needed time to recover. Maybe he should ask Raolo to go alone, talk to the chief first; Kellen should gather his lawyer and his shrink and show up as a committee. He must see Wally Mandelbaum right away. And find Sarah – when had he last tried to reach her?

He flicked his butt into the gutter.

Three men in a Toyota Land Cruiser: avuncular, smiling, talking, strangers yet familiar. The vehicle approached slowly, dawdling, holding up traffic.

Kellen felt a lurch. That odd, awful disorienting sensation that had been tormenting him came to him now like a gust of sick wind. The subliminal voices, shouting.

Raolo was reaching across to flick up the lock button on the passenger door. He held the film canister in his other hand.

"Raolo, get out of there!" Kellen shouted, looking at the Land Cruiser, at the front passenger window, at the bald-headed man in back, at a pocket-size radio transmitter he held.

"Hit the street, Raolo!" He backed a step toward some concrete pipe and struggled through coat and suit jacket to get his service revolver out.

133

Reaching for the lock button with his left hand, Raolo looked up to see Kellen moving back, going for his gun, shouting words drowned in the jackhammer's roar. He turned quickly in his seat, staying down beneath the windows in case there was someone out there with a gun. He went for his own.

The men in the four-wheel saw that Kellen had spotted them, and the bald-headed man quickly looked down at his transmitter, and Kellen knew he had one second to live, and hurled himself toward a break in the rows of concrete pipe.

The car flew apart – steel and chrome and glass and flesh shooting into the air, a searing white light going yellow, flames on the street, a hot sick smell, and the jackhammer screaming, choking, dying.

Kellen had been hurled back across two concrete pipes, his back arched over one of them, his head lolling, his eyes closed. He was dimly aware he was stunned, something important had happened, something very tragic. He felt an incredible sense of loss.

Try to wake up, try to get up.

Two of the sewer crew, thrown down by the blast, were on their hands and knees, looking around in fear and wonder.

Eddie the Cube braked in front of the remains of the patrol car.

"Okay, Bill," said Crowder from the back, quickly dropping the transmitter, picking up a machine pistol. "Fourteen seconds and counting."

Alabama Bill was already out the front passenger door – his specialty had been sacked quarterbacks – he was fast for his size.

A few strides to Kellen's supine form – the cop looked comatose, maybe dead – and Bill was frisking him tight with both hands, pants pockets to shoulders, feverish in his haste. He recognized wallet, house keys, must've dropped his revolver somewhere, don't fucking bother looking for the chunk, just get the film.

A bulge in Kellen's inner coat pocket. Alabama Bill pulled out the brass case and recognized it; O'Reilly had smuggled

134

the film out of the bank in this thing. As he turned to show it to the men in the car, Kellen opened his eyes and darted his right hand out, two fingers stabbing at the big man's eyes, connecting off-center with the index but true and hard with the middle.

Alabama Bill swung a wild, blind fist, his right eye already flooding, and it easily missed as Kellen rolled over the side of the pipe sections, spotted his gun, and dove for it. Kellen was performing on training and instinct, but not full awareness; he suffered a deep and hurting emptiness, and didn't know why, didn't know the explosion had tripped a switch intended by Satorius to block memory of the death of a person loved.

Through a tunnel of pipe, he saw a new four-wheel-drive vehicle with two excited, shouting men in it, one in front, one in back, pulling guns. A big man coming into view from his left, ten feet away, yes, the one who'd patted him down, and he was clutching a gun and a brass box; Kellen thought he remembered it from somewhere. The man's eyes were flooding but open, searching right, searching left, his automatic moving with his eyes, and he was backing quickly to the Land Cruiser.

Kellen jumped, his head cleared the top row of pipe, and he fired at the Land Cruiser's gas tank, two shots into it, but no explosion, fuel spilling out as if from a tap. He went back down as Alabama Bill sent three rapid shots ricocheting off the concrete pipe.

Buffets of freezing wind, like slaps in the face, were bringing him to. Recent past began to catch up.

Radio-detonated bomb under the car.

Raolo . . . Raolo was in it!

He was dead.

They'd murdered Raolo.

He crouched, raced behind the pipe to the sidewalk. In front of him: faces from behind the plate glass, faces staring. Big Al, Ruthie, their customers, noses flattened against the glass.

From behind the last stack of pipe he had a broader view,

135

more of the street. Traffic was stopping, snarling – the front passenger door of the Land Cruiser was swung wide open, trying to accept the big, bull-necked man, but the car was moving, accelerating in reverse toward a hole in the wall of vehicles. Alabama Bill was running with the car, trying to pass the brass box to someone in the back, a man with a machine pistol, but their hands not connecting.

Brass box . . . the film. No, the film was gone; Raolo had taken it.

Raolo. He's dead.

The car's exit was suddenly cut off – a brave city worker had reversed his five-ton truck, blocking the opening.

Eddie Comacho jammed his boot on the brakes, slammed the gearshift into forward, and Alabama Bill, who was trying to get in through the open back door, still holding the brass box, spilled to the pavement with the change of direction.

"Brakes! Brakes!" Crowder shouted.

But Eddie smelled the leaking gas and wasn't waiting. He whirled the steering wheel hard right, smashed the wooden barricade, veered past the tangle of metal that once was a police cruiser, and mounted the sidewalk in front of the delicatessen, skirting the last row of concrete pipe and O'Reilly.

Furiously, Kellen waved to the people behind the deli windows to duck.

"Down! Down! Everyone down!"

He had to stay down himself so as not to draw fire upon them, and waited until the car straightened out onto the sidewalk, swiping a pole, accelerating north to the corner.

Then he jumped up and fired three times through the back window, trying for the driver's head, but hit the ground as the machine pistol fanned out fire from the shattered rear window, fusillade low, into the construction site, a foot above his prone body.

The Land Cruiser clanged off the generator trailer, bounced onto and bent a pair of parking meters inset from the street, winning leverage to spin between a parked car and a fire plug. It careered back to the pavement and fishtailed around the corner, popping out of the bottleneck at the corner, and disappearing.

Gasoline had ignited, flowing into a blazing pool by the wreckage, a small bomb crater in the street.

Kellen hesitated a split second: Don't bother with the car, he had easier game – the wounded buffalo isolated from the herd.

Alabama Bill, clutching the brass case with one hand, his gun with the other, ran down Saint-Laurent, fell on his rear on the ice, got up, ran again.

"Everyone down! Everyone down!" Kellen shouted hoarsely as he sprinted after him, across the construction site, over planks.

The man fired several times over his shoulder, wildly, slowing Kellen, forcing him to use cover.

Alabama Bill had a hundred yards on Kellen, and disappeared, rounding a corner fifteen seconds before Kellen skidded around it and saw an incredibly empty vista west on a cold, bare street.

SOCIÉTÉ JEAN-BAPTISTE, said the sign beside him, *BINGO TOUS LES APRÈS-MIDIS*.

Kellen carefully opened the door, and a plump matron looked up at him and smiled, a stack of bingo cards on the table in front of her. People murmuring in the auditorium behind her, numbers being called out.

"A man just come in here?"

"Who . . . what, a man?"

"I'm a cop!"

"Why . . . yes, a big man, he – "

Kellen bolted past her, into the hall.

Alabama Bill was halfway down an aisle, a card in his hand, about to take a seat at a crowded table.

He looked up and saw Kellen bearing down, and drew his gun from his coat and fired. Kellen ducked, ran in a crouch – he couldn't fire back, too many panicking people.

"Down! Down! Get down!" Kellen screamed.

Alabama Bill jumped over a row of tables, scattering cards, tokens, and five elderly screaming women. He clambered over other tables, toppling them, firing behind him wildly, reaching a door, disappearing behind it.

Kellen dashed around the room, kicked open the partially shut door, saw no one, raced into the shadows, down the stairs. Outside would be a one-way alley, running behind Tailleur Glazounov and the little Jamaican grocery store, then the Banque d'Epargne, and the Ukrainian Greek Orthodox Church; after that the man would be back on the street.

Kellen raced into the cutting cold. There: the target, disappearing through the back verandah door of the church residence, knocking aside old Father Tchaichuk, out stealing a smoke on his pipe.

That meant the priest's wife was still inside. Nail him before he can take hostages. But nail him alive.

Kellen was gaining steps, lots of them, the big man couldn't have that much left.

He ran past Father Tchaichuk, who was sitting in a bank of dirty snow beside the door, his pipe firmly clenched in his mouth.

The house was ornamental, icons on the wall, full of little rooms; Kellen had been here for social functions. "Get *down*, Mrs. Tchaichuk," he said as he ran by the stairs – she was descending them, looking alarmed.

Shortcut through the dining room leads to the front door. He swung around a hallway in too broad an arc; Alabama Bill was at the open front door, and firing, and Kellen sprawled, returning fire wildly.

Outside, back on the street, The Main, Alabama Bill knew he had to wing the film, get rid of it. He hurled the brass box toward the roof of a poultry store and as it arced, saw it open and disgorge not a movie film, but a necklace, which disappeared along with the box into a puff of snow on the roof.

Freezing, wheezing, drawing great drafts of air, gagging at the wind's chill bite, he turned his head to see O'Reilly coming again, out the door of the priest's house, gaining fast.

Knowing he was dead meat on a straightaway, an easy target, he zagged left into another store, trays of white gleaming staring fish, and lobster, octopus, shrimp, then barrels of herring and olives, and halvah and noodles, and Alabama Bill in the middle of them and no way out and the cop coming through the door.

But Kellen didn't see him right away, he was distracted by a hysterical woman shouting foreign words. He looked to the left too late as Alabama Bill poked his head above a barrel of salt herring.

Bill pressed the trigger as Kellen turned.

The gun clicked empty.

Kellen's mind clicked back in time.

You run out the door, you run, you run, greenness and sunshine and trees' distorted shapes, and the big man in white is diving for your legs, tackling you, your body crumpling under his weight . . .

When Kellen returned to the market seconds later he was firing bullets through the herring barrel into Alabama Bill's chest.

Monday, three p.m.

School closed early because of the cold snap, the weather so severe that Thérèse had picked up Mario at the Ecole Saint-Anselme to drive him the three short blocks to their home, which was on a pleasant, boulevarded street in the east end.

She didn't expect Raolo home after his shift, because he would be going to Ile Sainte-Hélène, for the policemen's sit-in. More loyal to Kellen O'Reilly than to any sense of union duty, he would spend most of the night there. A night alone for her and Mario – but this time the cause was just. She fervently supported the union's campaign for shorter working hours.

She was feeling bad about their fight. Last evening, following their ruined Sunday outing, she hadn't been bought off

139

by roses, and had treated Raolo to a punishing Sphinx-like silence that continued until he left for work today.

But her hurt would mend. She would conquer her constant fear for his safety, her loathing of his chosen career, and she would carry on loving him and he would carry on being a cop.

Thérèse knew she was going to miss him badly tonight and start reproaching herself. *You're supposed to be his father. When the hell do you ever see him?* She shouldn't have said that, it was cruel, untrue; Raolo tried so hard.

She was expecting some people from a church committee she chaired, and wasn't surprised at the doorbell ringing.

Mario was boiling through his homework on the living-room table, anxious to get back to Inspector Maigret. He'd become an all-consuming reader of whodunits and police procedurals, and, of course, this worried Thérèse.

"Get it, honey," she said. She was in the kitchen, making tea.

Mario rose from his page of fractions to be simplified and walked briskly to the door. From the window he saw a taxi on the street, its motor running.

He opened the door and saw Kellen. His suit was torn and grease stained. There were smudges of black on his forehead, and blood from a scratch on his cheekbone. His face was torn with pain. When Mario looked at his face he knew. He knew absolutely.

But when Thérèse came from the kitchen door and saw him, she refused to believe it.

Monday, three-thirty p.m.

Sarah sat tensely in Wally Mandelbaum's office, sipping his tea and answering his questions. The office was relaxed and careless: a fridge, a TV set, a hotplate, tea, and coffee makings. Dr. Mandelbaum seemed a perceptive and friendly man, and fond of Kellen. He had explained he couldn't breach confidentiality, but would be glad to hear her own comments about Kellen.

She wanted something to relax her, a tranq, but it's impossible, the Labour Court will be in emergency session in an hour and a half, the union sit-in tonight, and, in a deluge of urgency that now engulfed everything else, there was Kellen to be located. Where the hell *was* he? He'd not reported back to Station Twenty-six.

She'd left messages, the station, his home; she had told her office to transfer him here if he called.

Was he okay? Had someone tried to kill him? The radio news had been sketchy, confusing. His partner had been murdered, plastic explosives apparently planted beneath a police car. Kellen had pursued one of them. He had shot him in a store. Later, at the scene of the bombing, he had struck a radio reporter seeking an interview.

Wally, too, was tense. And scared. Because he was pretty sure someone had been into his papers on the weekend – today he'd found Kellen's file mussed and slightly out of alphabetical order. So maybe Kellen *had* seen someone watching his office. One of those cold-blooded killers. And Kellen O'Reilly, his friend, was their target.

But Wally's attention now was riveted on something Sarah had said. Something Kellen had told her.

"Let's retrace some steps here, okay?" he said. Kellen, magically, had opened up to this woman. That he had talked at all about his father was extraordinary; what he said was more surprising. "You asked him why he became a cop."

"Yes, he said he wanted to carry on the tradition. His father was on the force."

"So what were his next words?"

"He said his dad was killed on duty, shot by someone. He didn't want to talk about it. Well, he couldn't; he didn't remember it clearly."

"That was all he said about his father?"

"He was at an impressionable age when it happened, I guess. He told me there was a kind of emotional crisis. It's why he went to Coldhaven."

"You're sure he said his father was murdered? That's what he said?"

Wally thought, it didn't make sense. Then he realized: maybe it made a great deal of sense. Part of the puzzle of Kellen O'Reilly clicked together.

She looked at him blankly.

"You didn't know?" he said.

She shook her head.

"In 1955, Kellen's father walked into his garage and put a bullet through his brain."

"What . . . why would Kellen lie?"

"I don't think we're talking about lying here. He believes it." As Wally talked, he pieced it together. "Satorius . . . I guess you're aware, he created an amnesia about his father's death. I wasn't sure . . . but yeah, now it's obvious, he made him believe his father was murdered. Part of the repatterning process. You know his methodology already, I guess. The famous sleep room. Satorius used drugs to keep his patients awake – LSD mostly, and curare, which acts on the nerves, immobilizes you. Then he built up new scenarios. With messages from under the pillow, on a looped tape."

"How could Kellen keep believing . . . wouldn't he have learned the truth? Later?"

The taboo subject, Wally thought. Kellen's constant fear of it and withdrawal from it were now made clear, decoded. He'd been programmed not just to forget the truth, but to deny it, to substitute another for it. But why?

And the words spoken by Satorius – Sarah had described Kellen's bedroom flashback in detail – instructing Kellen to remember that the scar-faced man had killed his father. Something out of *Clockwork Orange*, a Pavlovian mind-conditioning? The firing of the gun: release therapy, psychocatharsis? There'd been nothing about this to be found in Satorius's published papers.

142

To say more to Sarah Paradis would break the rule of confidence. But he felt impelled; there were puzzles to be solved together, and this was very much a time of emergency – a solution to Kellen O'Reilly could even, perhaps, help save his life.

"Me he doesn't trust," Wally said. "I've known him since we were kids; we shared a cell in student housing. He's known you – outside of union meetings – for three days. He keeps secrets from me, a therapist. You he pours out his guts to. I take it there's an attraction here?"

She smiled. "Yes, I am attracted. Very much. But he scares me, too."

"Let me tell you: he's a good guy. And smart, brilliant. Loyal to his friends. Loves kids and animals. He can cook. He's a catch."

"Okay."

"I'm not supposed to say stuff like that, it's not professional. I'm not supposed to talk about Kellen."

"I know how it works. I'm a lawyer, Dr. Mandelbaum."

"Wally. I like you."

"Same to you, Wally."

He smiled, felt some of his tension lift. "So let me give you the background. Brian O'Reilly was this extraordinary hero figure to Kellen. He was a brave cop, and there were stories of heroism. Things like going into houses to talk to husbands with guns to their wives' heads. And what happened is that Sergeant O'Reilly apparently – no one knows the details – but apparently he shot an escaped convict in the back. Tried to arrest him, there'd been a struggle, the man tried to run ... Anyway, he committed suicide the day before a formal inquiry. It was Kellen who found his father's body, with a service revolver in his hand."

"Oh, no," she said softly.

"He was eleven, pre-adolescent. Lot of separation conflicts, lot of avoidance. Denial functions as a very effective buffer against unacceptable truths. Usually a person learns to mobilize defenses that are a little less radical. Kellen wasn't allowed to. Satorius destroyed what mental records Kellen retained of his father's last days. He built upon the denial, bricked it up until it became an impenetrable wall."

"Haven't you talked to Kellen about his father?"

"Every time I try to confront him, he blocks, denies, freezes up. When I mention the suicide my words seem to bounce right back at me like rubber balls. As if he can't absorb what I say. And he says he gets a headache – which I'm sure he does – and the discussion ends. Margot . . . his wife . . . she encountered a similar problem."

Too many dark rooms, Sarah thought.

"Satorius built some kind of rejection device into his mind." Wally wondered if he had the strength to dismantle it. There were no shortcuts – unless one went to chemotherapy. In one experiment Satorius had reported successful repair of memory with LSD. But a careful reading of his paper suggested he was glossing over bad psychotic episodes suffered by some of the patients in his test group.

Wally believed therapy was all about helping people discover themselves, through their own logical, intuitive processes. But the traditional means had been wrong for a person whose mind had been sealed shut by forces outside him. Kellen had needed harder stuff than he got from Wally.

And now it would be painful. He would have to be confronted – newspaper clippings, the inquest evidence, everything. And be pushed beyond the barrier of those implanted headaches into a repaired state of health.

Sarah guessed what he was thinking. "I'll help," she said. "We'll both be with him."

Monday, four p.m.

"I know how it feels, Kel."

Borko, polishing a rifle with a cloth, looked down at Kellen

144

with an unctuous sympathy. He had cleared a corner of his desk for a roost; his swivel chair had been commandeered by Emile Lachance, the director.

"The fucking hell you do." Kellen sat stiffly on a straight-back chair, on the edge of it, as if ready to fly.

"He was more than your partner," said Lachance. "He was a friend."

"I'm staying in," Kellen said.

Borko gently stroked the cloth along the barrel of his bolt action, magazine loadable, butt-length adjustable folding bipod Fusil Model F-1, former IRA sniper's rifle.

"Three months," said Lachance. "The Caribbean if you want. Full pay and a bonus."

The chief and the captain seemed vaguely unreal, cut-out figures. Kellen felt numb. He was on the sloping edge of a nervous breakdown, one minute crawling back up, regaining his senses, the next slipping again toward the edge, the abyss below.

"Hit the street, Raolo!" he'd shouted. The jackhammer had drowned his words. What more could he have done to save his partner's life? He remembered, as if from a slow-moving dream, his struggle to pull his gun, his backing away from the car, abandoning Raolo to his death.

He'd revisited the scene, snarling at reporters, chasing them away, then staring in long morbid contemplation at the wreckage: a twisted frame, slabs of metal, bent and clinging. He'd felt swallowed up, a monster digesting him. He'd suffered another sensation of things going askew, a mental gear slipping its cog.

Big Al had joined him for a while, and put his arm around him, and wept, and later Kellen realized his own tears had frozen on his face. He'd had strength enough to get to Thérèse's house, to speak the cruel words that had to be said, to wait for the reality to seize her. To hold her and Mario while the pain poured through them.

Borko and the chief had waited for him at Station Twenty-six, getting their act together. This act. They wanted him to go on holidays.

"We'll of course, ah, review your account about this film," Borko said, glancing at the chief. "And about these experiments with, ah, guns and mirrors you think you were involved in. And, well, look, I think we want some medical tests."

Kellen blew.

"Eugene, you mother, you son of a bitch," he yelled, standing, his face in Borko's. "You dumb one-track officious bureaucrat! I *saw* the fucking film! Experiments I *think* I was involved in? *Think? I saw* it!"

Eugene put the rifle down and slowly slid off the desk and stood, gaining seven inches.

Kellen's fury was uncowed. "Medical tests – they can check my ass! Check yours! See if that's where your brain is!"

"Lieutenant!" Lachance barked. "Get hold of yourself!"

The command bounced off one wall, then another. The pistols in their glass cases looked like hands pointing. Yeah, O'Reilly, get hold of yourself.

"The bomb was Semitex plastic, by the way," Lachance said. "The lab has already got that far."

"IRA stuff," said Borko.

"And assuming there was this film in the vehicle," said the chief, "the scientists can probably find chemical traces of that, too."

Kellen sagged back into his chair. The chief didn't believe him either.

He had told them almost everything: Coldhaven, psychic driving, LSD and electroshock, his loss of memory; and he had watched their faces swell with incredulity. He'd held back some things: his treatments with Wally, his recent flashbacks, his current feeling that he was becoming unglued – but maybe they could see that, he couldn't hide the aura of madness coruscating around him, dancing, resting, dancing again.

Borko hung his rifle back on the wall, stood back, studied it. "That play on the trust company wasn't exceptionally brilliant," he said. "When they find out, they'll – "

Lachance waved him off impatiently. "Never mind. The important thing is, Kellen, someone wants to kill you."

"Someone? The C-fucking-I-A."

"I think that may be a little extreme, Kellen," said Lachance.

"You're sure you don't have this, ah, so-called film," Borko said. "Your victim was seen taking a metal container from you. But it disappeared somehow. We want to make sure you're not keeping any secrets from us."

"And who don't *you* keep secrets from?" Kellen hurled at him. "The whole world and Hugh McVeigh of the FBI. Or whoever he works for."

Another glance passed between the senior officers.

Maybe Kellen had told them too much. Maybe Borko and the director were part of it.

Lachance swiveled toward Kellen and put his feet under the desk. "Let me be straight with you."

"I know. The guy was out of bullets."

"And he and his chums just took out your partner."

Borko's voice went oily again. "We're not saying it wasn't a tricky call, Kel. But we want you to enjoy some time off."

Tricky call. Kellen hadn't made the call. He had wanted the man alive, but when the flashback ended someone else was in charge; some surrogate executioner was master. He realized afterwards: the big man in the flashback who tackled Kellen on the grass was the guy he'd shot behind the herring barrel.

Maybe Borko and Lachance were right; he should take time off, collect himself. No, don't be fooled by them.

"I don't know if I can avoid an inquiry this time, Kellen," Lachance said. "How do I explain that you were supposed to be off this case? And that now a cop has died?"

Kellen was nearly overcome with rage. "A *cop* has died? It was Raolo! Don't you guys care? I'm *on* this case. I'm going to bury those bastards!"

The chief sighed. "Eugene?" he said.

Borko wouldn't look at Kellen. "All right, Kel, here's the

bottom line. We know you're seeing a psychiatrist. Dr. . . . "
He was looking at his notepad. "Wallace Mandelbaum."

Kellen blinked. "You had me followed?" he said softly.

"Kellen, we were getting some . . . odd intimations of, you
know, things weren't quite right with you."

Kellen wanted to say something; words wouldn't emerge.

"We've, ah, come upon information that you've been hal-
lucinating. Seeing visions of people being blown apart.
Rather like the film you . . . think you saw."

"You sent someone sneaking into his office." Kellen put a
period between each word: "You low prying suck."

"We had cause," Borko said. "We also had a warrant."

Kellen wanted to move on the captain, smash him into the
metal phalluses on the wall. But he seemed frozen again,
numb.

His superiors were like impassive toy soldiers, and their
voices rang hollow in his ears.

Borko: "We think you're having a nervous breakdown."

Lachance: "If that's the problem, Kellen, we should know."

Borko: "You should consider a programming course, Kel.
You'll probably want to come off the street when this is over."

They were a part of it, part of the conspiracy, it was suddenly all very clear. Kellen saw Borko's hand reach out. He
stared at it, long bony fingers gliding toward him.

"We'll need the service revolver," Borko said.

Kellen wasn't sure why for a second. For his collection?
He looked at Lachance.

"You're suspended, Lieutenant. Give him the gun." A
voice one uses for the family dog. "Now give him the gun."

Sarah and Wally talked urgently until the sun started to disappear into the whirling clouds in the west. She talked about her court case, about the role she hoped Kellen might play in it. Any decision to take that unalterable step was Kellen's, Wally said. If made, he would support him fully in it. But first Kellen had to come to grips with his distorted past.

Sarah phoned Station Twenty-six again, only to learn he'd come and gone; someone in homicide said he'd been taken to a hotel.

As she was about to excuse herself – Labour Court was soon to enter into emergency session – the door buzzer sounded.

"Dr. Mandelbaum."

No response. Then, "Uh, yeah, it's me."

A few seconds later Kellen was at the door. He looked like a vaguely familiar stranger to her at first: shaved, a suit. Then she saw he had a cut on his cheek, and the suit was ripped and soiled. His eyes went around the office, not seeming to settle, to focus.

He finally turned to her, as she moved toward him nervously.

"What are you doing here?" he said.

"Kellen . . . are you all right?"

"What are you *doing* here?" he demanded.

She froze in front of him. "I . . . came to help. I . . . God, Kellen, you're scaring me."

He studied her, and slowly put a hand to her face, touching her as if to make sure she was real. When he seemed satisfied of that he nodded his head, and spoke softly. "I'm sorry. I wasn't expecting you. I'm sorry, Sarah."

He suddenly looked so sad. Sarah put her arms around him tightly. She felt his body racing, trembling, finally softening in her embrace.

"They killed Raolo Basutti," he said.

"We know," she said.

149

"And they're trying to kill me." She felt him stiffen again, all his muscles.

"Sit down over here, Kellen," said Wally, who was standing beside the couch.

"They've been spying on you, Wally." Kellen pulled away from Sarah and walked to him. "Borko and the Chief." A sudden shift of subject: "It was some kind of experiment in revenge therapy. Or kill-testing. With mirrors. I saw it on film."

Wally could see Kellen was barely holding it together. He listened to his scattered, urgent flow of words:

"It must have miscarried, the experiment; they're trying to hush it up." His voice went dry, cracked. "They've done something foul to me, induced a need to kill."

"Sit down, Kel," Wally said.

A mirthless, tight laugh. "I'm the guy in the mirror now. I'm the target."

Suddenly Kellen did another swift mood swing, and again was loud and angry. "The department is going to cover up Raolo's murder! I've been suspended because they're afraid I'll find the killers! Borko's working with them! So is the goddamn police director!"

"Kellen –" Wally said.

He grabbed Wally's elbow. "The film's gone. I had Satorius on film. But they think I've still got it. They saw that big bastard try to take it from me. But it was Bob Champlain's necklace." He let Wally go and turned to Sarah. "Borko thinks I've got it. He's told McVeigh that."

Sarah tried in vain to piece together the disordered history Kellen was relating. She wanted to go to him again, to hold him, to still him, but was afraid; she wasn't sure she knew him.

"They're going to keep coming after me." He laughed coldly. "But that's my advantage, I don't have to go to them, they have to come to me."

"Kellen, can you sit down and, ah, talk to us calmly a little bit?" Sarah asked.

"There's something else on that film. But I don't *have* it."

His voice became subdued. He walked slowly and purposefully to the window. "I don't have anything now. I have my own word and no one else's. No evidence. Only broken pieces of memory." His voice cracked again.

"Sarah, please get him a glass of water," Wally said. "Washroom's down the hall."

Sarah backed away a few steps, staring at Kellen, then left.

Kellen's tone became hushed and urgent. "You said my memory is trying to come back, Wally. Through flashbacks. How do I trigger them? There's something there . . . Or someone." He closed his eyes tight, and his fists. "I think it's someone I know. It's as if I almost have him, and then he fades." His eyes opened, raw and red. "How I do I bring it all back?"

"We're going to work on some hard therapy, Kellen. Sarah's going to help."

"I've no time. I need a quick fix of memory. Must be some kind of drug . . . "

Wally saw Kellen's expression change.

"How many mikes would it take?" he said, low, almost a whisper.

"I *don't* advise that."

"Would it work? It could, couldn't it? We could do it clinically, you'd be there to help me through it."

Wally hesitated. "To start with, LSD is on the banned list. Second, you're in no condition – "

"But it *could* work! Satorius did it; you told me."

"It also triggered some dangerous psychoses. You need to get to someplace safe, Kellen, and lie down and rest."

Wally watched Kellen stare long and contemplatively out the window at Coldhaven; it seemed, oddly, to settle him.

"Yeah. They've got someplace safe. Full of CIA. I'll get another hotel. I'll be okay, Wally; I'll be all right."

He smiled wanly at Sarah as she returned with the glass of water.

"I hate to ask, Sarah, but can I get a lift? Cabs are pretty busy with this weather. I had to wait half an hour for Alphonse."

Wally wondered if he should be reassured by this new rational voice. "Main thing is his safety right now."

"Listen, I know I'm a little disjointed, it's not been just your average day. I'm basically okay. I just need to sleep this off."

Sarah saw he was getting over it, his little breakdown. She knew about breakdowns. She'd been there. She couldn't remember why for a moment. Marcel.

As he took a long drink of cold water, she reached a hand to his face and wiped off some dirt. "Sure. I'll drive you."

She put on her coat and took Kellen's arm and told Wally she'd call him.

He shielded her from the whipping wind as they walked to her car. The engine churned grudgingly into life, and she let it idle, turned on the hot air.

"They have a safe house for you?"

"Yeah. Mine."

"I sincerely doubt it."

"No, really, they'll have guards posted all night, some of the guys have volunteered. SWATers – trained killers – they love to break necks in the dark. It's all cleared with the union. Oh, by the way, can you go down by Ontario Street first?"

"Why?"

"I'm going to bring them up some pizzas. There's a really good place there."

As she drove him, he talked – lucidly – about the scientific film he saw, the experiment with mirrors, his code number on the blackboard, O/14, his attempt to flee. His flashbacks had been memory's echo of some of the events filmed.

Then he asked her questions about her examination today of Gregor Satorius.

"He said he burned everything?"

"Yes."

"But he didn't burn a certain film marked '47-02.' Wonder why."

When they got to Le Pizza Parfait, Kellen told her to wait in the car, he wouldn't be long, and he got out and bent into the wind, walked up the sidewalk, and disappeared into the restaurant.

She huddled in front of the fan. Grungy pizza joint, grungy neighborhood, on a tough street. But it was quiet in this weather, no creature was stirring, not even the bums or the street dealers.

Kellen had turned sane and purposeful. He'd be safe, and she could turn to other crises, the *tribune de travail* in an hour, a strike that could fall apart, a long night coming.

In Pizza Parfait, Kellen called, "Four specials, medium, extra anchovy on one," then glanced around, and quickly moved to a table at the back.

Two of the customers at the table froze and went white. Freshmen, Kellen guessed, hash for the toga party. The man across from them was fortyish, had braided graying hair, wore a smelly old sheepskin and a floppy raccoon hat. Bennie DeMer; the Pizza Parfait was his sales office.

He yanked him up by his collar; Bennie was light, spindly, unresisting.

"I want to borrow you."

Bennie seemed resigned. He told his customers, "You're witnesses. I ain't got a scratch on me."

Kellen took his wrist and pulled him to the back, past the washroom door, up a flight of stairs to the rented rooms. Bennie didn't protest, said nothing at all until Kellen had taken him into the piss-scented hallway, to his door.

"Wanna see the warrant."

"Open it."

"Wanna see – "

Kellen splintered the lock with the heel of his boot. He pushed Bennie inside, thrust him against the kitchen wall, and turned and looked over the stock on the table. Small bags of white powder, a dozen plastic pill bottles with yellow pills, white ones, red. A set of scales, a Bunsen burner, and some test tubes to the side.

"Eye-proppers, truck drivers," Kellen said, examining the pill bottles. "Speedballs." He sniffed the white powder. "Smack. What else have you got?"

"A lawyer."

Kellen grabbed him by the shoulders and rammed him

153

back against the wall. "I don't have any time! This isn't a bust! You got acid, LSD?"

"Hey, man, easy, you know I got it all. In the fridge, in the fridge."

Kellen released him, took two fast steps to the refrigerator and opened it.

"If this isn't a bust, what is it?"

"A buy."

"I see, uh . . . Under the baloney."

He found it, about a dozen books of ten Canadian forty-three-cent postage stamps.

"How fresh is it?"

"Vitamin A-plus, lab fresh. Two hunnert mikes a hit. Just lick the glue off the back."

"I'll take a book of stamps. Send me the bill."

He stuck it in his wallet and ran downstairs and back through the Pizza Parfait, where he paid for his specials, then carried them back to the car.

"Like anchovies? I forgot to ask."

"No, I'm not hungry." She pulled out into the traffic. "Kellen, I'm sorry, I won't be able to come up. I've got to be in Labour Court."

"Oh, yeah, that's right, you mentioned."

"I'll drop back later."

Kellen hesitated. "Maybe I better just try to get through the night alone. Not that I don't – "

Their words collided. "Yes, really, that's best."

"And, you know, I've got these bodyguards in the apartment."

She laughed. "Makes it awkward."

"Yeah."

He was so much better, she thought.

"I'll be at the meeting in spirit," he said. "Tell Ouimet that, tell everyone."

"They may decide to go back to work, Kellen. With a policeman just murdered . . . I don't know. That rule-bound bigot, Taillefeur? He's organizing some kind of anti-strike caucus."

154

Kellen became stern. "Sarah, tell them not to bend. Tell them they are striking for guys like Raolo, family guys like him. Please, tell them I said that."

The trees on his street were bending to the wind as she pulled up to his building; the weather had turned overcast and a light snow was falling. She thought of the policemen inside, watching, maybe aiming their sniper's rifles at her Yugo, waiting to see who emerged.

"I'll see what we can do about the suspension," she said.

"Yeah, well, the union has other things on their plate. When do you continue with Satorius?"

"Next week."

"Ask him about MK-ULTRA project forty-seven. Ask him about Subject O-fourteen."

"That's you?"

"Ask him about it. Tell him you have a new witness."

"You mean it?"

"I'll give evidence."

"Oh, God, Kellen, that's wonderful." She kissed him hard on the mouth. He drew back from her, then they kissed again.

He opened the passenger door and a whirlwind of snow gagged him for a moment. "Jesus. The Chief wants me to find a tropical beach. I think I'll take him up."

She watched him hunch into the wind toward his staircase. It was five-thirty, the sun was setting somewhere behind the foaming western sky.

Monday, five-thirty p.m.

From his balcony, Kellen did a careful scan up and down the street as her car disappeared behind a trail of exhaust. No frozen watchers, no idling engines, no menacing shadows, no footmarks on the new powder snow outside his building.

155

He entered the apartment quietly, and turned the heat up but not the lights. All was empty and still, just the creaking floorboards and the moaning wind outside.

The department had reserved a room for him in the Bonaventure Hilton, under the name of William Johnson. Borko would have told that to McVeigh, or whatever was *his* real name, who would have told his pals, ex-CIA, or whatever *they* were. They would be waiting at the Bonaventure, waiting for him to check in.

They would think he would be crazy to go home. Therefore he wasn't crazy; he was being smart, staying a step ahead of them. He'd been a little out of touch with himself, off and on, but contact with Wally and Sarah had grounded him. He was okay now. He was okay, just fine.

And he would be safe here for a while, until they realized he wasn't in the hotel. Later he could go out into the greater safety of the streets, and into the all-night bars and blind pigs. He would be up all night anyway.

He wished he had a gun. He'd always believed people shouldn't keep them in their homes for thieves; that was the American way, quite unCanadian. But maybe tonight, after his journey into memory, he'd find one on The Main.

Mao padded softly up from somewhere and followed him, purring and insistent, as Kellen moved with slow deliberation around the apartment, which was darkening in the slow winter twilight. He turned the oven to warm, put one of the pizzas in it, and scooped some cat food into Mao's dish.

As he turned on the bathtub faucets the phone rang and he heard his recorded voice. Then another voice. Margot. Buoyant.

"Hi, darling. I got the film! I don't *believe* it. I'm still in shock."

The movie audition must just be over; she hasn't heard the news of the bomb, the deaths.

She hung up. He'd wanted to talk to her, to congratulate her, to share her joy. Something was going right for someone for a change. Not for me, Margot, not for Raolo. Not for the man behind the barrel. I killed the son of a bitch. It was a tricky call, Margot, that's what Borko said.

Kellen suffered a sudden recall of Raolo ducking down onto the seat of the car and the car belching flames. Raolo. A searing knife rode up his spine. He saw Thérèse's crumbling face, and saw Mario, struggling, trying not to cry, his thin arms stiff by his side, and then the grief bursting through.

He ran to the toilet and retched.

It took him several minutes to recover, but he felt purged, and he undressed in darkness and sank into the deep old claw-foot tub, down to his neck, his two feet over the rounded edge, and felt the healing warmth of steam drifting up his face. He felt a settling now, a knitting together. He was okay, he told himself again, but inwardly he knew his mind was as fragile as glass, ready to shatter.

Tonight wasn't exactly a felicitous time for him to be playing around with a psychoactive drug. But there would be no better time – because there was no time left. Wally thought it might work, you could see it in his face. Just a little, he'd do only a half.

He had to slow down, mentally prepare himself.

First there would be queasiness, and then the famous psychedelic rush, and after a couple of hours of that, the leveling off, and a period of intense clarity once the brain reassembles itself. His memory of his LSD experiences at Coldhaven was misty at best, but he had researched the drug, had studied the encyclopedia of lysergic acid diethylamide with morbid fascination during those capricious years when Dr. Leary and Sergeant Pepper reigned.

The books spoke of profound insights following the rush, and of gates opening to obscured memories.

Concentrate. So what was the Coldhaven project? Was it therapy or was that merely a pretense, a cover? Was it a fascist adventure, a study of the dark forces within men, a loosing of the uncontrolled id to free the feral beast?

Or something of more immediate practical use.

Satorius was a practical man.

Depatterning, curing neuroses through narco-hypnosis and electroconvulsion, that was his métier.

Destruction of unhealthy memory systems.

Then reprogramming new patterns of behavior.

And in so doing, testing one's ability to kill a man one hates.

Couldn't you program assassins that way? Send them into Central America, Eastern Europe? If captured: no recall of their training, of who their masters are; their memory cells are locked, untenanted, no torturer can get at them. And when they return from assignment, the memory of their deed is wiped as well.

Hold on – could Satorius, even with his moral illness, his sociopathy, have been a part of that?

Unlikely.

Yet . . . And musings even more tenebrous rose from the gloom of his mind.

Had they wound Kellen like a time bomb, prepared him to execute a dignitary, a visiting KGB agent?

Would he receive a signal, a few words in a spoken phrase that would put him into kill mode?

Maybe this paranoia was psychotic; maybe he was truly ill, and refusing to accept the fact. How does one ever know?

Whatever they'd been up to, they were prepared to murder – and chance their own deaths – to keep it secret.

They had succeeded in a way. They didn't know it. No hard evidence now. Only Kellen's dubious hearsay.

MK-ULTRA 47 / PHASE 02, FINAL TEST / SUBJECT O/14. MK-ULTRA sub-project number 47. Kellen had been Subject O/14. What else had been on the film?

Sloukos and Champlain – how had they come across that little movie? Blackmailers, but what role had these small-time jobbers played in MK-ULTRA 47?

Kellen found his terrycloth robe hanging by the bathroom door, and donned it, wrapped it tied, then felt his way through the darkness of his apartment.

Through the side window he saw the glow from old Saint-

Yves' windows, a comforting buttery light filtering through the blowing snow, which was gushing from the skies now, the wind swirling it, pummeling it, explosions of powder on the windows.

He told himself again that he felt well; things were calming. He'd get through it. He retrieved his pizza, and then moved Mao off his easy chair and lowered his weary body into it, and clicked on the remote control for the news.

"We take you on location, to the scene of the bombing, Carolyn McAllister."

"Police believe the gang planted as much as fifty pounds of plastic explosive beneath the car while the police officers and construction crew were in a restaurant. I have with me Captain Eugene Borko, commander of Station Twenty-six, who has taken personal charge of the case."

Kellen tore one forty-three-cent stamp in half – one hundred little micrograms on the sticky side of a tiny rectangle of paper.

"Inspector, do you have any leads?"

He slipped the rest of the stamps between the pages of *The Plague* and began shredding his half-stamp, sprinkling it on the pizza.

"Well, Carolyn, we have a few aces up our sleeve, but in a case like this you'll appreciate we have to hold our cards close to the vest."

His phone rang, and again he heard his voice. A five-second silence from the sending end. Click.

Monday, seven-fifteen p.m.

"The contract is specific. All members are entitled to attend any duly called extraordinary meeting. Quite legal. Monsieur Lamartine wails his lament about anarchy in the streets, but

159

of course there will be nothing of the sort. I don't see any of our local anarchists venturing out in *this* weather."

Sarah got a smile from Judge Rheaumé. She had him.

Half an hour later, Guy Lamartine led his clients dejectedly from the courtroom, followed by Sarah and the Brotherhood executive.

He drew Sarah aside.

"Have your little duly called extraordinary meeting. If you dare. It will be on your heads."

"What will be?"

"The fact that law officers sit down on the job when cop killers are free on the streets. I suggest you call the thing off."

"Are you prepared to reopen talks?"

"I have no such instructions."

She turned from him, and felt troubled. Now, because of Raolo's murder, many union members were expressing loud second thoughts about the token walkout. Shop steward Taillefeur, the company fink, was in full cry in his opposition to it, rallying supporters. Sarah – who had so vigorously urged the action – was now in doubt herself. But there seemed no way back. It was a question of solidarity.

She gathered her clients around her. Ouimet shook her hand vigorously. "*C'est sensas!* Good work, brilliant."

"Yes, very good work, Comrade Paradis," said Taillefeur. "Now we have painted ourselves into a corner. You should have let them win this one, and we could all save face."

"I don't *let* people win," Sarah said.

"The whole thing is fucking stupid," Taillefeur hissed. "A police car blown up, a detective killed. We're like goddamn fucking women, walking out. Cowards."

"*Fourre-toi-le dans le cul,*" said Ouimet through clenched teeth, his high spirits now doused by Taillefeur's cold water.

"Stuff it up yours, too, Fernand. You'll be hearing from some of us at the meeting." Taillefeur strutted away toward the door.

"He's a prick," Ouimet said. "*Un barbeux,* a disturber of shit." He turned to Sarah. "I hear they have suspended O'Reilly. By God, we'll show those arrogant bastards."

160

Sarah read his doubt, though, behind the passionate bravado. Taillefeur, by being such a *barbeux*, had made it hard for this stubborn union leader to alter course.

Monday, eight p.m.

Kellen's face glistened damply, glowed many colors.

"Hollywood Squares," little ego-filled cubicles. Three seconds. Click. "*Insolences d'une caméra.*" Click. "Dating Game," culture from below the border. Ford trucks are built tough. You can count on the Commerce.

He pressed buttons haphazardly, an experiment in flickering images, a futile attempt to induce the flashbacks.

He felt a qualmish feeling at his center, felt his anal muscles clenching. It was coming on.

He was not denying his fear. It wasn't fear of the drug itself but the memories the drug might bring, a fear of being joined with the past, a fear of reliving. But he had nowhere else to go but back in time.

He knew he had to sustain an awareness during the coming hours that his perceptions could lie, that he was on a drug. Don't confuse the real with the unreal. This is the famous trip, the ride on the psychedelic roller coaster; you can't get off, you're on it for the run. It's not dangerous unless you are.

He lit another cigarette. Colored light fluttered across his somber face.

"*Les Muppets.*" "*Il y a une fille dans ma soupe.*" February sale at The Bay. Mr. Spock, the controls not answering, Spaceship Enterprise shaking violently.

A softness at his ankles, and a purring. Creaks and clicks. The whine of wind. Distant anxious whispers from the set.

Beam me up, Scotty.

His phone rang again. He listened to his recorded message. Did he hear whisperings? A click. This wasn't wise, staying here. Later, they might come.

Jumpy, feeling prickles of paranoia, he got up and walked to a window and studied, through the blur of snow, the untracked whiteness of the street below.

Concentrate.

What was the lever that would send memory flooding back? How could he return to that house of horror?

Simple. It was fifteen minutes away by taxi, still perched there on the edge of the mountain. Saw it from Wally's window . . . was that today? When was he at Wally's? That's right, Sarah had just driven him home from there.

Her face came swimming to him, and he felt his heart beating; maybe it was her and maybe it was the acid as well.

He turned off the TV and listened to all the silent sounds, the apartment buzzing. The drug seemed to be pouring through his system.

Concentrate. If this one reel of film had survived, might others be extant?

Satorius was proud of what he did. A scientist – would he have destroyed everything, all the records?

What is hidden within the nooks and niches of Coldhaven?

Kellen pictured the manor building and a memory came: Satorius's office on the fourth-floor tower, Kellen's first interview by him twenty-five years ago, Kellen signing a release. A wall of filing cabinets in his office. A neat stack of files on his desk, lovingly kept.

A soft voice came from the surrounding silence. *Go there,* the voice told him. *Go to Coldhaven.*

"Who's that?" He heard his own voice, loud, startled.

Coldhaven – another distant voice. *The secret is there. Go there.*

It's a drug talking to you. Don't listen.

Go there. More voices, in chorus, louder, more urgent. *Yes.*

He would just stand outside the building, maybe walk

around it, hoping that the nearness would ignite remembrance.

He got up, found his way to his desk, and felt for the telephone, and picked it up. A little machine that could connect him with the outside world. The concept distracted him, lines to the world from his living-room desk.

He wiggled a finger into a hole in the rotary dial.

"Top Dog Taxi."

"Uh, Michelle, can you get me Alphonse?"

He sounded like someone else, a voice he knew, an acquaintance.

"It's cold as blue murder outside, he'll be forty-five to an hour."

"An hour's fine."

He was doing okay. How cold is blue murder?

"So where are you?" Michelle said.

"Ah . . . how do you mean 'where'?"

"Where. Like to where the heck you want the cab sent?"

"Oh, my place. Home. Avenue Ducharme."

"Gotcha down, Kel."

He could handle this. He could go outside and manage it, deal with people. There was no alcohol-like clouding of senses, just the opposite, a crowding of them, all sharp and focused. Energy. He could see in the dark.

Like Mao. He picked up his cat and stroked him, felt one with him, two old tomcats waiting in the dark. All the friendly shapes of his apartment. He could be secure here, in his terrycloth robe, anonymous in the darkness. He didn't have to go to Coldhaven.

He would just go for a little while. He would stand outside the manor house, and let the building's silent pulsing jolt his memory back.

He went to his bedroom, and it seemed to take an eternity to find everything, but from deep in his closet he pulled out his fur-lined parka, and from drawers he laid out long underwear, cotton shirt, pullover sweater, fleece-lined mittens, and found woolen socks and moccasins.

Monday, eight-thirty p.m.

Sarah emerged from the Ile Sainte-Hélène Métro station, into the fierce winter night. She'd left her car near the Labour Court on Cremazie, in an illegal zone and halfway onto the sidewalk. Its engine had frozen.

The wind streamed off the frozen river as she shouldered against it, found shelter behind the skeletons of pavilions and fought her way to the Hélène de Champlain, leased for the night to the Brotherhood, a great rambling stone structure near the site of Man and His World, Expo '67.

Just behind the building, the wind had set up an unholy wailing through the metal tress-work of the former American pavilion, Buckminster Fuller's geodesic dome, the world's largest, now an abandoned two-hundred-foot high monster of triangles and platforms, an epitaph for America, for her declining grandeur, 1967, the apogee, just before humiliation in Vietnam.

The structure frightened her, a metal carcass, skinned of its plastic covering.

Outside the restaurant, pounding mitts together and stamping feet and swearing, were several reporters. The TV people were better off, had vans.

She hurried inside, into the warmth, the air fueled by the breath of at least a thousand police officers, standing, seated, or squatting on sleeping bags. Many hundreds of the less-than-militant had stayed home, to protest from the comfort of their living rooms and beds. Others, Sarah guessed, had broken ranks and reported for work – how many, she was unsure, perhaps a couple of hundred.

The meeting seemed tumultuous already, a half hour into it. On the stage, President Ouimet was shouting into a microphone. Members were standing at floor mikes, demanding to be recognized. Someone kept yelling, "*Undémocratique!*" Ouimet was banging his gavel.

The skirmish was over something technical, a procedural ruling. She could already tell that Taillefeur, the foul-mouthed malcontent – there seemed to be one in every union – was orchestrating it, taking full revenge against Ouimet for telling Taillefeur to stuff it up his ass.

She walked briskly up the center aisle to the stage and joined the president.

"Sorry, my car conked out."

"Where's Kellen?" Ouimet asked. "Order! Order! You're out of order!"

"He's not coming."

"I thought he was."

"He's spending the night . . . he said he arranged with the union to have some men stay overnight at his apartment."

"Oh. Good idea. Some of the guys don't know that. I'll pass the word out." He banged the gavel. "You brothers and sisters in the back, let's have some quiet! And you, brother, sit down, we have a heavy agenda!"

Taillefeur refused to sit and yelled into one of the floor microphones: "Point of order, Brother Chairman, you haven't heard my motion to adjourn!"

"And I'm not going to!" He turned to Sarah. "He calls everything a point of order. He knows the rules. Help me out of this mess."

Monday, eight forty-five p.m.

Kellen stuffed a flashlight into a pocket, and tied on his moccasins. He walked out into the cold and locked his door. He was fitted out for a polar trek, belted and buckled. A team of dogs would be good.

He saw himself mushing toward Coldhaven. Mushing. He liked that word. Mushing.

Mushing on Bafflin' Island.

He heard himself laugh into the wind, crazy acid-laughter.

165

Energy seemed to be pouring through him; he was a river.

But a few minutes ago it had been wildly different, nothing was funny, paranoia reigned – they were coming, they had a wire on his phone, they knew he was at home. They. The conspiracy.

But they didn't come. And when he heard Alphonse honk the horn outside, a surge of high spirits swept through him.

He was aware he was drug-intoxicated, not processing; his anarchic moods and his turmoil of perception were unreality, not to be trusted, and he would keep that constantly in mind. He surely hadn't done enough acid to hallucinate – although when he had closed his eyes he'd seen, in addition to swirling neon shapes, a row of advancing eyeballs, and, later, what looked like a parade of squirrels carrying placards.

But this was reality: Alphonse Bague behind the windshield, familiar, a connector from the inner world to the outer, a guide, his eyes white beacons on his dark face.

"Let's go for a spin," he said as he sat beside Alphonse. Spin. He liked that word.

Alphonse stared at his passenger's huge dilated pupils. "You say a *spin*? What kind spin?"

Tires spin. Tailspin. Spin control. Out of control. Concentrate.

"Uh, south, toward the park." Kellen could hear the squeaky radio voice of the dispatcher. The taxi was a hot cocoon on a cold night.

"Where, 'zackly?"

"Coldhaven Manor."

"I hear sometime about dat place. Where they used to had the white man's voodoo."

"Mush me there."

He laughed. Alphonse glanced at him.

"Maybe I don' hear you rights, Lieutenant." He pulled out onto the street, tires spinning. "Mush?"

"It's what they turn your head into."

"Who do?"

"The voodoo. 'Who do the voodoo' – catchy dance number, eh, 'Phonse? Yeah, who do the voodoo and why do they do it?"

"Don' ast me."

Alphonse kept glancing at him strangely, and Kellen forced himself not to babble. For a while he watched the streetlamps swoop out of the darkness, and glow past him and away. He had a sense of being pulled to Coldhaven, a magnet sucking him there, its secrets impelling him.

Secrets that were struggling to come out; he could feel turmoil in his brain, an imprisoned past demanding release.

He was intoxicated, but his senses had been flung open by the LSD; he felt his mind expanding, growing. But sending too many images, too many thoughts and plans, all crowding around, demanding attention.

He couldn't unscramble Alphonse's weather report. "We down to minus fifty on the chill wind factor 'cause a con'inental polar mass is occluding with unstabled air."

Concentrate. Factor: the weather. Okay, nobody could possibly be tailing them. The Coldhaven grounds should be deserted. Factor: no cops working tonight. Factor: you're on a drug.

The taxi twisted and slid along snow-thick Pine Avenue, past the buildings of the hospital and university somewhere out there in the gloom.

Satorius's voice seemed to whisper words to him just below the threshold of his hearing. Words about his father, words repeating endlessly as if from a tape somewhere buried in his brain.

Everything started to swirl around him, and he fixed his attention hard on the lights and buttons of the dashboard, the meter clicking, clicking.

And he was looking out now, into the white maelstrom, the world outside whirling like the world within. What makes sense out in the occluding air mass?

"Let me out the next corner."

Alphonse stopped at Peel and Pine. "You feelin' okay, man?"

"Never better." Kellen felt uncontrollably generous, wrote

fifty bucks on the chit. He got out. The cold wind slapped him, restored him.

He watched Alphonse's taxi slither down the steep street and vanish, gobbled by a blizzard, vehicular whiteout. After two hundred yards, nothing, the city doesn't exist, just you exist within a halo of streetlight, you and the chill wind factor.

A young couple came out of the gloom, bending to the wind, ghostly figures who loomed and passed and dimmed and disappeared.

A car struggled up the hill into view, slashing through the unpacked snow, and stalled, and slid backwards slowly, and was gone, sucked back into the non-world.

Up the street, somewhere in that whirling oblivion, the home of the white man's voodoo.

Chill wind, ill wind, a walk with the wild wind, a leeway sail across the street, and a wire fence appears, and the skeletal arms of elms, and the flapping wings of spruce boughs.

Here was the high stone gate. He knew it. Two-and-a-half decades ago he had walked out through it. After three months inside.

He had sudden brilliant recall of that September morning – not a flashback, but clean, clear memory of a day until now forgotten. He had a picture of himself standing at this gateway in the rain. Trying to remember who he was and where he lived, and then a young man joined him, his face worried and familiar, explaining things, insisting: *Hey, pal, I'm Wally.*

And weeks passed before his life came back to him. His life minus three months, those months confused, mist-laden.

Snow shaping into drifts over a hillock in front of Castle Coldhaven.

He passed through the portal onto the grounds.

Up the slope, moccasins sinking, feet disappearing, reappearing, snow caking the parka's round fur window, he had a clear memory again of this, the Coldhaven grounds, the rolling lawn, a June day, young Kellen walking up here with a suitcase; but tonight's was a dark and abstract version, blacks and grays, no blues and greens, a canvas in motion with dancing trees and darting arrows of gusting snow.

Kellen stopped and stared. The building held its secrets. *We have to hold our cards close to the vest.* Someone just said that. Eugene Borko. Aces up his sleeve.

I know how it feels, Kel.

We're not saying it wasn't a tricky call, Kel.

Aces up your ace-hole, Eugene. He laughed wildly at his joke.

He looked down to his mittened hands and saw his pack of Player's in one, his lighter in the other. It must be time to smoke, the addict inside was making wage demands. He moved to the lee side of a thick maple tree, and fumbled a cigarette from the pack and cradled the flame.

It tasted synthetic, like smoking plastic; the LSD was telling him to kick the habit.

He looked at the cigarette, then broke off the charred filter, lit the other end, and drew on it, and still it tasted odd.

In front of him was the front door of Coldhaven, a door through which he must have passed at least twice. Once in. Once out.

Or maybe twice more.

Yes.

And a flashback came.

You try to fly, an escaping wingless bird, and the door opens onto the sunswept lawn, maple-leaf arms reaching out to gather you in . . .

Cigarette smoke made a whip-turn across his eyes, and brought water from his tear ducts. The wind carried him toward the door.

And he staggered to a stop as a second image blinked on and off. But the same one, a *reprise*, he was again running out the door into the day, but it continued . . .

You look behind, at the keepers of your mind, who are coming, men in white, intent, relentless as jungle cats, bounding out the door and down the grassy slopes . . .

He shot forward to the present – Coldhaven a vast, black shape in front of him. And he went back again.

The big man dives at you, and you buckle upon a rise of clipped lawn and into the green, prickly lake, rolling, smelling your sweat and your fear among the sweet odors of grass and earth, and the men are upon you, their arms pinning you, their soothing voices in your ears . . .

Summer's day switched in a blink to winter's night. And the night stayed for a few moments. Kellen took a butt hit, dropped the cigarette, and stared at the building from this hot spot in front of the door, a place where the flashbacks were coming like sparks from a bad connection.

Another.

You struggle, but your arm is twisted behind your back and you buckle forward and move with them. "We're your friends, we want to help you." Voices dripping of syrup and lies . . .

The building sucks you inside, the door closes, entomb-ment . . .

And the visions stopped, and there were just the snow, the wind, and the night. Kellen was left breathless, and he waited, expectant and afraid, but the episodes had ceased, as if the door to Coldhaven closed upon them as it closed on his drug-panicked remembered-self.

He had shot and killed two of them, those men in white. Older versions of them, thicker-faced and jowly. The drug-store, the market on The Main – violent events rippled through his memory.

He stood there a long time, trying to commune with him-self, assess. Then he found himself moving toward the door the men had dragged him through, a cyclopean door, an oval window, a glowing glass eye; soft voices were directing him there, yes, telling him to enter.

He shone his flashlight into the eye. The view was abstract. A dead spider behind the pupil, dangling from its dusty, wilted web, a many-legged Dr. Luk. The waiting room was bare walled, empty of furniture.

The fat, brass doorknob turned five degrees, then denied him.

He looked about at all the boarded windows. He plowed through deepening snow around to the side, not doubting his mission now. He'd been asked to come inside, he'd been invited to follow a trail, the flashbacks were the spoor of memory.

Monday, nine-thirty p.m.

Eddie Comacho was in O'Reilly's duplex once again, searching.

Around the corner off Avenue Ducharme was parked Comacho's latest vehicle – a hot-wired, four-wheel, three-quarter-ton '79 Dodge to replace the bunged-up, shot-up Land Cruiser. He'd hot-wired the pickup earlier this evening in a deserted car lot.

O'Reilly's house was familiar ground now, complete with obnoxious cat. Eddie Comacho figured he didn't need to toss the house with a fine-toothed comb for something as big as a film canister, and no point in being tidy, so he threw clothes and junk over the floor.

No movie picture.

Rudy said O'Reilly didn't turn the film in to his bosses at the cop shop; he kept it for himself. Rudy says O'Reilly was suspended for that. Rudy claims to have inner knowledge. Rudy is black belt fourth Dan. Rudy would kill Eddie the Cube if he knew what he was thinking. He was thinking: Rudy's done a real bag job here. He was thinking of Panama, maybe change his name and buy a little *finca*.

In the living room, he took a break and ate the last two cold slices of pizza from the box on the arm of O'Reilly's TV chair. Anchovies, Eddie loved anchovies.

The phone rang. Eddie heard his absent host's recorded message. Whoever, he or she just hung up.

171

Comacho went to the answering machine and rewound the tape for a bit. He heard a woman's excited voice: "Hi, darling. I got the film! I don't *believe* it. I'm still in shock."

Monday, nine-thirty-five p.m.

His flashlight found an alcove and a recessed basement window protected by only a woven metal screen, loose at one corner, and he knelt and pried it away. He'd be in trouble again with Borko, no search warrant. But hadn't he been suspended? He was free to do this, he was as free as a criminal.

No glass here, just boards nailed to the window frame, and he kicked them out and caught the scent of musty warm air from inside.

He slid to the floor, knocking something over with his legs, something tall and flat and smooth, and it fell with a sound of shattering glass that echoed fiercely, an avalanche of bright, shiny sound.

Then, for a while, he heard just his own breathing and beneath that, the deepest silence. The blackness which had flowed around him lost its power, and he could see ghosts here, unmoving watchful dark shapes in the mildewed air.

He took a careful step. The ghosts moved, too. He stopped, they stopped.

Ghosts of himself, reflected shadows of Kellen O'Reilly.

He reached out tentatively, and the ghosts reached too, and his fingertips touched the cool smoothness of glass. He turned his flashlight on: a mirror, tall as a man, and other mirrors, mirror upon mirror, stacked haphazardly against a wall, leaning, wayward, the beam of his flashlight reflecting, echoing from pane to pane, sending flickers and jabs of yellow light through the room.

To the side, a wall thickly padded. Furniture stacked under blankets. Dust, cobwebs.

Spotlights suspended from the ceiling and this, over here, is where the camera must have been. This is the room. Closed and silent and dark.

This is the room of mirrors and fantasy and murders acted out. Mirrors . . . multiplying Kellen O'Reilly into infinity.

The room flashed back from darkness into motion and light.

You enter into the padded room and see the camera mounted behind a screen, white frocks moving, a thin lank-haired man with a gun . . .

Don't fight it. Let it happen.

"Remember how he beat your mother. Do you hate him?"

Memory, don't stop.

The man in a T-shirt scratching his stomach, smiling . . .

The flashbacks accelerated now, popping like firecrackers, and the room flickered between the before and the now, peopled and active, then empty and silent; he felt himself being shredded between past and present, he'd set a flame to the fuse of this horrible previous time . . .

The man raises the gun, it bucks, spits flame, glass shatters . . .

What awful things are being done here? You want desperately to understand, but their drugs do not permit that.

"Not, yet, Mick."

"He walked in b-before I could stop him."

"All right, bring him here."

He closed his eyes but he couldn't close his sparking brain.

"Remember that he killed your father."

Father . . . father, echo and re-echo. His mind is shredding, he must escape from this haunted room. He turned and crashed into the mirrors and covered chairs, and churned toward the door, and clawed at the knob, and it wouldn't give.

The gun is hard as hate and you aim it at the man the doctor says has killed your father . . . A popping and the smell of cordite, and the man fragments into a thousand reflections . . .

And you suddenly know it's a lie, everything they said is a lie – they want to make a monster out of you . . .

With the remembering of that insight of twenty-five years ago, the flashbacks stopped, and were replaced by memory – distorted, unclear, but memory.

A memory of a drugged young Kellen O'Reilly being told to hate and kill, and obeying, and undergoing then a massive revulsion, throwing the gun down and screaming obscenities, waving his fists at the doctor and his men.

It came back in ragged patches. He'd run from the building, Satorius's men pursuing; he'd been carried back in . . . and there was a blank . . . no, he'd been sedated, he remembered Satorius coming toward him, a syringe.

Yes, he recalled a straitjacket, recalled being taken to the sleep room, Dr. Satorius hooking his brain into the ECT machine. There'd been convulsions and blackness, memory cells sealed off, arc-welded shut.

But something important was missing from this mutilated tableau of memory. He had been a witness to an event still beclouded; a secret was nudging him in the ribs, craving his attention.

With the cessation of the flashbacks, he felt a stilling, a focusing. The acid rush was done, its fever broken. He felt stronger, in control.

He put a beam of light on the transom above the door, a wooden panel on hinges.

He moved a table to the door. He hoisted himself up and pushed the transom, which opened, its rusty hinges complaining, and he climbed through it and jumped down onto a tiled floor.

A corridor, dimly lit at the far end.

Yes, here was the staircase up which he had fled, and afterwards was dragged back down.

And here at the end of this basement hall was the ECT ward, the sleep room where minds were wiped, where had been kept the portable electroconvulsive machine, which Satorius wheeled from curtained bed to curtained bed. Here is where they took him. For the last big jolt.

But there was something else, someone else. Rewind the tape of memory. The mirrored image of a man. The gun firing. Kellen's own screams, his escape . . . He'd seen something else. What was it?

At the end of the hall, a door to another, a weak bulb illuminating it. A wide stone stairway, switching back from floor to floor, finally giving way to some narrow winding steps to Satorius's office in the tower. Where the files had been.

Only three doors up here, three rooms. He remembered again the day of his first interview: Satorius had invited him into a lounge next to his office, and they'd had coffee.

The first door: that lounge. The middle door had the doctor's brass-plated name on it. Kellen used a credit card to slip the lock, and was astonished that he retained a deft touch. He was quickly inside, and he sent out a flashlight beam on a slow arc, left to right.

No cobwebs here, no boarded windows. White wicker furniture. Geraniums in pots. Books and magazines. A large stone fireplace. A wall of mirrored glass.

Within a semicircle of curtained windows sat an oval table and a swivel chair, its back to Kellen. He envisioned Satorius sitting there, godlike, staring out across the downtown skyline.

But no filing cabinets. Kellen remembered – clearly – racks of cabinets where now were bookshelves: books floor to ceiling. If the files had been burned, what is it that Satorius has recently been working upon here? The room smelled of mental sweat.

No sound except the battering of wind upon the windowpanes.

Kellen did a reality check. It was . . . Monday. It would be about midnight now, he was well past the rush, rolling downhill. Still high, but coming down. He checked his watch.

Only ten minutes to ten. No, his watch hadn't stopped.

Focus. Monday night, almost ten o'clock. Fairly stoned but processing. Some gentlemen are trying to kill you. They're ex-CIA or something. Connected to MK-ULTRA, sub-project 47. They'd worked with Satorius. You're in his office. According to Wally he's been toiling alone up here, every day.

Then the spot of his light caught a printer near the edge of the oval table. Beside it a computer, and beside that a stack of paper.

He sat on the swivel chair and swept his light across the tabletop. Writing tools. A box of blank computer paper, an English dictionary, a Thesaurus, a Fowler, something called a *Manual of Style*. No files.

Kellen looked at the stack of papers on the desk, squared and tidy. The top sheet read, in bold capital dot-matrix letters: "IN SEARCH OF THE MIND," and beneath that, "THE LIFE OF DR. GREGOR SATORIUS."

On the second page was printed, "VOLUME ONE: THE EARLY YEARS. COPYRIGHT GREGOR SATORIUS, M.D."

Kellen laughed softly to himself. He didn't try to analyze it, to ask himself what was funny.

The first chapter began:

"My first remembrance was a remarkably early one – at the age of two and a half – and it was of a pig being stabbed and gutted by a German soldier beside my father's barn. It was 1915, and the world seemed a brutal place, full of war and privation."

Good start, Kellen thought. Scarred for the rest of his days by the gutting of a pig. Where does the gutting of Kellen O'Reilly begin? He riffled through the pile. Page 283.

"She asked me in to tea. After a time she commenced to cry. But she expressed herself as being in a state of relief. 'Oh, Doctor,' she said, 'you have brought me to a realization that it is not my real mother that I fear, but some evil construct of my mind.'

"I knew then that I had chosen wisely into this demanding career. I possessed the correct instincts of a psychiatrist, the ability to thrust home, to find the truth. But seven months of enduring the outpourings of Baroness Tolna! Was there no quicker way to healing? Were therapists to be bound forever to the tedious dialogues of Freudian and Jungian analysis?"

Kellen felt a primal shudder run through him, a message from the LSD that it was not finished with him. It felt odd to look at this vile and arrogant man's life in his own arrogant words. He turned to the end of the stack. Page 327.

"As the war clouds darkened – already the Nazis had walked into the Sudetan – I found myself – still in my impressionable twenties – imbued with a sense of political purpose. The cafés of Budapest were thronged by such as I – Socialists, and we looked East for our Gods. How bitterly they failed us!"

End of Chapter Seven. How many more chapters were still in the computer? Would there be rough notes about MK-ULTRA? Had he punched in some of his research, his source material?

Okay, Kellen knew something about computing, he had his own desktop Monster; he'd not missed all of Borko's lectures. No diskettes anywhere, both disk drives empty. That meant a hard disk inside the machine, a memory bank. The computer bore a label: Northrup 386. What did he know about a 386? A big chip, lots of power.

He switched on the computer and the monitor, which became a staring eye, green-glowing, godlike.

A fan blew softly as the computer clicked through a test and told Kellen its RAM was good, then a message about a 65MB hard drive, and then a directory rolled onto the screen. Files named as chapter numbers, "CHAPT01.BIO," to "CHAPT13.BIO," and some software programs.

Sixty-five million bytes of coded memory in this machine. There would be more files. Somewhere here were all of Satorius's secrets. The library of his past: he'd never been able to destroy it, he believed in himself too much. *In Search of the Mind. The Life of Dr. Gregor Satorius.*

But how to access Kellen O'Reilly?

His head buzzing and racing and going nowhere, he stared mesmerized for a long time at the blinking cursor, until the room began to swirl gently in the background. Essential working parts of his mind seemed unable to slip into gear, to give him a coherent plan.

He typed "O'REILLY," and pushed the Enter key.

The monitor responded laconically: "O'REILLY?"

He heard Borko's voice: *I didn't see you gentlemen at the last data management seminar . . .*

Monday, ten p.m.

To enter the lobby of the Bonaventure Hotel, Hugh McVeigh had to show his badge to a scowling Royal Canadian Mountie. The NATO defense ministers were convening here tomorrow, and some had already arrived. RCMP all over the lobby in suits. He'd always pictured them as on the tourist ads – white men in red serge on black horses.

Must be the only country in the world that advertises cops as a tourist attraction. CIA should do that. Over here, ladies and gentlemen, Hugh McVeigh, in charge of waste removal.

His was the only black face in here. People continually slid looks his way, too polite to stare. The Elephant Man just walked in. No wonder all the cold fronts come from Canada. He'd get his butt back to Langley tomorrow and unfreeze it.

At the desk, he asked a woman for William Johnson, no *t*.

She looked for him. "I'm afraid he hasn't checked in. We're holding."

The Police Brotherhood meeting seemed the next likely place. If this were Detroit, say, or Philadelphia, people would be out trashing the town tonight. He remembered lawless Saigon, in the final days.

Kellen finally began executing some of the commands he knew, and some of them worked. He started to thread his way through the information bank, seeking the vaults of the MK-ULTRA years, the fifties and sixties, and minutes ground slowly by as he chain-smoked and crawled among the branches of an infinite tree of files with names like "KZ-506.RES" or "QX-1312.FIL" or "JF-16XX.DUP" – the names coded in some scientifically arcane way in subdirectories that seemed to divide into infinite branches.

No file named MK-ULTRA. No files under other code words used by the CIA for their brainwashing programs: ARTICHOKE, MK-DELTA, MK-SEARCH, CHICKWIT.

From time to time he brought up files at random, read them on the screen. Columns and figures, test results, treatment synopses, patients without names but code numbers: "F/33, M/24, T/09." Kellen had been O/14, and he searched for combinations of file names using that letter and two digits, and failed to find one.

Finally he located five files whose names commenced with "MK." And one read "MK-4763.CLO." MK-ULTRA sub-project 47, 1963?

When he tried to raise it on the screen he got a message: "ACCESS TO THIS FILE DENIED."

Concentrate. He had actually read through the manual Borko gave him. Wasn't there something about a program that would bring up all files containing a few keywords? You search for a . . . string.

He fought his way back to the subdirectory of command files. Here was a program called "LOCATE.EXE."

He ran it, and it asked him some simple yes and no questions, and then asked him for the "KEYWORDS(S)."

Kellen typed "O'REILLY."

The computer whirred and whispered, thinking.

Then it grunted and went silent, and several file names

appeared on the screen, all but one bearing the message, "ACCESS TO THIS FILE DENIED."

One file promised no such resistance. "SLX-477.NDX."

Kellen brought it up, and the screen filled with small single-spaced lines.

NDX. Index.

An index of patients. Halfway down the screen the cursor flashed triumphantly on top of the capital O in the name "O'REILLY."

"O'REILLY, KELLEN LAWRENCE, MALE, 23-4-44, B. MONTREAL, CITIZEN CANADA, STUDENT, NOT MARRIED. CODE: O/14. 09-06-63/03-09-63. MK-47, REJECTED PHASE 02. SEE MK-4763.CLO."

That was all about Kellen O'Reilly. For his period of enforced service from June ninth to September third he'd been subject O/14 in MK-ULTRA sub-project 47 – nothing new to be learned. But he'd been rejected at Phase 02.

"SEE MK-4763.CLO." That file had already been denied to him. "CLO": closed?

The cursor blinked, nagging him. The file that lay open to him was an alphabetical catalogue of Satorius's patients; these were the names Sarah so desperately sought.

Maybe he would take a printout of the index. Or, better, pinch the whole computer. Find a fifteen-year-old kid to break the code, get into those MK-ULTRA files.

The screen began with "OBEROFF, G., FEMALE, 17-10-26, B. KINDERSLEY, SASK., CITIZEN CANADA, MARRIED (JOHN), THREE CHILDREN. CODE: O/33. 20-01-57/31-10-58. SEE JYO-112.BIX."

Poor Mrs. Oberoff, who'd been almost two years at Coldhaven. She'd graduated well before his time.

He scanned down the page, Oberoff and Ogden and O'Reilly and Oswald and Proud'homme and Proulx and Pulgar.

He smoked the last in his pack to the butt as he morbidly contemplated the scant information against his name. "REJECTED PHASE 02." A phase of what?

Something was desperately clawing at him, hungry for his attention.

Oberoff, Ogden, O'Reilly, Oswald . . .

He felt his surroundings warp.

And he flashed back once more to the padded room in the basement, the room of Phase 02.

You walk unguarded into the room, dazed, fearful. You see the young man fire, glass shatters . . .

"Not, yet, Mick."

"*He walked in b-before I could stop him.*"

And the young man turns to you, sallow and flap-eared and smiling and stupid with drugs . . .

And he was staring at the screen again, at the grinning face which seemed to glow from behind the phosphorescent words there, a face pulled savagely from subconscious into memory, as his name screamed silently from the monitor.

"OSWALD, LEE HARVEY, MALE, 10-15-39, B. NEW ORLEANS, LA., CIT-IZEN U.S., MARRIED (MARINA). 15-06-63/29-08-63. SEE KWI-515.CLO. CODE O/13, MK-47. ACCEPTED PHASE 03. SEE MK-4763.CLO."

And it was Lee Harvey Oswald who was the feature player in the film that Sloukos and Champlain had spirited away. The man seen from behind in the footage that he and Raolo had watched. Doubtless he'd been in better view in the earlier frames.

He sat motionless, the computer still beaming its information at him.

The hit of '63.

November 22, 1963. He'd been sitting near the back of a Number 61 bus. He'd come home from the police academy to find his mother crying. The American president had been a living saint to the Irish of Point St. Charles.

Remember that he beat your mother . . . He remembered dimly from the newspapers, the evidence at the Warren Commission. How Oswald had been emotionally stunted by unhappy childhood years, his mother brutalized by his abusive stepfather.

MK-ULTRA, sub-project 47. The candidate for this position must be motivated by a sincere desire for revenge. Kellen had flunked the final test of Phase 02.

Oddly, Kellen suddenly wanted a coffee. He could smell it.

We looked East for our Gods. How bitterly they failed us!
He silently asked Satorius: Why Kennedy?

Satorius's voice answered.

"In 1949 they summoned me to Budapest. They asked – not asked, ordered me – to break the mental defenses of Josef Cardinal Mindzenty. I did. He confessed to his crimes."

Gregor Satorius flicked a desk lamp on beside Kellen. He was in his cape, holding a mug of coffee, looking at the screen. Kellen stared at him, stunned.

"His crimes." A hard, caustic laugh. "You want the story brief, yes? You will not wait for the book. Brief, the Company rescued me from Hungary. The Company gave me Coldhaven and money and the tools to fight Communism. And I gave twenty years of my life to the Company."

Kellen watched stiffly, motionless, as Satorius put the coffee down and shrugged out of his cape and hung it by the door, still talking, his voice becoming loud and strident.

"Hard years! Hard work! On the frontline of the Cold War! This Harvard playboy planned to emasculate the Company. And end my work. And sell out the world to the Bolsheviks, one little country at a time."

Satorius picked up his coffee, sipped it, glowered at Kellen fiercely, and at the screen. His voice became more controlled.

"How stupid of me. I left that file unprotected. I must be getting old."

"Stay away from it," Kellen said.

Satorius raised his eyebrows as if in surprise, and stepped back. "Winning without killing, Mr. O'Reilly. Is it not humane? To alter minds rather than take lives? That is how all wars will one day be fought. It is how we should have fought the Cold War, yes?"

"You talk of winning without killing?" Kellen said. "You killed!"

Satorius shrugged. "Please do not give me too much credit. I was in charge of screening and basic training. After that they took Oswald to Mexico for the, what do you call it, final prep?"

Kellen was assessing, working this through. Satorius held no weapon, but he evoked a nameless fear in him.

"But even in a war of minds, to kill the body is sometimes necessary, yes? What is one life, even a president's, compared to the winning of a war? Mr. Kennedy wanted to choke our funding off. MK-ULTRA, all our projects, all our work, all our hard and beautiful work."

"How many other assassins have you programmed?" Kellen said softly. "Did you kill his brother, too?"

Satorius made himself comfortable on a chesterfield in the far shadows of the room, and sipped his coffee.

Kellen guarded the computer; it would leave this building with him even if he had to tie Satorius to a chair.

"Your pupils are extremely dilated, it is very odd. Are you well?"

He was not. Hot flushes, prickles.

"You came close to making history, Mr. O'Reilly. Kellen? I can call you that? You could have been the chosen one. By the middle of Phase Two there were the only two candidates left. But instead of you, with your vigor and intelligence, it was Lee Harvey, who had the brain and the personality of a toad, who now has his name enshrined in every textbook of modern history. Yes, this is fascinating, isn't it, how the world brings us around, how the circle closes, and we meet again to talk history in a place where so much history was made."

He shook his head. "We worked so hard with you, so hard. But you failed the psychic driving, Kellen. The rebel in you wouldn't die. A policeman now – I would not have believed it. But it's a debt to your father, yes?"

His cold eyes fixed on Kellen's hot ones.

"That you probably still think you owe."

Kellen felt another little acid shudder.

"Are you aware that he shot himself?"

Kellen was programmed not to listen to this. He felt panic swarming through him, his mind slamming the door, barring the truth, denying.

"You're under arrest," he said hoarsely. "I'm charging you with being an accessory to murder."

"Sergeant Brian O'Reilly. Such a reputation for bravery. But he killed a man. He shot him in the back." His words were blunt and hard as stone.

"It's my duty to warn you that you don't have to say anything – "

"He took his own life – a bullet through the brain – a day before the inquiry was to start. You found his body."

" – but anything you do say – "

"You came to me with a most interesting case of denial syndrome."

" – may be used as evidence at your trial." He felt a terrible headache.

"Finally you talked about him. Under deep narcotherapy."

"Shut up. Do you understand the warning?" He kept shaking his head, listening and not listening, pain radiating into the center of his head. Satorius was trying to destroy him with his words.

"We created for you an amnesia about the suicide. Then we built a new truth." Satorius spoke with a cold and confident ease. "It wasn't so difficult, you wanted this very much. One month of sleep-teaching, repatterning, and your father was gone. And another month of autopsychic driving to block you from processing new input." He smiled. "Plastic mental surgery."

Kellen stared at him in horror, in total revulsion. He stood up and screamed, "You're under arrest, you fascist shit!"

"Does what I say cause you pain, Mr. O'Reilly?" Satorius said calmly. "It's meant to. You've been a headache to us. And you've interrupted my work."

"Your work!" Kellen shouted. "Your *work*! Your work is finished!"

He picked up the swivel chair and raised it over his head and threw it with force against the mirrored wall, and when it shattered he saw, behind it, two men, one with a bandaged hand, and they were ducking from the spinning glass.

He saw their guns.

184

He turned and dived toward the door, colliding with Eddie Comacho, who took him to the floor, pinning him.

"A headache," Meyers said. "That you surely are, Lieutenant. Well, Gregor, you said you would elicit information from him the easy way. Now it becomes hard."

Kellen sensed Meyers above him, his boot coming swiftly at his head, and he plummeted into darkness.

Monday, ten-thirty p.m.

Sarah stood, holding the microphone, waiting patiently for the chanting to stop. Ouimet had introduced her as the lawyer who today had fought the Communauté Urbaine to a dead stop. There'd been cheers, but the dissenters were still shouting: "Adjourn. Adjourn. Adjourn." An organized group, seated near one of the floor microphones.

Ouimet added to the tumult by banging his gavel. "Order! *Tabernac*, order!"

"A police officer is fucking *dead!*" Constable Taillefeur was at the center of the protest, at the floor mike.

"Sit down!" Ouimet yelled.

"I don't sit down when cop-killers are free on the streets of Montreal! Goddamnit, I have a motion to adjourn! Do you accept it or not?"

Cheers from the dissidents, boos from others.

"Let her speak!" someone yelled.

Sarah waited until the chanting subsided. Ouimet had called on her for help to quell Taillefeur's mob. She had skills in oratory, forged before juries and Parti Québecois rallies. She started softly.

"Brothers. Sisters. I know I'm only here as your legal adviser. I'm not a cop. But I've gotten to know one very well recently. Lieutenant Kellen O'Reilly."

185

A roar of approval. He was a tremendous hero. His name could become a rallying cry. The chanters – a group of about a hundred – were silenced, but Taillefeur remained belligerently standing at his microphone, his arms folded.

"As you know, Kellen can't be here, but I talked with him a few hours ago, and he said he will be here in spirit."

Even louder applause. Her voice slowly rose in pitch and vigor.

"He told me to tell you that you are doing this for families like Raolo Basutti's. He said if cops on the job had more support and more staff and less overtime – so you're not always tired, taking risks – then brave men like Raolo Basutti may have a better chance. Our urban government helped kill Raolo Basutti – they made it easier. That's what Kellen O'Reilly said."

He hadn't, but what the heck. She was starting to feel in control up here, comfortable now with her cheering audience.

"Kellen said this is about pensions and welfare benefits and shorter hours. You are fighting to give parents time for their kids. Raolo never had enough time for his only son – which of you do for your children? Do you want a statistic? Fifty-one broken homes among police families last year. That's up from thirty the previous year, and there'll be seventy this year."

She hoped she wasn't getting too puffed up with her eloquence, but they were all listening.

"Kellen said his partner planned to be here tonight. He believed in solidarity." Now slip the knife to the traitors. "Raolo was not a deserter; he was a fighter."

She paused for dramatic effect, but Taillefeur ruined the moment, shouting: "He's a *dead* fighter, murdered on duty! While we debate, the killers fucking *laugh*. Who else is going to die tonight because we're here and the streets are deserted? I have a motion to adjourn!"

The chant began again, and Sarah tried to shout above it. "Kellen O'Reilly said we can't give up! Raolo's partner, his best friend! He said we can't bend! Kellen O'Reilly, who they suspended because he fought for this union!"

But the invocation of his name seemed to have lost its magic.

"Point of order! I have a motion to adjourn!"

"Let her speak!"

"A motion to adjourn is non-debatable!" Taillefeur shouted.

Ouimet now rose massively beside her, clenching his microphone, red faced, his voice quavering – her speech seemed to have infected him with emotion.

"I'm not accepting it! I tell you we are not going to quit! I tell you, like Brother O'Reilly, we will never bend to the bureaucrats of the Communauté Urbaine! No, we do not bend! We keep our backs straight! There will be no motion to adjourn!"

Howls of outrage. Accusations of dictatorship. Demands to resign. "Challenge the chair!" someone called.

His words punctuated by shouts and heckling, Taillefeur said, "I stand here representing a group of almost one hundred men, who, like me, have sworn to uphold the law and protect the citizens of our community – "

Boos and hisses drowned some of his words.

"And I therefore challenge the chair. Under Roberts Rules of Order, the chairman must give way and a vote be taken to uphold his ruling."

Sarah slowly sank to her seat in the deluge of sound that followed. Half the members were on their feet, Ouimet was banging the table with a swinging gavel, and the mob with Taillefeur was chanting again, "Adjourn! Adjourn!"

Suddenly Sarah didn't care, and was disgusted at her puerile demagoguery. The strike was not important. The union was not important. She wanted to be with Kellen, not at this hateful meeting. She should phone him, make sure he's all right. Wake him up and tell him she's in love with him and then tell him to go back to sleep.

As Sarah looked over to the bank of coin telephones near

the front door – a dozen people were lined up behind each one of them – she saw Thérèse Basutti and her son Mario enter, under the escort of two ushers and Father Vauthier, the police pastor.

Thérèse seemed overwhelmed by all the sound and energy, and hesitated, but proceeded forward, and they walked slowly toward the center aisle. And when they gained it and started moving to the platform, heads began to turn to them, and the room began slowly, magically, to hush.

One of the ushers ran up the steps and whispered to Ouimet for a few moments, and he bent to Sarah. "She wants to speak."

Sarah looked at Thérèse, now standing at the bottom of the five steps leading to the platform. She was pale, and wore no makeup. Her eyes were downcast. Mario's roved around the room. Sarah could tell he was being a brave soldier, his head held high, his eyes dry but raw.

"Well, then, let her speak," Sarah said.

"Brother and sisters, I want to present to you Mrs. Thérèse Basutti," Ouimet said as he hurried to her, to escort her up.

He kissed her on each cheek, and offered a hand to Mario, who took it, but shook his head and backed up when Ouimet tried to urge him to come up with them. Thérèse kissed her son on the forehead, and took Ouimet's arm and they went up the steps to the stage.

Everyone was standing and applauding. Sarah went to Thérèse and gave her a little hug and a word of condolence.

"Thank you," Thérèse said softly.

She stood at the end of the table, without a microphone, and waited until the clapping stopped. Then a rustle of seat-taking. Even Taillefeur, when he saw he was standing alone in the middle of the hall, retreated to his chair.

"I . . . just felt I had to say something. We've been with my family all evening, but you are family, too . . . I have many friends among you. I know you are worried about us, about how we are."

Her words were thin and fragile but somehow crisply audible through the quiet hall.

188

"We will mourn him for a long time, but we will recover. I . . . guess I prepared myself mentally for this a long time ago. I know that's an awful thing to say."

She was struggling with each word. Sarah wondered why she was doing this, how she'd found the courage.

"One of the worst things is we just . . . we had a fight . . . about his work never stopping. He worked yesterday, Sunday; it was supposed to be his day off. I want to tell him . . . I mean I wish we could have our last words to say over again . . . The last day to do over."

Thérèse took a deep breath. "Anyway, I want to say this to you, to all of you, to my friends here, that I love you. I respect you. You should be proud of what you are doing here tonight. You should be proud of who you are. Raolo was proud to be a cop."

She began to fragment.

"And I was . . . am . . . proud of him . . . for being a cop . . . for everything."

Thérèse burst into tears and she put her hands to her face.

"But I swear to God my son will never become a policeman."

She was shaking furiously and in a rage of tears as Sarah and the usher hurried to her, and slowly walked her to the back. There was total stunned silence in the room.

Ouimet looked around the hushed room, and said, "Père Vauthier will offer a prayer."

After the priest led them in prayer and a minute of silence, Ouimet called the next item on the agenda, a report from the negotiating committee, and the business of the meeting resumed uninterrupted, in funereal quiet.

When Rudy Meyers first looked at the computer screen there had been tremors of anger at the periphery of his still center, but he had willed them to dissolve.

"All files were to have been destroyed; you said it had been done." He observed that Satorius couldn't seem to look at him.

"I transcribed the significant work. It was for no one's eyes but mine."

"And this?" The manuscript.

"A hobby, something to amuse me."

"You are lying to me," Meyers said, smiling, calm. Inner peace, his master taught, shows as outer composure. Satorius hesitated, then said abruptly, sharply, "Some day the world will have to know what we have done."

"The world was *not* to know. Records were not to be kept. Books not to be written."

"We have a duty of truth to history," Satorius said, and then, looking at him, he hesitated, unable to read Meyers through his smile. "I would only publish posthumously, of course."

"It will be published, Gregor, over *my* dead body."

Satorius turned testy again. "I do not take orders from you. Quite the reverse."

"We are equally servants of an oath."

"An oath. Save America from herself. What a bloody trail has been left in the honoring of this oath. You should have trusted my work; Oswald's memory of Coldhaven was gone. Bringing the criminals in, the sloppy business with that Mafia cancer victim, Ruby – it was an insult to me and to science."

"The Mafia was already in, Gregor. Do you think we could have funded MK-ULTRA 47 on the crumbs the Company was throwing to us? Langley was threatening to close us down."

"The result was that too many people knew."

"They died." This was a tiring argument, an old one. There was work to do.

"And more spring up like weeds. The result has been deaths, blackmail, more deaths."

Meyers could tell that he would not be portrayed as the central hero of the doctor's manuscript. If history were to be written, Meyers should be entitled to his accurate and rightful place in it. Yes, too many knew. But the looser-tongued among them had terrible accidents. Although some preferred suicide. In 1967, David Ferrie died that way, after being called in for questioning by the New Orleans District Attorney. So had De Mohrenschildt. Johnny Roselli, however, ended up in a barrel floating in the ocean. Sloukos and Champlain had been robbery victims.

These were deaths all artfully conceived. Meyers took pleasure from them. And in a way it was sad that so much mangled history had been written about these episodes: so much Company disinformation, so many theories. But truth doesn't matter; theater does.

Comacho walked in as Satorius was bundling up his manuscript and putting it in a briefcase. "Mick says our friend is coming around. What next?"

"An oral examination," said Meyers. "It seems clear, Eddie, that Ms. Sarah Paradis is in possession?"

"My theory – he stashed the movie, probably in that store where he cooled poor old Bill, and he told her where to pick it up. That's when she phoned in to him."

"We will test that theory. Do you have any of the good drugs, Gregor? Sodium pentothal?"

Satorius shook his head.

"I will use the pressure points." Meyers flexed his fingers.

"I don't want his blood on my hands."

"There will be very little blood, Gregor. And you need not fear it being on *your* hands."

"I have rank and I have authority. I want no killings here. Do you understand?" His voice sharp, waspish. "Yours is a simplistic, brutal mind, Meyers, and uncreative. Two hundred volts for one second will permanently erase the last twenty-four hours of his memory."

Meyers thought about this. "The portable unit still functions?"

"Yes, it's in the sleep room. It worked with him before. You know what I can do. I can return him to childhood."

"Yes, ah, very good idea, Gregor. Eddie, please help the Doctor. Fetch the ECT unit and help him set it up."

After the two men left, Meyers sat down to the computer and typed a command to reformat the disk.

The screen warned: "ALL FILES WILL BE PERMANENTLY ERASED. ARE YOU SURE?"

He informed the computer he was. He listened to it click, wiping its own memory, then watched the glow fade green to black as he turned the machine off.

Monday, eleven-ten p.m.

"You *are* talking to the precinct captain, madam. I'm *sorry*, lady, I'm only human. Police . . . Sir, unless it's an emergency . . . Well, just tell them to turn their amplifier down. Police . . . Yes, ma'am, that's very rude language . . . Maybe you should just hang up your phone next time."

Exhausted, Eugene Borko hung up his, and sat morosely at the receptionist's desk and caught his breath.

Only two constables had reported for duty, both out now on urgent calls. How is it that at most of the other precincts at least half-a-dozen officers showed up?

Where was the woman from overload that headquarters had promised?

And where was Kellen O'Reilly, who hadn't checked into the Bonaventure?

Not at the Brotherhood meeting. He'd called there: one of the shop stewards said he'd heard Kellen was at home under armed protection. But no answer at his residence.

Psychotic, wandering the streets?

What in Sam Hill was going on, anyway? The FBI man, McVeigh, had said with assurance: Mafia. He'd not, however, been candid – those hit men never did return to Fort Lauderdale.

He'd called Miami, talked to the senior agent of the Drug Enforcement Administration Bureau, one Jessica Flaherty. Yes, she knew Meyers. Too well, she said. Guns for dope. Used to run a contra camp on a State Department contract. Millionaire right-wing crazy. Ex-private investigator.

And ex-CIA. Quietly removed from the Company over something in 1972, the year of the Watergate break-in.

McVeigh had told him nothing of this.

Kellen O'Reilly had ranted about the CIA. Maybe he wasn't as crazy as he sounded.

The switchboard lit up again.

Monday, eleven-thirty p.m.

Kellen lay on his back on an examining bed and stared up at these men and knew he was soon going to die. He was held to the bed by straps at his ankles, shoulders, and forehead. His arms were pinned to his sides. He was in a small room lit by a bare ceiling bulb.

Satorius was doing the talking, a lecture about electroconvulsive therapy. The man with the bad hand and the good foot, Meyers, stood beside him with a smile that stopped at the lips. The man they called Eddie was against the wall beside Mick. The stutterer.

"Ultimately a long series of shocks such as I describe can cause brain death. Or more likely the heart will crash first. But you would lose consciousness quickly; we are not here to torture you."

193

The portable ECT unit was on a wheeled cart beside Kellen. He was connected to the machine by wires, to two stainless steel electrodes set onto electrode jelly on his temples, and held there by a rubber strap. Blood had congealed on his face; Meyers' boot had broken the skin above the hairline.

Adrenaline had burned away much of the lysergic acid in his system, but enough was left to make this a bad trip in hell. The head throbbed, a deep bass voodoo drum. The faces were sallow and sick in the yellow light.

Satorius adjusted the voltage dial. He flicked up a click-switch on the face of the small machine. Dials and buttons lit up.

"Death is an extravagance, Kellen," Satorius said. "All we must really extinguish is a day of your memory."

"A bad day, Mr. O'Reilly," said Meyers, "you won't miss it."

A pause.

"If you help us, there'll be no more killings," Satorius said. "No one need be hurt. It doesn't make much sense, yes, to be stubborn like this?"

"Okay, let's start again," Meyers said. "We know Miss Paradis has the film."

They had told him this earlier. Where the bloody hell had they got this idea? If they held to it, they would target Sarah next. He felt an incredible helplessness.

"I have more patience than time, my friend." Meyers put an index finger on Kellen's chest. "Where did she hide it?"

"Let me handle this," said Satorius. "I have more than a little training in this field."

"Please move away, Doctor." Meyers put a hand to Satorius's arm and pushed him aside. The doctor shrugged his arm away from him. "Did you instruct her to hide it someplace?"

"I told you she doesn't have the film," Kellen said.

"Where is it?"

"I don't know."

"It pains me to do this." Meyers jabbed.

A knife-like stabbing shot through Kellen, head to foot. He

gasped and smelled a mingling of Meyers' after-shave and his own clammy deathbed sweat.

"She doesn't *have* it!"

Meyers' thumb came to rest beside Kellen's right eye. Kellen felt the fingernail cutting. He couldn't move his head.

"No blood," said Satorius. "They can trace – "

"Shut up, please."

Kellen's mind raced like an accelerating engine. He looked up at Satorius's pale, shining, nervous face. The weak link, bad blood between Meyers and him . . . And Kellen sensed something more than bad blood.

"Mr. Sloukos suffered," Meyers said. "Before he passed away."

Sloukos, Kellen thought. It came to him then, a possibility, maybe a probability: Sloukos and Champlain had not been alone. He started talking fast. "Meyers, I'll let you in on something. Your two blackmailers had a partner."

His eyes went from Meyers to Satorius, who was standing shock still.

He felt the pressure of the thumb lessen.

"You really must be strapped, Satorius, if you're putting Coldhaven on the block. Going to be able to sell it before the banks foreclose?"

Satorius issued a high-pitched snort. "Now see what he is trying to do."

Kellen thought he just might be able to take Satorius with him to wherever in heaven or hell he was going.

"Only one way Champlain and Sloukos could have gotten hold of that film. The profits were going to be split three ways. One for the silent partner."

"This is outrageous!" Satorius shouted, with a vehemence that surprised Kellen; he was onto something, a chance hit in his dying hour. How far could he stretch this?

"Yeah, we found your name in some notes Champlain made . . . "

"It is a total lie!"

"In his apart – "

Kellen saw Satorius's hand move, and all he saw after that

195

was an infinity of colors, and his body arched from the bed, jerking spastically, then subsiding as Satorius released his finger from the ECT button.

Eddie the Cube coughed. Otherwise there was silence.

Satorius began to talk as if through a clogged throat, and he cleared it, and started again. "When he comes to he'll be disoriented. He won't be playing these games."

"But will he remember where the film is, Gregor? You said two hundred volts would wipe the last day from memory." Meyers contemplated Kellen's prone form. "He's useless to us now."

He turned to Satorius with a look not of annoyance but speculation.

Monday, midnight

Meyers watched fascinated as he rapidly punched the button with his index finger, and as the body continued to dance and kick, mouth open in a bloody tongue-bitten rictus of horror. Finally, after what seemed a lifetime, a last kick and a shake and a quiver. He felt for a pulse and was satisfied.

Tell it to the world now, Gregor.

He turned off the power and listened to his own soft, controlled breathing. Breath without emotion, his master had taught him. Breathing is power.

Never be sorry. His master had taught that, too. The seventh rule.

Still, there was sadness as he looked at Satorius's crumpled form. Such a great event had been shared.

He switched off the lights and returned to the tower office. Comacho was burning the last pages of *In Search of the Mind* in the fireplace. Mick Crowder was adjusting a micrometer screw on his M21 sniper's rifle, fine-tuning the trigger pull. They were in their boots and ski jackets, ready to depart.

"It was a difficult thing," Meyers said. "I admired him, but he suffered from pride."

Mick nodded and hefted the rifle. A few years ago Meyers had taken him on staff at the Contra training camp near Fort Myers. Crowder was a fine teacher, and he hadn't lost his deadly eye.

Mick aimed through the superscope at Eddie Comacho's head.

"B-bang."

"Don't screw around," Eddie said. "I'm not feeling too good."

Meyers saw that Comacho was pale. "Don't do this to me, Eddie. You had better be in condition to drive." He was their wheelman; Comacho had raced in the Southern dirt-track circuit.

"Don't know if it's something I ate, or what."

Kellen had been fetched, and his unconscious body was tossed loosely over Satorius's big desk, face down, arms tight to his chest in a straitjacket. Drool ran from the side of his mouth.

Meyers looked into his satchel. "What do we have that can't be traced?"

Mick clamped a battery-powered nightsight onto his rifle. "The Landman-Preetz," he said.

Meyers picked the handgun up with his gloved hand.

"What's the d-deal now?" Mick asked. "Bump him and run, or what?"

Meyers had thought about leaving O'Reilly alive and electrically depatterned. All memory gone, his fingerprints on the panel of the ECT machine. He himself would never be sure he wasn't guilty of murder. At the least, it would be apparent he came in here maddened and revenge-seeking, and performed on the person of Satorius a symbolic sacrificial rite.

The scenario appealed to Meyers' sense of ironic drama.

197

Observe life as theater, and play your finest part in it. From Sloukos to Satorius, the theater of death.

But one shouldn't fall prey to one's sense of fun. One of the primary twenty-one rules: Let your heart be light, but do not be seduced by pleasure.

He had a safer way to direct the scene, safer in the sense that Satorius's exact science may not be so exact, and O'Reilly was dangerous with or without recent memory.

"This is how the plot will read. The demented detective did in the dastardly doctor. Then he followed in a great and honorable family tradition. He shot himself in the head as a good law officer should. Like father, like son. Ironic tragedy."

"Where do we do that c-card-carrying lawyer lady?"

"I feel sick." Comacho started walking toward the door. "Where's a washroom?"

Distracted, Meyers and Crowder didn't see that Kellen was now sitting up, on the edge of the desk, almost somnambulant, staring at them through dazed eyes.

"Feels like things are movin' around inside me. Bugs or amoebas or something."

Kellen looked around, tried to comprehend. Three strange men with guns.

"There's a facility off the lounge," Meyers said. "Let's see you put yourself together quickly, Eddie. This isn't in the game plan."

Kellen was gripped by a sense of closeness to death. He wasn't sure where he was; the room seemed familiar from a time long ago. He was strapped into a straitjacket. He seemed drugged, was having a hard time focusing.

"I got this anchovy taste in my mouth."

"Go with him, Mick. I will, ah, execute the plan."

As Meyers turned he caught a flash of movement: O'Reilly, propelling himself violently toward one of the big curved windows.

Before Meyers even raised his Landmann-Preetz he realized the chamber was empty and he heard it clicking uselessly as Kellen flew head first into the curtain, tearing it from its fasteners and carrying it through the broken window.

198

The curtain sheltered him from a rain of glass as he flew armless into the cold night, unable to see that he was four storeys above the ground, and he felt himself go over a ledge and into empty air, and he fell ten feet to a roof outcropping cushioned by thick freshly fallen snow.

He slid helplessly over the edge, the snow boiling around him, and plummeted another storey onto a longer sloping roof, and from that he fell with an avalanche of snow deep into a drift upon the lawn outside Coldhaven, choking, gasping, struggling to raise his head from the tangle of curtain, to crawl from the snowbank, to find his feet. And without use of his arms he somehow drove himself free, and stumbled forward again, rolling down an incline.

He knew killers were coming; echoes of a long-ago summer day sounded deep within his burning brain: 1963, a young man running to freedom from Coldhaven, the orderlies in pursuit. Was this a flashback recalled, or true memory? Recent events overlapped, were shuffled into disarray like a deck of cards; there'd been gunfire and murders, and somewhere and sometime not long ago there'd been a bomb and flames and wreckage, and an overwhelming grief.

And once again he gained his feet, plowing with aching slowness through the snow, and he turned and saw Coldhaven, and although he had no knowledge of why he was here, he guessed he'd been taken captive, drugged with some potion that caused his vision and hearing to be distorted. What day was it? What time?

Snow was falling only lightly now, and the sky was lifting and was transfused with the glow of light from the city's heart, south, down the hill.

He was aware that a woman he loved was in danger. Sarah. Sarah Paradis.

He urged himself toward the gate, the street, and heard shouts from the men running out the front door of Coldhaven.

He lurched to the cover of some thickly white-matted spruce trees, and worked behind them to the fence, the gate, and he remembered the sniper's rifle – don't move into the streetlight. He crouched and jogged along the fenceline.

They had murdered some people. He'd been working their file. Why couldn't he remember what had happened to him, what they'd done to him?

Pine Avenue, freshly plowed, a pair of headlights moving up it, toward him. He darted out from the shadows toward the car, and it swerved, and he saw the frightened faces of two young women inside, and he shouted, "Stop! Help me! *Aidez-moi!*"

Rear tires spun on the frozen street and it accelerated away.

"Call the police!" he screamed after them.

He dared the street-glow – he could run here, he could get distance on them – and followed the snowplow's recent track, padding furiously east, sure-footed on moccasins. When had he put them on? What had they done to his memory? What drug had they used? Something psychotropic – his skin tingled, colors were vivid.

His head throbbed, regular beats of pain. He felt the itch of fresh-dried blood in his hair and on his skin.

He darted out in front of another car, a Co-Op taxi, and it swerved, careered to the side, and almost struck him before racing away.

"Call the police, you bastard!"

He realized his pursuers must have a vehicle. He left the street and scrambled down into the deserted McGill campus. The paths were heavy with snow. All but an occasional flutter fell now from the sky; the air seemed lighter, softer, the cold spell broken.

Some of the earlier fragments began to settle into place. The drugstore shooting, the accountant's murder.

The smiling moon-faced man with the bandaged hand. Was he the one, then, whom Kellen had wounded, the happy-face ski mask in the drugstore – how many days or weeks ago?

The episode came fully back then. Sarah Paradis had been held hostage. Her face filled his mind. Sarah whom he loved and with whom he'd made love: Sarah, where are you? Sarah, you're in danger.

Where do we do that c-card-carrying lawyer lady?

The words he had awakened to in Coldhaven's tower.

And someone else he loved had already been killed. And it hit him like a steel pipe. Raolo. My God, he thought. Raolo, his partner. The car bomb on The Main.

On Prince Arthur: a young man and woman trudging along a beaten path on the sidewalk.

"Help me!"

They turned and saw him and began to run.

"Stop. I'm a police officer!"

They ran faster.

A corner *dépanneur*, still open – BIÈRE ET VIN, EXPORT A's, LOTTO QUÉBEC, lights and warmth.

He saw himself in the window glass, wild-eyed in a straitjacket, blood caking one side of his face, and he leaned on the latch and it gave, and suddenly he was inside, a warm fountain of air.

An elderly man at the magazine rack, stepping back in fear. The Oriental shopkeeper reaching below the counter.

"Call the police, please. And help me out of this."

"Go away," said the store owner. "All police on strike."

Kellen shouted hoarsely, "Someone's trying to kill me. Untie me, get me loose."

He looked at the shopkeeper's revolver, and backed and wheeled and ran outside again. Toward The Main, the world he knew, nine blocks to Boul Saint-Laurent, twelve to Station Twenty-six.

And if the police were on strike – this, then, was Monday night. They were all on Ile Sainte-Hélène. And so, thank God, was Sarah.

No cops tonight, no prowling cruisers. A ghoulish chuckle rose from his throat. Ironic justice. He'd swung the vote in favor of the strike, and now was a hunted cop in a lawless city. Unarmed. In more ways than one.

He kept to the alleys now, and the little streets where no one walked. He slowed to a trot, drawing drafts of breath. Be calm. Reassemble the recent past. On Friday, the flashbacks

201

began. Ignited in some preternatural way by the arrival of killers in this city. Their victims, Mafia hired hands: Sloukos, Champlain and . . . yes, Dr. Luk.

But this wasn't a Mafia operation. It was a CIA death squad – how did he know that? A safety-deposit key . . . Kellen had got into the vault.

More recent events began to settle into place; there was a chronology to them. Man behind the pickle barrel. Kellen shot him. There'd been a problem over that.

He came out onto Saint-Laurent, walking now, but quickly, looking up and down a street which was nearly empty – except for a few men who came from a bar and saw him and walked quickly to their car, then began to laugh and gesture at the dazed man in the straitjacket: this was The Main, bizarre the fashion.

He saw the sewer construction machinery in front of Big Al's, and the events of the explosion and foot chase came gushing back, clear, ordered. He'd stood here later, weeping. He'd gone to see Thérèse and Mario . . .

And afterwards, some kind of confrontation with Borko and the chief. What next . . .

Wally's office. He seemed to remember that Sarah was there. But what had they talked about? At about this point in the mid-afternoon, all the threads and patches of his memory faded into nothingness.

But as to the later hours of this day and night there remained a strong circumstantial case: he'd been taken captive; he'd been drugged and tortured, and probably questioned about the film. Some kind of CIA ability-to-kill experiment that Satorius was running; ruthless men were spilling blood to keep this secret buried.

How had he got to Coldhaven? He seemed to remember there had been a hotel room reserved for him . . .

But he had a faint recall of Sarah driving him home.

Why do they want to kill her? Had he said something under drugs or torture to endanger her?

The sniper's rifle: they were on their way to Ile Sainte-Hélène to assassinate her.

BIG AL'S HOUSE OF SMOKED MEAT. WHERE THE ELITE MEET TO EAT. Kellen walked in as a customer walked out, looking sideways at the snow-wet armless bloodied apparition.

A stillness as the half-dozen late-nighters stopped talking. Big Al, at his meat slicer, looked Kellen up and down before turning it off and wiping his hands on his apron.

"You want a menu?" he said.

Tuesday, one a.m.

Rubbing his arms, wearing an oversize coat Al had lent him, Kellen raced up the street toward Station Twenty-six, starting the day yet again, from the top. The lawyer's office and the wills. He'd gone back to the station. Eugene Borko had introduced Agent Hugh McVeigh with his lies about the Mafia.

Then the Essex and Edinburgh Trust. Then Juley's porno theater. Where they'd viewed that strange film: an experiment by Satorius with guns and mirrors. Some floppy-eared, short-haired guy shooting at someone's reflection first. And his own nineteen-year-old self coming onto the screen and doing the same thing.

Remember that he killed your father.

What was that about? – it didn't make sense. His father hadn't been murdered . . . Had he wanted to believe that? Maybe he had. He remembered telling Sarah something about his father being shot, and didn't know why he would lie.

Or was he programmed to believe that? There'd been headaches . . .

Recent memory was gone, but it wasn't hard to reach back to 1955 and bring back a day that seemed cruelly etched into memory. His mother bringing him home from hockey practice. Then asking him to look in the garage to see if his father's car was still there. Finding the car, and his father in it, his service revolver in his hand.

He thought then of Mario Basutti, his godson, and he was eleven now, too. Would it take him as long as Kellen to recover from a father's death? No, because Kellen would be there, God willing, and help guide him through it.

He forced his mind back to the events of the day. Okay, the movie. He'd been rattled after seeing it. Some kind of breakdown. He and Raolo then went to Big Al's; he gave Raolo the reel of film. Then the men in the Land Cruiser . . . yes, the same men he'd just escaped from.

Then the bomb, and they'd taken out Raolo but missed Kellen, and they all escaped except the fat guy behind the barrel. Borko and the chief had roasted him over that. That's right, he'd been suspended. And then, somehow he'd found his way to Wally Mandelbaum's office. But at Wally's all he could remember was his friend's face, and something of his own incoherence. And Sarah . . .

He had to get to Ile Sainte-Hélène quickly. He'd tried to phone there from Al's deli, but all the lines were tied up.

Kellen flexed and rubbed sore muscles as he peered through one of the front windows of Station Twenty-six and watched Eugene Borko at the helm of his deserted vessel, at the switchboard phone, scribbling notes.

Eugene, you're no member of any plot. You're just Eugene. Bork the Stork, straight and tall, the honest soldier. No, they hadn't gotten to Borko. They merely slipped past him.

As Kellen will try to do. And down those stairs to the weapons locker. He was feverish with anxiety: get a gun and get to Sarah. Before they do.

Borko's head was bowed to his pen as Kellen quietly entered and found cover behind the stairway wall.

"Sir, I think you've had one too many. Now collect your thoughts. Tell me what he did to you."

Kellen stepped lightly down the stairs.

"He dragged you into the bathroom."

Kellen swore softly: the armory's steel door was padlocked and chained. It would take a cutting torch. Someone had to have left a gun behind in this building, Station Twenty-six cops are notoriously careless. In unlocked closets: uniforms, commando gear, riot gear. No guns; he can't go armed with a wooden club or an electric prod.

He grabbed a flak jacket and a heavy white sweater, and struggled into them as he ran down the hall to the back stairwell, and up its narrow staircase to a second-floor landing.

Borko was below him on the ground floor, still on the phone, facing away. "Where the bloody heck is that girl you said you could spare?"

The lights were on in Borko's office. Kellen pulled the Beretta Model 12 submachine gun from the fasteners holding it to the wall, and buckled its clip belt diagonally across his chest. He pushed a clip in, and he turned to the door just as Borko walked in.

"Oh, my God." Borko stopped dead, frozen. He was sure he was going to die. "Let's talk about it, Kellen, whatever it is, maybe you've got a legitimate grievance, we were probably a little unfair."

"Move away from the door, okay, Eugene?"

Borko edged into the room. Kellen had the barrel pointing down, but he was cradling the gun, ready.

"I've been thinking about some of your theories on this case, Kellen, maybe you – "

"Shut up and listen hard, Eugene. They tried to murder me again tonight. I think they used some kind of drug to question me – I don't remember. They are going to try to kill Sarah Paradis now. She's surrounded by cops, but these guys don't care. They're professionals and they're desperate."

Borko observed a massive bandaged welt on Kellen's head. "Would you mind telling me – "

"Phone her. Keep trying, I couldn't get through. Tell them it's an emergency. Tell Sarah not to move from there. They have a sniper's rifle."

This seemed a rational voice, Borko realized.

205

Kellen went to the door. "Give me time, twenty seconds. Think of it as a career move."

He raced to the stairs, skidded to a stop just past the fire pole, hesitated a split second, then clamped his knees around the pole and rode it swiftly down.

From a wall downstairs, he grabbed a set of keys for one of the cars in the garage.

Tuesday, one-thirty a.m.

They were finally on Ile Sainte-Hélène, on an unplowed road, circumnavigating the rocky islet, getting the lay of it. Eddie the Cube's gloved hands were tight on the steering wheel, and the cold silence was screaming at him.

He had forced himself to throw up – the anchovy pizza, he'd decided, was the culprit – but he still felt a little jacked-up on something, felt like he'd been hot-wired just like this old pickup truck. His bald spot was tingling, and there was a sound like little hornets buzzing past his ears.

Also he was getting inklings of major disaster, hot tips he should be heeding.

He was concentrating hard at the controls. Eddie could feel energy radiating from Rudy Meyers beside him, an energy angry and sick.

They'd got lost. It wasn't his fault. Crowder had got him all mixed up with his goddamn map and his Porky-Pigged directions, and they went over the wrong fucking bridge. Meyers had barked at him. Meyers doesn't bark. He's losing his cool, his glorious, mother-fucking, ice-cold control.

Evergreens drooping under the snow. Montreal shining across the frozen river. A circular road to nowhere. Round and round we go, we never get off Rudy's merry-go-round.

A series of small parking lots, and they came into a lit area, cars in front of a big stone building, a TV van, four or five reporters hanging around.

"T-too much action," said Mick Crowder, who was squeezed between Eddie and Rudy.

"Don't slow down," said Meyers.

Eddie drove carefully, anonymously, past. He wanted to say: Let's go back over the bridge, Rudy. It's time to go home.

Meyers looked up through the windshield at something above them. "There it is. Find a place to park."

They pulled off into a lot out of sight of the restaurant, and when they got out, Eddie saw, beyond a grove of trees, a high network of steel ribbing rising above the trees.

"The American Pavilion," Meyers said. Eddie stared at him; the man was standing at military attention, shoulders back, arms straight. Why don't he salute? Old Rude was definitely becoming a little lunched-out, maybe like an Iranian fanatic on a suicide mission.

The blizzard had whirled off toward northern New England, and a nearly full moon above them was struggling to show through the sky's haze. The snowdrifts were grimly gray. Eddie could hear a rumbling of voices. It was coming from the restaurant. *Muchas policias*, he thought. *Rudy esta loco.*

"There's good available light," Meyers said. "Watch for taxis, Mick, especially the Hot Dog Taxi Company – O'Reilly uses a jigaboo driver from there." He pointed to an eighty-foot-high platform inside the geodesic dome. "Up there, Mick. Just like in Dallas."

Tuesday, one forty-five a.m.

Though it was nearly two o'clock, Mario told his mother he wanted to stay. Thérèse didn't want to go home, either; she

207

preferred being in this place of high energy to being at home with weeping sisters, weeping mother. She was gathered with friends at a table in the kitchen, and they were telling stories on each other, keeping it light.

They tried to comfort Mario, but he felt smothered by them, and quietly told his mother he'd be happier just being by himself. He went to a corner and opened a Hercule Poirot, and read for a while – the first page of Chapter Six about five times.

Everyone seemed to understand his need to be alone, and although the kitchen volunteers brought him sandwiches and cans of pop and ruffled his hair, they didn't try to break into his silence.

He did, though, want to see Kellen, his godfather, but wasn't too disappointed that he was not here. Kellen was going after those guys; he was going to get them.

Mario went back to the hall with his book, and pretended to read there – so no one would bug him – and listened to the men and women talk about drafting a statement for the press. He tried to concentrate on what they were saying, tried to understand the issues – the detectives in his books never seemed to have to deal with this kind of stuff.

He wasn't so sure now that he wanted to be a cop. His teacher told him he could be a writer. Straight A's in composition; his dad had been proud.

He kind of covered his face with his book so no one could see him wipe the wetness from his eyes.

When the meeting broke for twenty minutes for coffee and sandwiches, he had to escape from everybody again, and he found a dark corridor leading to a side door, a staff entrance. He pressed his nose to the window of the door, and stared out through its melting ice into the grayness.

Beyond the trees, shining silver under the moon, he saw the dome of the U.S. Pavilion.

Sarah was next in line for one of the pay phones outside – the ones inside were impossible. Two dozen cops were out here, smoking or catching the air, a warming night air now; barometers were rising fast.

Sarah knew it was ridiculous to call Kellen at almost two in the morning, but she'd started worrying again, and begun asking around, and for some reason no one could tell her who'd made the arrangements for his protection. "Oh, I heard that somewhere," was what she'd got from various shop stewards.

Inside the Ile Sainte-Hélène restaurant, Taillefeur was in caucus with his troops; they'd been quiet since Thérèse's speech, but were reorganizing.

Sarah heard Ouimet's amplified voice from inside, calling the meeting to order. The man in front of her hung up the phone.

She stuck in a quarter and quickly dialed Kellen's number.

She got his recorded message.

"Kellen, are you there? Is anyone there?"

No one came on the line.

"Miss Paradis?"

She turned: a smiling man with a round balloon face. In a long coat with its collar turned up, his hands in the pockets.

"I'm Agent Herb Trotter, FBI." A hand came out of a pocket and held up a badge. Agent Herb Trotter, FBI, it said. She didn't like the look of him.

"Press invited in for this session," someone called out at the door.

"Lieutenant O'Reilly asked me to leave a message that he's safe and secure."

He turned and walked away toward one of the parking lots, and Sarah hung up the phone. "Wait."

The man stopped. "He'll be in touch with you in two days. He said you're not to worry."

He turned again, and Sarah ran toward him, untrusting of him, but there were still some people out here. "Just a minute."

She caught up but he didn't stop, strolled placidly forward.

"You'll have to do better than that," she said. "Where is he?"

"I'm sorry I'm under instructions not to say more."

"Where *is* he?"

209

The man stopped. "Okay. We've been running an on-going investigation, ma'am, into this MK-ULTRA business. We had to bring Kellen into our confidence before he accidentally dismantled it. Please protect this confidence. Good-bye, Miss Paradis."

He began walking again. Sarah paused, then took ten steps to catch up to him, and, as he abruptly turned to her, she felt something very hard and sharp against her breastbone. She felt it rip the fabric of her blouse – a knife.

"No talking, keep walking. I don't want to hurt you. I just want information." Meyers burped those short phrases like a machine gun, fast, before she could react. "Try to scream and I will cut your vocal cords."

She stopped, frozen with fear. The point of the knife was now touching her lower throat. He was slightly behind her, with his arm across her chest. She wanted to glance back quickly to see if anyone was still outside but dared not.

"Move."

She walked forward like a zombie.

In a few seconds they were in the shadows of the building, heading in the direction of the geodesic dome.

From behind his darkened window, Mario saw them come distantly into view, a big man in the long coat huddled around a slight woman, both of them walking stiffly away from the restaurant. The lady, he thought, was walking like she was sick or something. It looked pretty weird; they were going away from the parking lot, toward the big dome.

Tuesday, two a.m.

The cross hairs quartered a La Salle Taxi, and Crowder waited. Two men came from the building and walked toward it. He lowered the rifle.

210

He looked down into the gloom, trying to make out Eddie Comacho on the tier beneath him. He called down softly, "Eddie, you there?"

"Yeah."

"You g-going to do surveillance, you got to be where you can see."

"I don't like it in the light."

Rudy had warned Mick: The Cuban would show cowardice under pressure. In the end there'd just be Rudy and Mick, the way it always should have been.

Tuesday, two-o-five a.m.

The silence was soft and heavy – shouts from within the meeting place came distant and muffled to Kellen's ears. A silver moon shimmered through the lattice of the dome as he moved from shadow to shadow along its fenced perimeter, keeping the ball of the moon on a plane with the platform.

There. No question this time. The man stood framed within the moon's penumbra.

At one of several breaches in the woven wire fence, he saw fresh footprints, and followed them in.

The walls of the burned-out ground floor theater were splashed with graffiti: YANK OFF! SCREW THE CRUISE. NICARAGUA SI!

Two hundred feet away, on the other side of the theater, Meyers had Sarah backed against the wall, his left hand holding the stiletto knife to her chin. She saw the bandaged right hand, and she knew who he was – Happy Face from the Pharmacie Lagasse.

"Where did you put the film, Miss Paradis?"

"Film . . . I have no film."

"Open your bag and empty it, item by item."

With trembling hands she did so: purse, notebooks, makeup kit, loose change sinking into the snow.

"Just tell me why you think I have this film. I've never seen it."

"Time is of the essence. You have thirty seconds of it – "

He heard a rustling in the snow and quickly turned his head to see what made the noise – there was nothing but snowbanks and shadows.

Mario, about to race back to the restaurant, had slipped and fallen into a hole in the snow, and was covered to his waist. He knew he daren't move or even breathe, because the man threatening Sarah Paradis was only ten meters away, behind a snowdrift.

He heard the man say, "And after thirty seconds, unless you tell me about the film, I am going to cut off your face with this knife."

And he began counting.

"A thousand and one. A thousand and two . . . "

Mario felt a gloved hand go over his mouth.

Tuesday, two-ten a.m.

Eddie Comacho clenched his hand tightly on his handgun, all his muscles held taut to fight his jitters. His body, by getting sick, had tried to warn him, he was free-falling toward Calamity City. Rudy was loony with stubbornness, he'd led them on a mission of endless disaster.

He would sneak down, run for the pickup truck, be the only one to survive.

He glanced up at Crowder on the level above, who was aiming his rifle at another taxi. He stepped slowly backwards deeper into the shadow of the upper stairway.

And froze when he heard Kellen O'Reilly's quiet voice behind him.

"That's fine, stop right there."

Eddie turned his head sideways, tried vainly to see into the dimness. But he recognized the voice.

"Now slowly bend, spread both arms away from the body, and put the piece on the floor."

"If you make me a deal," Eddie said, "I'll talk."

Tuesday, two-eleven a.m.

"Thousand and twenty-nine."

She opened her mouth to scream and his middle finger darted at her throat, and she gagged and closed her eyes and tried desperately to catch her breath.

"Thousand and thirty. Miss Paradis, this isn't personal, but you won't talk and I have to kill you."

He drew the knife blade back for a sharp hard thrust, but his arm didn't come forward – it was caught at the elbow in an iron grip.

Hugh McVeigh said from close behind his ear, "It's bad for the image, Rudy." He let the elbow go.

Sarah opened her eyes. Meyers was whirling away from her, quickly positioning the knife between him and the tall black man who'd come up from behind him, and who stood calm and serious, weaponless, tamping tobacco into a pipe. Frock coat and a small-brim hat with a feather.

"McVeigh," Meyers said. The tone sounded of sadness.

Sarah took a step to the side, then another.

"You pathetic old crackers haven't kept up with the changes. We have this *new* corporate image, my man. We don't kill indiscriminately." He caressed the word, syllable by syllable.

Sarah started moving away quickly.

"Don't go too far, ma'am, he's not alone."

213

She stopped near the wire fence, uncertain, twenty feet away from them; she could hear their voices but not their words.

"Her daddy's a big player in this country," McVeigh said softly to Meyers. "That makes it *flagrantly* indiscriminate."

"Hugh, this is about project forty-seven; it sprung a leak." Meyers put his smile back together but his voice cracked.

"Who asked you to plug it?" McVeigh put a lighter to his pipe and got it going.

"We were being blackmailed."

"By a couple of Mafia paper pushers," McVeigh said. "I don't see how a Mafia factor works its way in here. This was sold to the director as a program to wipe foreign agents' memories."

"You have it exactly, Hugh. I've been out here protecting the Company's name, you should thank me."

"Thank you, Rudy. Now toss the knife off to the side. It has a cooling effect on our relationship."

Meyers hesitated. He held the stiletto loosely in his good hand, the left one, belt high and up.

"To be fair, Rudy, you need two good hands against me." McVeigh smiled. Meyers watched his eyes.

McVeigh darted to the side and his hand flashed toward the wrist of Meyers' knife-hand, and as Meyers drew it quickly back, a boot drove at full acceleration into his groin. He dropped the knife and clutched himself there, in terrible agony.

Mario saw this lightning skirmish just as he finally pulled himself from the snowpit and came scrambling to his feet. The black man had whispered to Mario: "Stay here and stay quiet," but he was going to do neither, he was going to go for that hole in the fence and raise the alarm. These are the men who blew up his dad's car. Everyone had to get out of the building. He slogged toward it as fast as he could through the knee-deep snow.

Meyers slowly straightened up, and grunted, "You're not going to kill me. I'm ex-Company. We're fighting the same war."

"Be forthcoming, Rudy. What were you meatballs up to with this Satorius? I have my private theory. The year was 1963. Crowder, who was like your personal valet and had a rep as the best rifle in the Agency, was posted to Dallas that year. Do I read it right?"

As Mario struggled through the snow to the restaurant, he heard shouts from inside, then boos and applause. He'd almost reached the car lot when a cruiser pulled in; Mario recognized it as the kind his dad used to drive. The driver got out and checked to see if the doors were locked. Mario ran toward him.

Meyers straightened, tried to stand tall despite his discomfort. His smile was gone.

"It was approved by some very senior people, Hugh."

"They're more circumspect than you. Brainwashing agents we can weather." McVeigh knelt and picked up the knife. "This we can't. Sorry, my man."

Meyers' smile returned. The twenty-first and final precept taught by his master was simple: Die bravely.

"He was a nigger-loving Commie cocksucker," he said.

Tuesday, two-sixteen a.m.

"I saw him lead her away from the phone and grab her," Comacho said, talking low, urgently cooperating.

Kellen's heart froze. He was still behind Comacho, his gun to his man's spine.

"Where are they now?"

"Somewhere below. I'll go state's witness, amigo, you name the terms. The whole story, from the top."

"Where's the guy with the rifle?"

"One floor up. Want me to call him? You can take him down when he comes into the light."

Mick Crowder was by now across a plank and onto the steel hexahedrons, climbing down, his rifle strapped behind him. He'd heard their soft voices, and now as he crawled lower he could see their legs, and now hips, now chests, Eddie and someone behind him, and Eddie was talking.

Kellen decided: ask more questions later; Sarah, first. Walk this guy down, deal with the one up there later.

"I'm going to be tight in behind you. Go fast, downstairs." He prodded Comacho in the back with his submachine gun.

As Comacho stepped forward, Kellen sensed movement in the far darkness. And just as he made out a human form on the dome's skeleton in front of him, a gun cracked, the bullet piercing Comacho's breast and exiting from the back with such velocity that Kellen felt the slug's impact against his flak jacket, and staggered back, stumbled against the stairway, as two more bullets came, popping and splintering off the concrete a foot from his chest.

Kellen slid flat onto his stomach near Comacho's jerking, dying form, and he braced his submachine gun and ripped off a fusillade, sweeping left to right, bullets clanging against tubing.

Crowder slid slowly onto a horizontal bar, and hung there like a Raggedy Ann doll for almost a second, then his weight carried his legs up and he went down headfirst toward concrete.

Kellen was already racing down the stairs, screaming, "Meyers, let her go! Let her go or I'll kill you!" Six flights, five flights, four.

He saw the doors of the restaurant open, people pour out.

Then he saw her, Sarah, standing alone, her hands to her mouth.

Two flights, one. And across the concrete walkway.

He stopped.

Around the wall, forty feet in front of him: Meyers' body was crumpled against a fence, head lolling. A black man in the shadows beside him, stuffing a pipe. He saw Kellen and nodded.

"It's all over, O'Reilly," McVeigh said.

"Over for you, pal." A familiar voice.

Kellen looked to his right, and first saw Mario Basutti, near the wire fence, and then saw Borko, a little closer, thirty feet away, down on one knee, his service revolver braced expertly on his left wrist.

McVeigh had taken his lighter from his pocket and he'd whirled at the sound of Borko's voice, the pipe in his other hand.

Kellen, when he thought about it later, figured Eugene must have mistaken the pipe for a gun. The captain nailed McVeigh with a marksman's shot through his temples.

Cops were running toward the fence, some with guns out, some shouting.

Borko slowly rose to his full six-six. "Is that the last of them, Kel?"

He came forward and bent to his victim's body. "Jeez, this is that FBI . . . "

Kellen looked over at Sarah; she was weeping; someone was comforting her. He looked at Mario, who was motionless, staring. They were within a perimeter of silent cops. Kellen turned sadly back to Borko.

"I'll tell the Chief it was a tricky call, Eugene."

Victoria Day, two p.m.

Spring had lasted its regulation two weeks. The snows had clung on into May under the conifers and in dirty roadside patches, and now suddenly were gone. Today offered bird-song and buzzing flies and blue skies, the hot crunch of coming summer.

Wally's oldest, Nickie, was romping with Mario – whom

Kellen had brought along – on air mattresses in the limpid waters of Lac Echo, a sparkling clear and lifeless lake. Acid rain.

The cottage of Wally and Louise Mandelbaum was in the Laurentian highlands; they'd bought it two years ago, along with its kitsch furniture and its velvet paintings and Popeye lamp and banana telephone. The sign at the mailbox said Snugglers' Cove. The place was true camp, therefore high art, Wally insisted, secretly knowing better, rationalizing, too cheap to pay for taste.

The Mandelbaums and Kellen and Sarah Paradis were on the verandah, playing Trivial Pursuit, a game Wally hated with a feeling akin to passion. Eight years of university, and he was bringing up the rear, sports and science his only slices of pie. Kellen O'Reilly, supposedly brain-damaged, was ahead, a lucky man whom Lady Fortune favored with easy questions.

To make matters worse, the Expos were down to the Mets six-two in the fifth – Louise had forced compromise upon Wally; he could listen to the ball game as long as he played the board game.

Kellen, beside him, was chuckling into the banana phone, talking to Margot.

"Sure, but you're *supposed* to look pregnant. It comes with the deal. You can't look like a pogo stick and be pregnant."

"Geography," said Louise. " 'Name the five countries bordering Switzerland.' Forget it."

"Germany, Italy, France," said Wally.

"Austria?" said Sarah. "There are no more."

"Trick question," Kellen said. "Liechtenstein."

"This game has absolutely nothing to do with intelligence," Wally announced. "The truly great minds don't wander around with their heads stuffed full of useless information. Einstein would wipe out."

Wallach fanned, stranding two. Wally heard popping noises across the lake – firecrackers.

Queen Victoria's birthday. He remembered going to riot parties with Kellen in Irish Point St. Charles – a Jew joining

218

joyfully in the general damning of the English. The holiday had a sense of revolution about it, fireworks at night.

But there'd be no such fun at Snugglers' Cove this night. "No fireworks," he'd told the kids. "Kellen is coming."

"It's just the pregnancy blahs, Margot. You'll perk up. Ciao."

When he hung up, Sarah gave Wally a bland, patient expression. "Isn't he adorable? Do you think that marriage will ever be over?"

"Yeah, it's a pretty sick relationship," Wally said.

Kellen grinned, Sarah sighed. From Marcel's frying pan into Kellen's fire: she loved him, perhaps, too eagerly. A much-changed man, most of whose dark rooms were now filled with light. Others, however, seemed too full of Margot.

Irrational jealousy. She should be thankful he was whole and well. The flashbacks had stopped. He'd spent many days and nights poring over the back issues of newspapers, reading about his father. He'd had a session with Wally, and had handled his father's death with astonishing ease. He had knitted together, but Sarah could see a twitch of his facial muscles when firecrackers echoed across the lake.

He hasn't much talked about that wintry night of terror three months ago, but would if pushed, and had done so at the inquiry. He was still amnesic for the seven to eight hours before he escaped from Coldhaven, but forensics had filled in the gaps. They had taken swabs from his forehead: electroshock jelly; and had recovered samples of his hair and blood on the ECT table.

His evidence and Mario's, before the special inquirer, exonerated Eugene Borko. The shooting death of Hugh McVeigh was ruled to be a tragic but understandable error of judgment on the captain's part. Kellen had testified to everything he could remember of that day and night; he had described the film that he and his partner viewed.

Headlines. COP ALLEGES CIA KILL-TESTING. Another scandal rocks Washington.

The FBI denied any knowledge of McVeigh. The CIA maintained its policy of refusing to confirm or deny whether he or any of the dead men had ever been on staff; although they leaked a story that Meyers was an agent gone bad who'd been fired. They'd frankly not heard of Meyers' associates, said the official leaker.

Kellen had been joined as a plaintiff in Sarah's suit. The defendants were already preparing their slanders against him, and demanding an independent psychiatric assessment. But he hasn't seemed perturbed. He has taken leave from murders, was working full-time for the Brotherhood, helping Sarah prepare submissions for the binding arbitration the government had forced upon them.

Sarah would be making these submissions all next week. The work never ends. But the Halcion days, thank God, are gone.

Wally picked up the dice. A six and a one. Entertainment. Louise read the card: " 'Which is the only one of the Seven Dwarfs without a beard?' "

Wally thought. "Snoopy."

Kellen and Sarah roared.

"Dopey, dear," Louise said.

"Dopey, Pokey, Sleazy, Guppie, Yuppie, who gives a shit?"

Martinez gave up a shot through the middle for a double and a run in.

Kellen rolled the dice. "History."

"This fills his pie," Wally groaned.

Another screamer and Buck Rogers was going to the mound to fetch Martinez to safety.

Louise read Kellen's question. " 'Who murdered John F. Kennedy?' "

"Didn't I say?" Wally threw up his hands. "He always gets the easy ones . . . Kel – you okay?"

You're sallow green in a halo of computer glow, and evil suffuses and poisons the air, and a voice comes haunting and distant from across the room. "You failed the psychic driving, Kellen. The rebel in you wouldn't die."

Printed in Canada